Introduction

Cup of Courage by Darlene Mindrup
In A.D. 49, Tirzah, a Messianic Jew, finds herself partnered with a pagan Roman in attempts t

ing his brother. Tirzah's life is in
ened by devout Jews who want Ch
have strength to sort out her attrac
hope from a Hebrew inscription c
worshippers use when partaking of the Lord's Supper.

Cup of Hope by Susannah Hayden
Christina's home in twelfth-century Jerusalem is under attack by the Turks. She turns to her childhood friend Lukas for wisdom in caring for a small band of orphans. When Jerusalem falls, the Turks ask for ransom in exchange for letting the people live. Christina and Lukas have nothing to help themselves. How will they save the many children in their care?

Cup of Honor by Marilou H. Flinkman
Leah and her brother were Jews raised in Europe prior to World War II. They are separated and sent to refugee camps in the Mediterranean. Leah longs to reach her brother in Palestine, and Joshua Ben Ami may be the one who can help her. But his zeal is for a Jewish homeland. Will Joshua have time for her?

Cup of Praise by Jane LaMunyon
Sarah Reuben works at a small museum in Jerusalem's Old City and becomes fascinated by an ancient chalice. Michael Van Gelder, who captured her heart years ago, has returned home with the announcement that he has embraced Christianity. He is able to explain the inscription on the chalice for Sarah, but will she believe in the chalice's worth when it is stolen?

The Chalice of Israel

Four Novellas Bound by
Love, Enchantment, and Tradition

Marilou H. Flinkman
Susannah Hayden
Jane LaMunyon
Darlene Mindrup

BARBOUR BOOKS
An Imprint of Barbour Publishing, Inc.

Cup of Courage ©2001 by Darlene Mindrup
Cup of Hope ©2001 by Susannah Hayden
Cup of Honor ©2001 by Marilou H. Flinkman
Cup of Praise ©2001 by Jane LaMunyon

Cover photo: ©PhotoDisc, Inc.

ISBN 1-58660-388-4

All Scripture quotations, unless otherwise noted, are taken from the King James Version of the Bible.

Published by Barbour Books, an imprint of Barbour Publishing, Inc., P.O. Box 719, Uhrichsville, Ohio 44683 www.barbourbooks.com

Printed in the United States of America.
5 4 3 2

The Chalice of Israel

Cup of Courage

by Darlene Mindrup

Chapter 1

A.D. 60

The hot Palestinian sun shone brightly on the earthen city landscape below, placing the silhouettes of two young women in sharp relief. Tirzah, the older of the two, brushed the beaded sweat from her face. She pulled her perspiration-dampened tunic away from her chest, shaking it slightly to allow the air to circulate beneath. Lifting the shawl from her head to permit the slight breeze to filter through her long dark hair, she stared impatiently at her younger sister, Rebekah, whose brown eyes flashed with anger.

Trying to relieve some of the tension that had risen between them, Tirzah moved to the stone cistern behind their mud dwelling place, patting the space next to her for her sister to join her.

At first it seemed as though Rebekah would refuse, but at last she relented, seating herself stiffly at her sister's side. For a moment, neither one said anything. Finally, Tirzah sighed.

"It's wrong, Rebekah, and you know it."

The brown eyes that turned Tirzah's way held a mixture of defiance and guilt. "What is so wrong with having a friend who is not of the Way?"

Tirzah stared steadily at Rebekah until the other finally dropped her gaze to her sandal-shod feet.

"Rebekah, this can only cause trouble. What I saw cannot be described as mere friendship."

The other girl's face colored brightly, but she refused to look at Tirzah. Tirzah had to lean forward to hear the softly spoken words.

"It was not meant to happen."

Tirzah sighed again, feeling suddenly much older than her twenty years. Though only two years younger, Rebekah often seemed more like a child.

"Rebekah, look at me."

Slowly, the girl complied. Guilt shimmered in the depths of her large, almond eyes. Tirzah took her hand gently, and to her relief, Rebekah didn't resist.

"Oh, my sister," Tirzah cried, "I would have spared you this if I could, but you are so headstrong."

A slight smile briefly touched Rebekah's lips. Tirzah's own lips firmed with resolve. "The man is a Roman. They have different ways. Different beliefs. They believe that for a man and woman to know each other physically is a part of worship of their deities. In their temples, women and men have physical acts together, often with other people's spouses. They think nothing of adultery and fornication."

Rebekah pulled her hand away. "We were only kissing."

One dark eyebrow lifted. Tirzah continued to watch her sister's beautiful face, which was a study in emotions.

"That kind of kissing quickly leads to other things."

Giving her sister a withering glance, Rebekah got to her feet and moved some distance away. She dropped her shawl to her shoulders, revealing the glorious mass of brown curls beneath. "And how would you know?" she asked, looking back over her shoulder.

Tirzah's face paled, but she controlled her expression, revealing nothing of what she felt. "Don't try that with me," she told her sister in a voice edged with icy calm.

Rebekah quickly looked away, her unseeing gaze moving over the many small homes surrounding them. Her shoulders slumped dejectedly.

"I apologize, Tirzah. You are right." She turned a beseeching look on her sister. "But I love him."

"Oh, Rebekah!" Tirzah moaned. She had hoped that things had not progressed that far between her sister and the young Roman.

Rebekah crossed quickly to her sister's side. She hesitantly laid a small hand on Tirzah's forearm. "But it's not what you think!" Rebekah argued. "He no longer believes in the Roman gods. He is a God-fearer."

Tirzah noted the younger girl's familiar, yet perfect features. Her bow-shaped lips were the color of a pomegranate, her skin flawless and smooth as a peach. It was no wonder the young Roman was smitten.

Taking her sister by the hand, Tirzah gently twined her fingers with the younger girl's as they had done so many times when children. "But he is not a Christian," she remonstrated softly, her voice firm. "Though it is wonderful that he at least accepts our God, he still does not accept our Lord."

Rebekah slowly seated herself on the edge of the sun-warmed stone cistern. She released her sister's hand, burying her face against her palms. Her shoulders shook with suppressed sobs.

Ever at a fault before tears, Tirzah dropped down beside her, rubbing the other girl's back gently.

Sniffing, Rebekah mumbled something, and Tirzah had to force the other girl's hands from her face to understand what she said.

"Now, what did you say?"

Hopelessness had replaced the defiance in the shimmering brown eyes. "I said that he wants to marry me."

Tirzah felt her body go cold all over. She opened her mouth to protest, but words failed her. She got up and began pacing back and forth in the small garden area, kicking up tufts of sand with each agitated step.

Finally, she closed her eyes, lifting her face to the bright blue heaven above. Silently she asked for Jehovah's wisdom in handling this matter.

"How long has this been going on?" she asked hollowly, her back to her sister.

"We've been seeing each other for several weeks," Rebekah answered softly, and Tirzah finally turned to face her. She tried to mask the anger churning inside her. Her sister had always been easily swayed. It was the one thing she and her mother had always feared: that some man would come and take her away from the teachings she had come to believe in. Like the seed that landed among the rocks.

Seeing her sister's woebegone face, she couldn't stay angry. Rebekah was, after all, but a child.

"It has to stop," Tirzah told her firmly. "Do you want to chance losing sight of the one thing that matters most—your salvation?"

"But I can bring Domitus to the Lord. If he has become a God-fearer, surely he can be made to believe in Jehovah's Son."

Tirzah sighed. "How many times have we been warned not to join ourselves to unbelievers? They don't have in mind the things of God."

Rebekah thrust her lips out in a pout. "You don't understand! You've never been in love."

Tirzah had no answer to that. It was all too true, but then, she had never had the opportunity. Beside her beautiful sister, she was but a brown moth, and men's gazes always went past her to follow after Rebekah.

Realizing what she had just said, Rebekah turned quickly to her sister, an apology ready on her lips. Tirzah shook her head. "No, don't say anything. It's all right. What you said is true."

A heavy silence hung in the air, almost as stifling as the summer heat. Tirzah was the first to break it. "You must tell mother."

Rebekah lifted horror-filled eyes, shaking her head vehemently. "I couldn't!" She shook her head again, even more vehemently. "No, I just couldn't. It would break her heart!"

Tirzah cupped her sister's chin with a gentle hand, lifting her face. "And what about yours? You must either tell her or break off this destructive relationship."

Sighing, Rebekah pulled her chin away, turning to watch the kites gracefully swirling in the air above them. So beautiful, yet they were carrion birds that lived off the dead. Shuddering, she looked back at Tirzah.

"What am I going to do, Tirzah? I don't know what to do."

Tirzah took her sister's two cold hands into her own, squeezing slightly. "Shall we pray about it?"

Rebekah gave her a half-hearted smile. "I would like that."

Tirzah knelt before her sister's seated figure, closing her eyes. Together they asked for Jehovah's guidance with their problem. As always, Tirzah felt a load lifted from her shoulder after such an encounter with the Lord. It was so nice to be able to leave the burden with Him.

When they finished, she told her sister seriously, "You must do your part, also, Rebekah. Remember what the disciple James told us. When someone knows the good he should do and he doesn't do it, this is sin."

Pain reflected in the younger girl's eyes, but she set her shoulders resolutely. "I know. I will have to tell Domitus that I can no longer see him." She looked hopefully at Tirzah. "Would. . .would you come with me?"

Tirzah was thrilled with her sister's reply but hesitant to do as she asked. Still, it would cause her sister much pain to break off this relationship, and she should be there to help and offer guidance if she could. Besides, Rebekah was so easily swayed, this young man would probably charm her into forgetting her decision. Tirzah unwillingly agreed to go.

Rebekah rose and started for the house, her body sagging as though she were many years past her age. She stopped halfway, turning back to Tirzah. "Please. Let's not tell mother."

Tirzah paused but finally nodded her head in agreement. There would be enough hurt for Rebekah. It would be foolish to cause mother to suffer as well. Especially since she was suffering enough from the rejection of her friends and family due to her belief in Jesus as the Messiah.

Tirzah watched Rebekah enter their little home, then seated herself against the edge of the cistern. Lifting her face to the sky, she once again petitioned the Lord on her sister's behalf.

Gallius warily watched his brother coming across the triclinium toward him. The soles of Domitus's sandals tapped against the cool marble tiles with firm intent. The set of his shoulders warned Gallius that his brother was about to offer some information that would not be to his liking. He sighed, setting his cup of wine on the table and pushing back an unruly lock of black hair that had fallen across his forehead.

Domitus took the couch across from Gallius, waiting until a servant placed a goblet of cool wine at his side before speaking. "Gallius, there is something I need to discuss with you."

Gallius's lips twitched slightly. Though his brother was a mere eighteen years old, his grave expression gave him the look of a much older man. He was a younger replica of Gallius himself, and his turbulent gray eyes spoke clearly of trouble brewing. Gallius lifted an inquiring brow, stifling a grin when his brother swallowed hard.

"I. . .I wish to get married."

The words were so unexpected that Gallius merely sat blinking at Domitus for several seconds. Finally, he let out a loud crack of laughter, causing Domitus to jump slightly in his seat.

Frowning, Domitus gave his older brother a cold glare. "There is nothing amusing about it. I don't see what you find so entertaining."

"And who is it to be this time?" Gallius asked him, trying to hold back the laughter. He reclined negligently against the couch, his intent look watching his brother's open face.

Domitus jumped to his feet, his hands clenching into fists at his side.

"I knew you would react this way! I'm serious this time. I love Rebekah, and I want to marry her."

Gallius lifted a supercilious brow. "Rebekah? That has a Jewish sound to it."

Color flooded Domitus's face. Crossing his arms defensively, his short red tunic pulled tightly against shoulders fast becoming as broad as his brother's. "She is Jewish."

Gallius leaned back against the couch, crossing his feet at the ankles. He lifted his cup, taking a quick sip. Anything to hold back the sudden misgivings flooding through him.

"I see." He gave his brother a look intended to quell the younger man's enthusiasm. "This has to do with that confounded religion you've embraced."

"It has nothing to do with that."

Gallius studied his brother's angry face, noting the sudden hesitancy to look him in the eye. Something was wrong here. He knew Domitus well, and the boy was obviously hiding something. Gallius stared ruthlessly at his brother and motioned to the couch. "Sit down, and let's discuss this."

Domitus glanced at the couch, then back at his brother. Some of his earlier bravado ebbed away, but he wasn't about to give in. "There's nothing to discuss," he answered belligerently.

"Sit!"

The command was meant to be obeyed. Domitus complied.

Gallius sat up, returning his cup to the table. Linking his fingers, he allowed his hands to hang between his knees as he leaned forward. "I assume she's beautiful."

Again, Domitus colored hotly. "What has that to do with anything? I would love her if she were not."

"Would you?"

Silence filled the room. Finally, Domitus admitted, "I know that I have behaved badly in the past, but this time it's different."

"Tell me how," Gallius commanded quietly.

Domitus absentmindedly took some grapes from the silver tray on the table, then just as distractedly put them back. It took some time before he could finally look his brother in the eye.

"It's true that Rebekah is beautiful, and that is what first attracted me to her. But after getting to know her, well. . .she's different, that's all."

Gallius snorted softly. "That is an understatement. Jews are a race apart from anything else on this earth. Their insane ideas of an invisible God who rules their lives and their confounded ideas of purity are foolish. Add to that their stubborn refusal to accept our gods. . ." Gallius shook his head, confused. "How on earth did you even manage to get together with this young woman?"

Domitus nervously pleated the gold trim on his tunic. He watched his fingers, refusing to look at his brother. "I met her at the temple."

"I assume you mean the Jewish temple," Gallius said wryly, and Domitus nodded, still without looking up. Gallius sighed. Not for the first time, he wished he had never been sent to this wretched Judean city. Though Jerusalem was beautiful even by Roman standards, still, it was not Rome.

Domitus turned a pleading facc to Gallius. "I ask only that you meet her and that you keep an open mind."

Gallius's eyes narrowed with speculation. "And has she agreed to be your wife?"

For thc first time, Domitus looked nonplused. He shrugged his shoulders slightly, once more turning his look away from Gallius's probing stare.

"She said that she would tell me tomorrow." He glanced up, his look hardening into one of determination. "But she will agree. I know she will. We love each other."

"And what of your service in the army? You know, as well as I, that there are only two reasons for ending that service. Death or demobilization." Gallius's voice held a warning that

Domitus couldn't miss. "I don't think you wish to contemplate the first option, and with Jewish rebellion against Rome rising every day, I doubt that we will be demobilized. It's forbidden for legionnaires to marry. You know that."

Domitus glanced at Gallius briefly before once again dropping his gaze to hide whatever thoughts he held. "I was hoping that you would use your influence to have me released."

Gallius took his time answering. Thoughts rushed through his head at an alarming rate. Betraying Rome's army was a serious matter. He had to do something to protect his brother from his own foolishness, but what? An idea suddenly occurred to him, and he smiled slowly. "Perhaps I could go with you when you next meet her."

Domitus expression was guarded, but even so it was obvious that he was loathe to arrange such a meeting. Seeing no other option, he finally agreed. After all, what could happen in a busy city like Jerusalem?

Chapter 2

The sun had descended to just above the hills when Tirzah, Rebekah, and their mother sat down to their final meal for the day. Tirzah took her accustomed place on the hard ground next to her mother, while Rebekah took the seat across from her.

The waning sunlight slanted through their open door, slicing across the low wooden table at which they were seated. The three women clasped hands, bowing their heads while Mother's sweet voice asked a blessing on the food.

After Mother had finished, she broke the loaf of bread and handed a piece to each of her daughters. She lifted the small pitcher from the table and poured some milk into a cup, handing it to Rebekah, her brief glance at the girl somewhat anxious. "Jacob brought us more goat's milk today."

Rebekah's cheeks turned a fiery red. She lifted frustrated eyes, glaring from Tirzah to her mother. "I wish he would stop! I do not care for him that way, and I certainly don't wish to marry him."

Dropping her gaze to the table, Mother picked at her own food. Her dark eyes were full of pleading when she next looked up. "Rebekah, he loves you, and he would make a fine husband.

It's not like I am trying to wish on you a man long past his prime. Jacob is young and handsome, and he has a way to support you." She sighed, leaning back. "I only want to see you both happy."

"Then give him to Tirzah. She is the oldest anyway and should marry first."

Tirzah choked on her food, gasping for breath between fits of coughing. She glared at her sister. "Leave me out of this. I am not the one whom Jacob loves."

Their mother's shoulders hunched wearily. Her sad smile touched Tirzah's heart.

"I want you girls to be settled with homes of your own. I am not getting any younger. I want to see you taken care of."

Tirzah glanced sharply at her mother. For the first time, she realized what a burden it must be for her to care for two grown daughters. Suddenly, she noticed the lines of weariness etched in her mother's face. Had their family not rejected them because of their faith in Christ, they would have had someone to provide for them. As it was, her mother had been added to the list of widows in the church to be supported by the Christian brethren in Jerusalem.

Her mother was proud, though, and didn't wish to accept assistance she felt should be given to those in greater need. Looking around the small home, Tirzah didn't see how there could be others in a worse situation, but she knew it was true. A famine had hit Jerusalem with disastrous consequences, and many people were suffering. At least Tirzah and her family had a home.

She sighed. And at least they still had each other. Her father had been killed by an overturned millstone in an accident three years ago, and they had lived from hand to mouth ever since.

"Rebekah," her mother said softly, staring down at the table. "I have already told Jacob that you will accept his proposal of marriage."

The color drained from Rebekah's face, and she stared at her mother in horror. Tirzah was no less amazed herself, though she supposed she shouldn't have been. It was the Jewish way to arrange marriages between children, but somehow, she had never supposed that her mother would do such a thing.

Angry color rushed back into Rebekah's cheeks, and she glared defiantly at her mother. "I can't!" Rebekah wailed. "I just can't! Mother, you don't understand."

The older woman met Rebekah's obstinate look with one of her own. "Jacob will provide for you, and he has insisted on providing for your sister and myself as well. We can't continue to live on the charity of others when there are so many in need."

Tirzah opened her mouth to protest, but her mother silenced her with a look and continued speaking. "Since we will be living with Jacob and his family, I can sell this house and give you both a small dowry. I couldn't do that before because we needed somewhere to live, but now that has been taken care of."

Rebekah's breast rapidly rose and fell in her agitation. Tirzah could see the storm coming and tried to prevent it. "Can't we talk about this, Mother?"

The older woman turned to her with a look Tirzah recognized all too well. Her mother expected obedience. Tirzah closed her mouth on further words.

"It is settled." Mother's voice was inflexible, and both girls knew that there would be no swaying her.

Rebekah jumped to her feet, her hands clenching into fists at her side. "I won't do it! I won't! You can't make me. I don't love Jacob."

Her mother sighed again, her eyes once more pleading. "You will learn to love him."

"Like you never did with father?" Rebekah asked bitterly.

Tirzah drew in a sharp breath. Before she could speak, her mother answered in a soft voice. "I loved your father in my own way. He was a good man."

Tears shimmered in Rebekah's eyes, her beautiful face filled with hurt and anxiety. "I want more than that! Don't you see?"

Tirzah held out her hand, wishing to comfort her sister, but Rebekah ran from their small home, leaving the door open behind her.

Tirzah glanced at her mother and noticed that though her chin was set stubbornly, her shoulders sagged as with some great weight. Getting to her feet, she followed Tirzah from their home into the darkening evening.

Tirzah found Rebekah huddled on the ground beside the stone cistern. She was rocking back and forth, and Tirzah could hear her quiet words escaping through her gentle sobs. "Lord Jesus, help me."

Tirzah settled herself next to her sister but refrained from touching her. Instead, she pulled her legs up to her chest, wrapping her arms around them. Lifting her face to the darkening sky, she fixed her gaze on a single star.

"She only wants what's best for us, you know."

A soft snort was her only answer.

Tirzah glanced at Rebekah's tear-laden face. "You know it's true."

Rebekah buried her face in her hands. "Oh, what am I

going to do? I can't marry Jacob. I just can't!"

"You once said that you loved him," Tirzah reminded her.

Rebekah glared at her sister through the gloom. Only the light of their single lamp, spilling through the open door of their home, allowed them any vision at all.

"I was a child! I did not know what love was until I met Domitus."

"How do you know that's love?" Tirzah rebutted. "You thought the same of Jacob just a short time ago."

Rebekah didn't answer for a long time. She sighed sadly. "I just know, that's all."

Tirzah clasped her sister's hand with her own, squeezing reassuringly. "You told me just today that you were going to give him up. Was that a lie?"

Biting her bottom lip, Rebekah pushed her palm against her forehead. "No! I mean, I don't know. I didn't mean for it to be."

Tirzah turned fully toward her sister, clasping her other hand that lay limply at her side. She shook her sister's hands gently. "Nothing has changed, Rebekah. Domitus is not a believer, and Jacob at least is. If you disobey the Lord's teachings and join yourself to an unbeliever, it will only cause you pain. The Lord doesn't want that for you."

Rebekah jerked her hands away. "Then why do I feel such pain right now?" she rasped. "How can it hurt to love like this?"

Frustrated, Tirzah shook her head slowly. "If this love was from God, you would not be in such pain. Rebekah, when we are in God's will, we are at peace and feel content."

"Will you still say that if Mother chooses a husband for you?"

Tirzah watched her sister's trembling lip and had nothing to say.

"I just don't know what to do," Rebekah said softly.

Tirzah noticed that her sister's tears had dried and would have offered a suggestion, but just then their mother's shadow crossed the threshold, and she called out to them softly. The two sisters rose, dusted off their garments, and walked back to the home in silence. Rebekah passed their mother without looking at her, going to her mat and curling into a ball. Her very posture spoke volumes.

Martha looked at Tirzah, her eyes pleading for understanding. Smiling slightly, Tirzah kissed her mother's cheek and retired to her own mat. Blowing out the lamp, their mother joined them. The silence was almost deafening.

Gallius strode along at his brother's side, fully aware of Domitus's anxious expectation. His own mind rushed madly about, trying to decide what course of action would best prevent his brother from doing something rash.

The sun was already intense, though it was only a few hours past sunrise. It was going to be a scorching day.

Although Domitus was not in uniform, Gallius was. The leather of his chest piece creaked with his movements, and the perspiration running in rivulets down his back and darkening his blood red tunic made him begin to regret his decision to dress so.

Domitus walked in silence, and Gallius followed where he led without interrupting his brother's thoughts. They had journeyed some distance from the Antonia fortress, the military garrison in Jerusalem where they lived, to the lower section of the city, where the poorer of the Jews resided.

Gallius glanced about him uncertainly, wishing the coming ordeal was already over. He would rather face an army in battle than a band of zealous Jews on the verge of rebellion. At least in battle one knew what to expect. In these Jerusalem crowds, sicarii assassins moved and struck without warning. The sicarii were notorious for their hatred of Romans, and they were expert at using their long knives to dispatch Romans and Roman sympathizers to the netherworld. They hid in the crowds, struck, and moved on before anyone was aware of what had happened.

Gallius breathed a sigh of relief when they exited the Essenes Gate and left the city behind, but his expression soon changed to a frown as he wondered just where his brother was leading him. "Where are we going?"

"Not far now," Domitus said without breaking stride.

Before long they entered a small stand of cypress trees just a short distance outside the city's walls. Other than the chittering of birds perched among the branches of the trees, absolute quiet reigned in the small glade. The sudden coolness of the shade was a relief after the long walk in the hot sun. Gallius relaxed slightly while breathing in the scent of evergreens, his eyes scanning the area briefly.

"This is nice," he told his brother in surprise.

Domitus nodded briefly, his gaze fixed on the road they had just traversed. Gallius settled himself on a log from a fallen cypress, wondering what would happen next. He hadn't long to find out. Voices could be heard coming up the path. Women's voices. Gallius noticed his brother tense.

"She's not alone," Domitus said softly.

It was only a moment before two women came into view. Gallius caught his breath at the perfection of the one in the lead. Rarely had he seen such a beauty, even among all his travels over the empire. Though her hair was covered by her shawl, her face glowed with youthful luminosity.

The other girl followed her into view, and Gallius had no doubt which one his brother had set his affections on. This girl was neither beautiful nor vivacious. She exuded a gentle serenity that instantly caught Gallius's attention.

The first girl hesitantly made her way to Domitus's side. He glanced at her briefly, then beyond to the other girl, his lifted brows asking a question.

"Domitus," the girl said softly, and it was like hearing the chiming of soft bells. "This is my sister, Tirzah."

Domitus barely nodded the other girl's way before fixing his attention on the woman before him. They carried on a soft conversation that Gallius couldn't hear, but there was no disguising the intensity between them.

Curious in spite of himself, Gallius allowed his gaze to roam over Tirzah, who stood watching the scene intently. There was something vaguely familiar about the girl, and he tried to remember where he might have seen her. Of course, having been in Jerusalem for more than a year, he had probably seen her among the crowds. Though not lovely, she had a face one would remember.

She met his look, her eyes brown pools of still water. His own eyes widened with swift recognition. Those unearthly eyes had haunted his memories. When he had first reached Jerusalem leading a troop of soldiers, he had had to interrupt a rather loud discussion between two Jews who showed every sign of turning to violence. This woman had been trying to intervene and had been thrown to the ground. After effectively dispatching the perpetrators and the swelling crowd of angry dissidents, he had helped her to her feet only to be met by those dark orbs full of uncertainty and some inner secret he felt drawn to. Many nights those eyes had tormented his dreams.

A flicker of awareness reached out to him from the depths of her eyes. It was some time before either could look away, and Gallius was surprised to find his heart rate accelerating and his breathing quickening.

Domitus's angry voice intruded into his thoughts.

"You can't mean it," Domitus choked. He reached forward, taking Rebekah by the shoulders. His fingers dug into her. "Why? You said you loved me." His eyes glittered with frustration. "I want to marry you!"

Tears sprung to Rebekah's eyes. She glanced over her shoulder at her sister, who nodded her head slightly. Swallowing hard, Rebekah looked at Domitus with eyes that begged his understanding.

"I. . .my mother has promised me to another."

Domitus's eyes widened. His grip hardened, but he quickly released Rebekah when she winced. Stepping back, he shook his head slightly. "You can't," he denied hoarsely. "You love me!"

Rebekah began backing away, her gaze never leaving his face. "I can't marry you," she said softly, tears clogging her throat.

When she turned to leave, Domitus stepped forward, intent on stopping her. Tirzah stepped between them. Her eyes were no longer so peaceful. They blazed with determination. "Rebekah has told you her decision."

Domitus glared at her, his dark eyes flashing a warning. "Get out of my way," he gritted.

Gallius thought it time to intervene. His brother looked ready to kill, and the Jewess looked like a she-bear ready to defend her cub to the death.

"Domitus."

The young man looked back at him.

"She has made her decision. If her mother has promised her to another, then by Jewish law it is the same as if she were already married."

Tirzah glanced at him sharply, obviously surprised that he should know something of their law. Frustration flowed from Domitus as he glared from one to the other. He looked past Tirzah's shoulder to where Rebekah stood at the edge of the wood.

"You told me that you wanted to marry me," he told her bitterly.

"Sometimes, we can't always have what we want," Gallius interrupted smoothly. He placed a hand on his brother's shoulder, squeezing a warning. All he needed right now was another reason for these Jews to be angry at the Romans. "Don't make a scene."

Domitus looked at each person there before pushing past Tirzah. He stopped beside Rebekah, staring for a long moment into her anguished eyes. "This isn't over yet," he warned ominously. Turning, he strode away.

For several seconds no one moved. Rebekah focused tear-laden eyes on her sister, her abject misery apparent to all.

Gallius felt a moment's pity for the girl. He glanced at Tirzah, and although she still looked composed and cool, her eyes revealed her feelings. She shared in her sister's misery.

As though she felt him looking at her, she turned, and as before, it seemed an eternity that they stared at one another before Tirzah went to her sister and, placing her arm around her, led her from the woods. Gallius stared after them for some time, his heart slowing to a steady beat. He had the oddest sensation that something monumental had just transpired.

Chapter 3

Tirzah took the basket from Jacob and set it on the table, trying not to look him in the eye. She had wondered what had sent Rebekah flying from the home and down the path behind their house. Rebekah had been avoiding Jacob for three days now, ever since their encounter with Domitus.

"Is Rebekah here, Tirzah?" Jacob asked anxiously.

Tirzah shook her head, angry with her sister for putting her in such a position. "No, Jacob. She left a short time ago."

Disappointment flooded his features. Shrugging wryly, he stood aside while she emptied the basket given to all the widows in the city by the deacons in the church. It would have been hard to survive without the support, but Tirzah was all too aware of her mother's increasing desire to no longer need such help, especially with so many families suffering from the famine.

Jacob's brown eyes glittered with excitement. "I am so pleased that your mother has consented to mine and Rebekah's marriage. I want you to know that it will be my pleasure to care for all of you until such time as you. . ."

He hesitated, and Tirzah tried not to smile. She placed the flat loaves of bread on a plate and glanced at him briefly.

"Until I marry?" she questioned. "That could be a very long time, Jacob. I'm well aware that I am a plain woman with no dowry."

His face flushed with color. "I did not mean. . ."

She smiled reassuringly. "It's all right, Jacob. I understand."

He reached into the basket, lifting out a sack of dried lentils. Tilting his head to one side, he studied her seriously.

"You are not so plain as all that," he observed, his honesty making Tirzah flinch. "And when your mother sells this place," he added, motioning around the home, "then you will have some dowry." He smiled at her, a kind, gentle smile. "A man would be fortunate to have you for a wife."

For some reason, his words brought an image of Gallius's face to Tirzah's mind. He had been in her thoughts often the last few days, causing her no end of frustration. She finished emptying the basket of the dried figs, olive oil, fresh fruits, and vegetables, then returned the container to Jacob, laying a palm gently against his cheek.

"You would have made a fine brother," she told him softly, appreciating his attempt at kindness, and he flushed lightly. "I will tell Rebekah that you came by."

He nodded, his face once more serious. "I want to set a date for our wedding, but she seems to be avoiding me."

Rearranging the fruit on the platter, Tirzah once again avoided eye contact. "I'm sure you will see her tomorrow night."

"I look forward to it." Glancing at the descending sun, he told her, "I must hurry. Sabbath will begin soon. Shalom."

Tirzah watched him walk down the path away from their home. Once he was out of sight, she lifted her shawl from the peg by the door and hurried to the marketplace. She hadn't much time before Sabbath, and she needed to find her sister.

Tirzah wandered through the market streets, becoming more anxious as time passed. Already most of the shops had closed for the night, preparing for the Sabbath rest. She was about to give up and return home when someone touched her shoulder. Whirling around in surprise, she clutched her tunic over her chest where her heart was thudding with fright.

Because Gallius wasn't in his Roman uniform, it took Tirzah a moment to identify him. She had recognized him in the wood as the soldier who had stopped the fight that had been brewing between Jacob and a man who was a devout Pharisee. That day had been imbedded in her memory for all time. When Gallius had looked into her eyes and asked her if she was hurt and she had lifted her gaze to his, something had passed between them that had left her shaken to the core. Something unexplainable that she had been afraid of even as she had been irresistibly drawn to it.

"I was hoping you would come here today," he told her without preamble, interrupting her thoughts. Her heart gave a slight thump in response to his words. "I have been waiting here most of the day so that I could see you." A sheen of perspiration from the intense heat shimmered on his bronze skin, and his dark hair clung damply to his temples. "I would like to talk to you, but I didn't know how to find you."

"You wanted to speak to me?" Her voice squeaked with surprise. His grave face seemingly carved of stone made Tirzah suddenly uneasy with mistrust.

Gallius's dark gaze fastened on her briefly before he quickly scanned the area. Noting the suspicious stares from those around them, he practically growled at Tirzah. "Is there somewhere we can go and talk?"

Tirzah followed his look, noticing the disapproving stares

she was receiving from the few remaining vendors. For a Jewish woman to talk to a strange man in public was improper, but to do so with a Roman was even worse. And despite Gallius's clothing, he was obviously Roman. His clean-shaven face stood in stark contrast to those around him, not to mention his considerable height. To be in the Roman legion, a man had to be a certain height, and Gallius far exceeded that standard.

She wasn't certain what he wanted, but the lengthening shadows warned her not to tarry. "I have to go home," she told him finally, hoping to discourage him. "It is almost time for Sabbath to begin."

Frowning, Gallius glanced at her again. He had lived in this wretched city long enough to know what that meant. There would be little for his troops to worry about tomorrow with these devout Jews in their temple and synagogues, not straying far from their homes in case they might desecrate the distance allotted by their prophets from old. "Have you far to go?"

She shook her head. "No, not far."

His face cleared. "Then I will walk with you." Taking her by the arm, he began retracing the path Tirzah had trod earlier. He allowed her to pull her arm from his grasp, grinning slightly at her obvious attempt to distance herself from him.

"You wanted to talk to me?" she questioned again. Her initial fright had given way to curiosity, and Tirzah studied the Roman discreetly. He was definitely handsome, enough to turn any girl's head, but he had an air about him that made Tirzah extremely uncomfortable.

"My brother hasn't eaten in three days," he told her without preamble, his voice filled with worry. "I'm beginning to be very concerned about him."

Tirzah sighed. "It has been the same with my sister," she

told him, gnawing on the corner of her lip in vexation.

He glanced at her briefly. "I had wondered." He took a deep breath. "I'm afraid that this time my brother is serious."

Tirzah stopped, and he turned to her in question.

She shook her head. "This cannot be. Rebekah is already promised to another, and if Domitus continues his pursuit of her, Rebekah could be accused of adultery."

"They aren't married yet," he said, a slight smile turning the corners of his lips.

Tirzah blinked her eyes against her growing anger. The Roman was mocking her. "I think you understand more of our laws than that. You already told your brother that her engagement was the same as marriage."

"According to your Jewish laws, but my brother is Roman, and despite what your people might wish, so is Judea." The arrogance in his voice was apparent. "Your laws are nothing more than a form of religion that should be abolished. Love knows no religion. When a man and woman come together, God, any god, ceases to exist."

Tirzah's eyes darkened, her embarrassment acute at discussing such a personal topic. "That's not true! When a man and woman come together with the blessings of God, it is a sacred thing."

Gallius laughed harshly, his eyes narrowing as he once more let his look roam over her. She might not be beautiful, but she certainly had enough curves to tempt a man. And he was tempted, though for the life of him he couldn't explain why. Still, her innocence was obvious, especially since it was such a rare thing.

"Spoken like a true virgin." His voice dripped with sarcasm.

Heat flooded Tirzah's cheeks at his audacity. Although he

didn't touch her, she felt caressed by Gallius's slow-moving eyes. She pulled her shawl tighter around her, lifting her chin a notch. She shuddered at his predatory look.

"Spoken like a true Roman," she snapped back, mindless of the fact that he could have her arrested for such insolence. She knew that she should be afraid of this bold centurion, but she couldn't let such arrogance go unchecked. Angry words spilled from her lips before she thought of their possible consequences.

"In Rome," she asked hotly, "how many people die because of wasting diseases brought on by the attitudes toward love you just expressed? God commanded my people to join one man to one woman for life. That is the way of my people, and with such attitudes we have no such diseases."

Gallius jerked his head back, staring at her defiantly. He pulled her to a stop, holding her wrist firmly while he cupped her chin with his fingers and thumb and forced her to look into his eyes. His action startled her, her eyes growing large with sudden fear.

"You also have no life," he growled, allowing his thumb to caress her bottom lip. Reflexively, her lips parted at his touch, and he felt the blood course warmly through his veins at the innocent gesture. "Your life is full of nothing but laws that take all the enjoyment out of life."

Tirzah met his icy look with one of confusion. It was very hard to remember just what they had been talking about with him so near. Her unexpected feelings gave her more reason to fear that something he had said might just be true. Would God and His laws cease to exist for Rebekah when she was overwhelmed by her feelings for Domitus? Would she truly turn her back on God for the love of a man? To Tirzah, such an idea had always been incomprehensible, but that was before this moment. Realizing her own reaction to a man she hardly knew, she began to sympathize with her sister.

"Rebekah will never betray her God," she finally told him, the uncertainty in her voice obvious.

His dark look did little to reassure her. "We shall see."

The morning dawned bright and clear. Tirzah woke before the sun was up, lying still and listening to the sounds of Jerusalem once again stirring to life. Today would be quiet because it was the Sabbath. Most of the activity would be centered around the temple and the various synagogues.

She lay thinking over the conversation she had had with Gallius the day before. His assessing gaze had left her frightened, not so much by him as by her own reaction. Ever since, there had been little else on her mind.

Aggravated with herself, she pushed such thoughts from her mind and concentrated on the day before her. The Sabbath. Special to God's chosen people. How was it that the Gentile Christians couldn't see that? It had sparked more than a little controversy between the two groups over the intervening years since the Lord's death.

As the sun penetrated the gloom of the interior of their house, both Tirzah's mother and Rebekah began to rouse. Tirzah shook herself. It was past time to get up and about the business of the day.

After the three women had eaten a cold, quiet breakfast of bread and dates, Rebekah surprised them with the news that she was going to take a walk. Her flashing eyes did little to encourage a debate on the matter.

Mother eyed the girl sternly. "You must not break the Sabbath."

"I won't. I don't intend to go far, but I would like some fresh air."

Both Tirzah and her mother glanced at Rebekah suspiciously but said nothing. There was very little fresh air to be had inside this crowded part of the city. They watched her leave, both quiet with their own thoughts. After Rebekah left, they sat down together, as was their custom, and talked quietly. By mutual consent they avoided the topic of Rebekah's marriage.

Hours slipped by before Rebekah returned home. When she came in, her cheeks were flushed with color, her brown eyes glowing with some inner secret. Although their mother, after taking one look at her youngest daughter, held her tongue, Tirzah did not. As soon as the older woman left the room to get some water from the jug outside the door, Tirzah hissed at her sister, "Where have you been, Rebekah?"

"I have been enjoying the sunshine. That's all."

Tirzah knew she should take warning from the look Rebekah gave her, but Gallius's words hung heavy in her mind, and Tirzah could not let the matter drop. "Where have you been?" she asked again, insistently.

Rebekah's eyes darkened. "Have you then become my mother?"

Before Tirzah could answer, their mother returned. She looked from one daughter to the other, anger still evident by her posture. That she was still upset over Rebekah's refusal to consider Jacob as husband was very clear. Tirzah bit her lip, wondering who would win this battle of wills. Perhaps she should be saying a few prayers on her own behalf because, if her mother had chosen a husband for Rebekah, might she not also have someone in mind for Tirzah? The thought unsettled her.

"It is almost time to go to Ephraim's house for the evening meal," Mother announced. "Sabbath will soon be over. Get yourselves ready."

Rebekah and Tirzah hurried to obey. While Rebekah pulled her shawl over her head, Tirzah prepared the lamp they would carry with them. Although the olive oil was precious, fellowshiping with other believers made its use a necessity. They couldn't travel until after the Sabbath, and it would be dark before they were halfway to Ephraim's home.

The triple blast from the shofar's horn blown by the hazan standing on the roof of the stone mason's synagogue announced the ending of Sabbath, and the three women made their way through streets dimly lit by the band of fading twilight. Other friends met them along the way, and their group had become a small party by the time they presented themselves at Ephraim's house. Ephraim was one of the wealthier Christian Jews in the city, and he shared his home and food as often as possible.

Inside, others had already arrived. The chatter was quiet as brothers and sisters in the Way visited together, sharing their worries and joys. Though the gathering was joyful, fear of others who were not of the Way hung heavy in the air. Persecution from other Jews had become intense over the last several months.

Ephraim led the group in the worship service. He began by asking them to recite with him the prayer given to the apostles by the Lord Himself. The words brought a worshipful expectation to the gathered crowd.

Jacob was late in arriving, causing a slight stir when he entered. Ephraim waited until Jacob was seated, then rose to his feet and addressed the small crowd.

"Brothers and sisters, before we partake of the supper in

remembrance of our Lord, I wanted to introduce you to a fellow believer who is now living with me." He motioned to the man at his feet. The other man shifted uncomfortably under such close scrutiny. His golden hair and clean-shaven face told the rest of the group that the man was a Gentile.

"This is Demas. He was living in Rome when Caligula had all the Jews expelled. Demas is a Greek who has found the way of the Lord."

A sudden murmuring rose from the gathered crowd at this news. Although the apostles Paul and Peter had long ago settled the matter of Jewish Christians worshiping and eating with Gentiles, many were still uncomfortable doing so. It was the one issue that still caused much unrest between Jewish and Gentile believers, this matter of the old law and a new one. Most of the Christian Jews in Jerusalem refused to give up their old ways, even after receiving instructions from the Jerusalem Council. Usually the Gentile Christians worshiped on their own.

Ephraim continued. "Demas was at one time an idol maker." The murmurs grew into loud whispers. Dark looks were thrown the Greek's way, but Ephraim hushed them to silence. "Many of you know that for an artisan to be admitted to a guild is a high honor. Many of you also know that to attain that goal, an artisan must first produce a masterpiece for his craft." He lifted a silver chalice from the table and held it aloft for their inspection. It gleamed brightly in the glow from the oil lamps.

"At one time," Ephraim told them, "this goblet was a silver idol of the god Jupiter."

Angry voices rose loudly, and Ephraim had a hard time hushing them to silence. He glared around the room. "Look to yourselves and see if you find perfection. How many of you were in the crowd that called for the Lord's death so many years ago? How many of you have denied Jehovah's Son and cursed Him with your own lips? You think Demas's sin is any greater?"

Those in the room exchanged quick, guilty looks before closing their mouths against further insults.

Ephraim fixed his look on Tirzah, and she quailed under the weight of his questions. His stern gaze passed on to others, and they must have felt the same. They squirmed under his regard. He lifted the cup again.

"Demas created a masterpiece that he was offered a fortune for. Instead, after he came to know our Lord, he melted that idol and fashioned this cup in honor of Him. The craftsmanship is exquisite, and Demas cannot be faulted for his earlier ignorance. He offered this cup to us for use when we drink the wine to remember our Lord."

Skeptical brows lifted around the room, but no more voices interrupted Ephraim. Instead, a hushed expectancy hovered over the crowd.

"Demas crafted words on the cup that we can all understand. He wrote them in Hebrew, in honor of our Jewish heritage. It reads, 'I will pour out my blood for you.' " Ephraim smiled sadly. "I believe we can all understand the significance of that."

Tears came to Tirzah's eyes. She glanced at Rebekah and was surprised by her sister's demeanor. Fear radiated from her eyes when they turned Tirzah's way. Tirzah opened her mouth to say something, but Rebekah turned quickly away.

Ephraim's voice interrupted her thoughts. "Let us first give thanks for the bread that represents His body. One day, we will partake of this with Him in heaven itself."

After asking a blessing, Ephraim passed the plate of bread. Everyone took a small section and ate, bowing their heads in reverence.

Ephraim did the same with the cup. It took longer than usual to receive the wine because everyone wanted to study the chalice.

When it finally reached Tirzah, she was no exception. Ephraim was certainly right. The craftsmanship was exquisite. Curling branches of thorns wove around the outside of the cup, and a flowing river sprang from the thorns, winding around the Hebrew words.

Tirzah understood the significance. The blood flowed from the thorns that had been placed upon her Lord's head. Those thorns represented sin, and only the Lord's own blood could take away that sin. She felt a great lump in her throat. The Lord had given His life for her. What had she ever done for Him? Would she be willing to pour out her life for anyone, much less an ungrateful world?

Pictures of Domitus and Gallius flashed through her mind. She was suddenly ashamed that she had looked down upon them because they didn't share her belief. Instead of reaching out as the apostle Paul had done to the Gentiles, she had only scorned them for their false beliefs. As she thought of her conversation with Gallius the day before, her heart felt heavy. In her arrogance, had she condemned them to the flames of Gehenna? Had she condemned herself?

Chapter 4

For the next several weeks, Rebekah went silently about her business, treating her worried family to sudden fits of tears and unexpected bouts of joy. Both Tirzah and her mother were confused by Rebekah's unusual behavior and more than a little concerned.

Tirzah suspected that Rebekah was still seeing Domitus, but she had no proof. Sometimes after Rebekah disappeared for awhile, she would return to the house elated, her eyes bright with some hidden secret. Tirzah had thought about following her younger sister one day, but that seemed an underhanded thing to do. Instead, she continued to pray that God would turn Rebekah's heart toward Jacob once again.

Since the meeting at the market, Tirzah often caught herself looking for Gallius among the crowded streets of Jerusalem. When she saw him, he was usually looming over the crowds, his Roman appearance making him stand out even when not in uniform. Each time she saw him, her heart seemed to skip a beat, and it bothered her that she was no more immune from his handsome presence than any other young woman might have been. She realized her folly in allowing her thoughts to dwell on the Roman at all, but daily her sympathy for her sister's plight grew. No matter how much Tirzah chastised herself, like her sister she seemed to be helplessly drawn to a Roman.

As Gallius strode through the crowded, noisy streets of Jerusalem, his alert eyes searched among the throngs for a woman with dark solemn eyes. He wasn't quite certain why he sought her, but he couldn't seem to keep his eyes from scanning the area around him. When he did spot her, she was usually hurrying away from his vicinity, but he knew it was her by the way she gracefully glided along the street even in her worn, homespun dress. She moved as though she were royalty.

He was increasingly filled with a desire to seek her out and get to know her. He tried to shake such thoughts away, knowing the futility of associating with a Jew, but they refused to be displaced. Perhaps he had been too long without a woman, but the thought of seeking out one of the women of the streets didn't appeal to him. He simply couldn't get Tirzah's gentle, innocent face out of his mind.

So it didn't surprise him when he came upon her suddenly one day as he strolled through the market in the lower section of the city. In truth, he had probably unknowingly been loitering in the area for just such a chance.

She had just exited a small house, turning to talk to someone inside who was hidden from Gallius's view. The door closed behind her, and when she turned around, she saw him. She stopped in her tracks, her eyes widening with surprise. Something flickered briefly in their dark depths, and Gallius felt himself quickly respond to the change.

He had just started across the street toward her when he noticed movement above on one of the building parapets. In a flash his mind recognized the danger to Tirzah, and he instinctively gauged the distance between them. For a moment, the blood seemed to freeze in his veins. He plunged across the street, wrapping his arms around Tirzah and shoving her back into the doorway from where she had just exited. He heard the slight whoosh of breath as his body pushed hers into the wooden portal.

A loud crash sounded behind them as a large clay urn smashed into hundreds of pieces where Tirzah had just been standing.

Gallius loosened his hold slightly, his heart thudding like a war drum within him. His searching look met Tirzah's wide, terrified eyes, and his voice came out more harshly than he intended. "Are you all right?"

She stood trembling like a leaf in his arms. Before she could answer, the door opened behind them, and if not for Gallius's quick reflexes, both he and Tirzah would have plunged into the owner's house.

Ephraim stared from one to the other, his mouth opening slightly when he noticed Tirzah still wrapped loosely in Gallius's arms.

"Tirzah?" the old man questioned, his look fixed suspiciously on Gallius. "I thought I heard a noise."

Gallius pushed Tirzah to the side. "You did, old man," he fairly growled, his eyes flashing with fury. He flung himself back out toward the street, hurrying toward the steps on the side of the house that led to the roof.

Ephraim noticed the smashed urn in front of his door. He lifted horrified eyes to Tirzah. "What happened?"

Still shaking, Tirzah shook her head slowly, her mind still

in a fog. If not for Gallius, she would be dead. Crushed beneath that shattered pottery.

Gallius returned quickly, his shadow preceding him into the room. He grabbed Ephraim by the front of his tunic, lifting him from the floor. "You tried to have Tirzah killed!"

The words spoken so coldly deprived both Ephraim and Tirzah of speech. Tirzah looked at the old man in alarm. Her voice was a horrified whisper.

"Oh, Ephraim. They thought I was you!" She pulled ineffectively at Gallius's clenched fingers. "Let him go! It's not what you think."

Ephraim shook his head slightly, giving Tirzah a warning glance. Gallius didn't miss the look that flashed between the two, and he slowly loosened his hold, dropping his hands to his sides.

Ephraim straightened his clothes, giving Gallius a small smile, although there was no warmth in the gesture. "I am certain it was but an accident. Yet I can never repay you for saving Tirzah's life. I owe you a great debt."

The cold look Gallius bestowed on him made Ephraim flinch slightly. In his anger, Gallius looked even larger than before. "Save your thanks, old man," he ground out. "It's answers I want."

Ephraim looked innocently back at him, shrugging his shoulders slightly. He held out his hands. "I am not certain that I can give you any. What can I say? An accident is an accident."

Gallius fixed his glacial look on Tirzah, and she shuddered. "That was no accident. Someone tried to kill you," he hissed. "That pot was too heavy to fall of its own accord."

Tirzah's face blanched even further. She glanced toward Ephraim before she turned her attention to the ground. Gallius realized that neither Jew would say anything more about the incident. There was an undercurrent of tension running throughout this city that would doubtless one day tear it apart—something to do with Jews and some others called Christians. He would have to investigate this further. Perhaps Tirzah would be more forthcoming if he got her by herself.

"I will walk you home," he told her flatly.

Tirzah knew by the sound of his voice that there would be no gainsaying him. "Have a care!" she warned the old man softly. With one last look at Ephraim's anxious face, she fell into step beside Gallius. Reluctant to allow him to see the expressions on her face, she pulled her shawl closer about her.

The attack on Ephraim had to have been perpetrated by the Zealots. There was no other explanation for it, and if the Zealots were trying to kill him, then the sicarii wouldn't be far behind, and they were far more lethal.

It was obvious that the Zealots were trying to increase animosity between the Hebrew Jews and the Christian Jews. The fact that Ephraim had a Gentile living in his home, and one who had been an idol maker at that, had probably caused them to direct their attack toward him—that and the fact that he was one of the respected leaders of the church in Jerusalem.

Her troubling thoughts were interrupted by Gallius.

"So," he asked quietly, "was it you or the old man who was the target of that assassination attempt?"

Her gaze swept up, only to be caught by his intense look. What did she see in his eyes? Fear? Anger?

"I owe you my life," she answered softly.

"That doesn't answer my question," Gallius said, feeling totally frustrated. He pulled her to a stop and stood staring down at her. She could very well have died from that "accident."

The thought made his insides go cold. He reached out, allowing his fingers to slide down her cheek, to feel the warmth of her. To know that she was truly alive and well.

He saw the response to his touch in the darkening of her pupils, and he felt his blood begin to heat. It amazed him, this reaction he had to this one woman. He must protect himself from such feelings.

"I will find out, you know," he told her, a dark challenge in his eyes.

He left her at the door to her house, striding away with purposeful intent. Tirzah watched him go, her heart sinking with each step he took. She had no doubt that he would find out the true cause of the accident. What would he do when he found out that they were all Christians? She would be hard pressed to decide which group Romans hated more, Jews or Christians. Somehow, for all their sakes, she had to stop her feelings for this Roman centurion from escalating, but unfortunately, she was not certain how to go about such a task.

Chapter 5

When Tirzah and her mother arose the next morning, Rebekah had already gone from the house. The two exchanged worried glances but said nothing about the absence.

Jacob came with his daily allotment of goat's milk for them, leaving dejectedly when he realized that Rebekah wasn't home. Tirzah's eyes followed his progress down the street with sympathy. She shook her head slightly, turning back to meet her mother's angry frown.

"Jacob will give up on her if she continues in this nonsense," the older woman stated, her irritation evident. Tirzah said nothing. What was there to say?

After her mother left to make her rounds of the ill, Tirzah, feeling restless, decided to go to the temple. Many of her friends met there each day, for it had become a gathering place of sorts, and she suddenly desired company. Perhaps Rebekah would be there, and they could talk.

Before she could reach the precincts of the temple, however, Tirzah was halted by an angry mob. The crowd was so large that there was no hope of making her way through it, even if she had wanted to, and with the shouting going on around her, she hesitated to continue in any event.

Roman troops appeared suddenly, shoving their way through the crowd with their shields, their spears effectively clearing a path for them. Tirzah recognized Gallius among them. He muscled his way toward a man being swarmed by the angry crowd. The man was being beaten mercilessly by the frenzied mob. Gallius cleared the people out of his path as though they were mere insects. He lifted the beaten man to his feet, and the man held out his hands in entreaty.

Tirzah drew in a shocked breath. She remembered the apostle Paul from the times he had come to speak with the body of believers that met at Ephraim's house. She hadn't heard that he was in Jerusalem.

The commander of the garrison joined them, and Tirzah watched as more words were exchanged. Paul was speaking with the commander, but the noise around her deafened her to their words. She watched a soldier bind Paul, and then, acting as a body shield, the troops moved with their prisoner toward the Antonia fortress. Tirzah was swept along with the crowd, her body aching from the prodding and jostling.

The crowd kept shouting, "Away with him! Away with him!"

When the soldiers were about to take Paul into the barracks, he said something to the commander who, after a moment of staring at Paul intently, finally jerked his head in affirmation. Paul addressed the crowd in Aramaic, and they instantly quieted.

Looking down at the scene from his unusual height, Gallius tensely scanned the crowd, ready for any further attacks. Among the hundreds of angry people surrounding him, one pair of dark eyes caught his attention. He identified Tirzah instantly, wondering what had brought her to be part of this mob. They stared at each other for some time before he finally forced his gaze to move on, searching the angry crush of people before him.

He didn't hear the prisoner's last words, but they brought a furious reaction from the already volatile crowd. People shouted and threw off their cloaks, flinging dust in the air. Gallius began to choke on the storm of flying sand.

"Rid the earth of him!" some people yelled. Others screamed, "He's not fit to live!"

Gallius stiffened, preparing for another onslaught. The commander yelled to the soldier next to him, "Take him inside!"

Although Paul disappeared inside the barracks and the gates were effectively shut behind him, it was some time before the crowd dispersed altogether. Roman troops stood ready, spears and swords glinting in the late morning sun.

Tirzah turned to move on with the still murmuring crowd, but Gallius stood in her path. His gaze moved over her quickly. "Are you all right?"

Remembering those same words from only days before, Tirzah flushed under his steady regard. Surprised at his concern, she nodded her head. "A little bruised, perhaps," she said wryly, "but other than that I'm fine." She glanced back at the fortress worriedly. "What will they do with him?"

Gallius shrugged, his eyes narrowing at the note of distress in her voice. "The commander has ordered him flogged and questioned to find out why the crowd wanted his blood so badly."

Tirzah weakened at the thought of Paul's coming interrogation. She offered up a swift, silent prayer for Paul's protection.

Feeling Gallius's gaze on her again, she reluctantly met his look. She wasn't certain what she saw in his searching eyes, but her heart started thrumming like a harp in response.

"Come," he told her, holding out his hand. "I will walk you home."

Sensing that he wanted to question her further, Tirzah hesitated. She ignored the hand, folding her hands behind her back. Chancing a quick glance at him, she saw his amused smile and knew that he had guessed correctly the reaction she had to him. Quickly looking away, she started back along the route she had come.

Gallius easily matched her stride. He tilted his head slightly, wondering what there was about this rather plain Jewish woman that so intrigued him. Her people were a blight on the earth—at least that's what he had always believed. But this one woman held intelligence in her large brown eyes, and when she smiled, she was completely unaware of how provocative the expression could be. Her eyes held an innocence that most men, most Roman men at least, would pay a fortune to sample. But there was something else. Something on the edge of his consciousness that he couldn't seem to draw into the light for further inspection.

"You know the man we arrested today?" he questioned.

He didn't miss the flicker of fear in her eyes.

"No. . .not personally."

Her reticence communicated more than the three words she spoke. Increasingly, Gallius was convinced that something was developing beneath the surface of everyday life in Jerusalem—and whatever that something was, he needed to understand it.

"Why were you at the temple today?" he asked, his narrowed gaze searching her face for answers.

She glanced at him, their gazes interlocking for several seconds. She tripped over a stone on the path, and Gallius reached out to steady her. Her warm skin against his rough palm brought unbidden thoughts to mind. Frowning, he quickly released her, though for a brief second he was tempted to do otherwise.

"I often go to the temple. Many of my friends go there as well. We sit and talk," Tirzah told him, her face reflecting her troubled thoughts. "I hoped to find Rebekah there." She paused and then told him quietly, "I'm sorry about your brother. I know Rebekah would never have done anything to deliberately hurt him. Is he. . .is he well?"

Gallius stiffened at her question. "I have yet to see him this day," he responded. "But lately he has been acting very strangely. I'm not certain what he is thinking."

His words had an unusual effect on Tirzah. She stopped abruptly, her face suddenly going pale.

Frowning, Gallius lifted a dark brow in inquiry. "What is it?"

Lips pressed tightly together, she turned away from him and hurried her steps onward. Catching up with her, Gallius abruptly pulled her to a stop, his grip gentle yet unyielding.

"What aren't you telling me?" he asked insistently.

Tirzah studied his unyielding stance and then stammered, "I. . .I'm not certain, but I haven't seen my sister today, either."

Gallius gritted his teeth. "It doesn't take much to guess that they are together, does it?"

"Perhaps not. Perhaps it is a mere coincidence."

"And perhaps the moon will be green tonight," he answered sarcastically. Heaving a sigh, he shoved his hand roughly back through his hair. "If he does something stupid, I will personally see him flogged," he gritted out angrily, frustration evident in his voice. He smiled wryly, taking the sting from his words. "I had better try to find him. Them," he corrected and saw the distress his words invoked. He thought of saying more, but closing his lips against the words, he told her softly, "I will tell you what I learn." Turning, he purposefully strode toward the barracks.

When Rebekah hadn't returned by late afternoon, Tirzah finally went to her mother and told her of her worry, but she kept silent about Domitus as she had promised. Though the two women could share their concerns, there was nothing they could do about the situation except hope that Rebekah would attend the meeting at Ephraim's home.

Each night, Ephraim opened his house to the believers, offering a meal that many could not afford on their own. Families already suffering from the famine faced further hardship because of being ostracized by other Jews for their Christian beliefs. Many Jews refused to do business with those of the Christian faith, causing the closure of many family-owned businesses. That was one reason Paul had come to Jerusalem, to bring contributions gathered from other believers. What amazed Tirzah was that most of those who had given to Paul were Gentiles.

Tirzah and her mother made their way to Ephraim's home together, partaking of the evening meal with other believers, but Tirzah's mind was far from those present. She leaned over to her mother. "Should we tell Jacob? Someone needs to search for her."

Her mother shook her head slightly. "No, we will wait a little longer. Perhaps she will be at home when we return."

After the meeting was over, the believers dispersed once

again to their own homes. Rebekah had not made it to the gathering, and Tirzah's heart hung heavy within her as she and her mother walked through the darkening streets. If Rebekah wasn't at home, Tirzah didn't know what she should do. Though it was possible that Rebekah was with Domitus somewhere, it was equally possible that something terrible had happened to her. They would have to tell Jacob.

When she and her mother reached their home, a lone figure stepped from the darkness startling them both. At first, Tirzah's heart lifted with hope, but just as suddenly, it plummeted to her toes as she recognized Gallius's tall figure.

Gallius barely glanced at Tirzah's mother before giving Tirzah his full attention. "May I speak with you?"

Tirzah ignored her mother's indignant gasp. She pushed her gently toward the door of their home, telling her reassuringly, "I will be in in a moment."

"Who is this man?" the older woman demanded, refusing to be budged.

Tirzah hadn't yet mentioned to her mother the possibility that Rebekah was with Domitus, and she somehow knew that what Gallius had to say would not be to her mother's liking. "Please, Mother."

Reluctantly, Tirzah's mother retreated into their home, but she left the door open behind her.

Gallius took Tirzah's arm and pulled her farther into the darkness. "Your sister? Is she not with you?"

Warned by his tone, she answered with a question of her own. "Domitus is still missing, is he not?"

Lamplight suddenly spilled out the open doorway, casting eerie shadows along the planes of Gallius's face. Tirzah saw a tick working in his cheek and knew that he was in a towering rage.

"I had hoped," he told her heavily, "that it wasn't true." He glanced down at her, trying to gauge her feelings. "I found a note from my brother saying that he was taking your sister and leaving for Rome."

He had to reach out to catch Tirzah as her legs buckled beneath her. He drew her close, lending support to her suddenly weakened limbs. She lifted a horrified gaze to his face.

"I can't believe it," she whispered. She closed her eyes tightly, hanging limply in his embrace. "Dear Jehovah, please, no."

Gallius shifted his hold, allowing her to sit on the ground. He settled himself next to her, one arm still around her shaking shoulders. Although he meant to comfort her, her nearness was having an unsettling affect on him.

When she opened her eyes and stared into his, he was suddenly lost in a world where the two of them were alone and everything else ceased to exist. He totally forgot his reasons for being there, aware only that her eyes held the secret to a peace he had long been searching for, a peace that the Pax Romana, the Roman peace, had failed to fulfill. He wanted to lose himself in the quiet, still waters of her gaze.

He allowed his fingers to rest lightly on her soft lips. He searched her face intently, frowning at his own reaction to her presence. "Tirzah?" What did he want to say? What could he say?

He wanted to kiss her, but he was afraid that once started he wouldn't be able to stop, so intense were the feelings flowing through him. Something of his thoughts must have been reflected in his eyes because Tirzah's eyes filled with panic, and she pulled back from him. Loath to do so, he slowly released her. His heart beat heavily. He turned away, taking a deep breath, his senses slowly returning to normal.

"I have to find them," he told her, his voice harsh. "If I

don't, my brother will be considered a deserter and will forfeit his life."

Tirzah barely registered his words. She was having a hard time concentrating when her thoughts were so scattered. She was frightened by all that this Roman represented, but she could not deny her strong attraction to him. At times, it was hard to ignore her body's traitorous reaction to his nearness. It was hard to remember why he was there in the first place. What he had just said finally penetrated her muddled thoughts, and she stared at him in horror. "And Rebekah?"

His forbidding look made her shiver. "You know your Jewish laws. You tell me."

Tirzah was offended by his patronizing tone, but what he said was true. Her sister could very well be stoned, maybe not by other believers, but surely by other Jews. The Sanhedrin would see to that, even though Roman law forbade such punishment. They would somehow find a way.

"I believe they might try to go to Caesarea," Gallius told her. "From there they would be able to get on a ship to Rome. Probably my brother intends to go to our estate there." His teeth gritted harshly. "The fool! Always impetuous. He can't have given this much thought."

"They were probably desperate," Tirzah said quietly, thinking of Rebekah's pain-filled eyes.

Gallius scowled at her, then noting the tears silently wending their way down her cheeks, he softened. He sighed heavily, watching her with mixed emotions. "Pray to your God that I find them before it's too late."

He lifted a hand and gently stroked her cheek. She was burned by his touch, and before she could pull away from him again, he closed his warm lips over hers.

"Goodnight," he told her softly, then quickly rose and walked away to be swallowed up by the night.

Gallius stood at attention before his commander, along with Antigonus, another centurion.

"Paul's nephew has warned me that there is a plot by some forty Jews to kill Paul before he can face their Sanhedrin," the commander told them. "I want you to get ready a detachment of two hundred soldiers, seventy horsemen, and two hundred spearmen to go to Caesarea at nine tonight. Provide mounts for Paul so that he may be taken safely to Governor Felix."

He handed Gallius a sealed scroll. "Give this to Governor Felix. It explains everything."

Gallius snapped a salute. "Aye, Commander."

As one, Antigonus and Gallius turned and left the room. Gallius left Antigonus to go his own way, thankful to the deities for allowing him to go to Caesarea. Perhaps he could find his brother before any harm was done. As long as Domitus wasn't late for duty, things would be fine for him. He frowned, stopping in the dimly lighted passage outside his bedchamber in the garrison. The same could not be said for the Jewess. If her people found out that she had gone away with a man, especially when she was betrothed to another, their teachings about purity would demand she pay for her folly.

He retrieved his gear and made his way to the courtyard. The troops looked fresh and ready, even after hours of drill, and they made an impressive sight. He felt a familiar thrill of pride in them. He mounted his horse, and they exited through the fortress gates and quickly made their way out of the city.

All along the way, Paul kept up a steady discourse on his

belief in his God until Gallius wanted to shout for him to be quiet. It surprised him that so many of his men seemed interested in what the man had to say, but then, there was something powerful in the words that he spoke. Gallius realized that even he was listening from time to time.

Could there really be only one God? And if so, why would His Son have to be used as a sacrifice to take away the sins of the world? Jewish ideas and Roman ideas of sin were far different. Yet something stirred in his soul as he listened to the heart-wrenching tale of the man called Jesus who died alone, buried in a borrowed tomb.

Gallius was suddenly less proud of the soldiers who had done their duty by hanging Jesus on a cross. That punishment was used only for the most nefarious of crimes, and what had the man Jesus truly done to deserve it? Crucifixion was so heinous a death that it was forbidden by Roman law for any Roman to be killed that way.

But this man Paul believed that Jesus rose from the dead. The thought made Gallius shudder. Surely Paul must be mad. Even his own people had turned against him. He remembered tales that he had heard about this man killing Christians with a zeal that most would admire, but overnight he had changed. What could possibly have wrought such a difference in any man's heart? Insanity? He pushed aside the thoughts and allowed his mind instead to think about Tirzah. Suddenly, he stiffened on his horse. Tirzah's concern over Paul. It suddenly made perfect sense. Tirzah was a Christian!

Chapter 6

When the group of soldiers reached Antipatris, they garrisoned for the night. Exhausted after their grueling trek, Gallius slept deeply, Antigonus snoring loudly beside him.

Early the next morning, the cavalry continued on, while Antigonus and the footmen returned to Jerusalem. Gallius and his troops kept up a hard pace until they arrived in Caesarea, thankful to reach their destination unhindered.

Gallius handed over the prisoner and his letter to the governor. For a moment, Paul's eyes met those of Gallius, and the Roman centurion felt drawn into their secret, fiery depths. Words that Paul had spoken sounded loudly in his head. *God loves all. His Son died for all, even the Gentiles.* Troubled, he turned away.

Released from his assignment by the governor, Gallius made his way through the city to the garrison. Since they had made steady progress, he was fairly certain that he had made it to Caesarea before Domitus would have been able to. Information he had received in Jerusalem told him that a caravan had left early the previous morning. He was fairly certain his brother had traveled with it.

After arranging for quarters at the garrison, Gallius left the military compound and wandered the streets of Caesarea, or Caesarea Maritima as it was known because of being a port city. Built by King Herod the Great less than seventy years earlier, the gleaming city was still fairly new by Judean standards. Here among the statues of the gods and goddesses Gallius should have felt right at home, but instead he felt oddly unsettled.

A notice painted on a wall informed him that there would be a chariot race that day at the Hippodrome. Normally he would have been thrilled to attend, but this day he hardly gave the notice a glance.

With massive shoulders set, he resolutely made his way to the harbor. He walked along the quay, taking note of arriving and departing ships. His alert eyes searched among the teeming throng for any sign of Domitus and Rebekah, though he doubted that they had had time to arrive.

He marked each ship that would sail in the next day or two and made his way to where the owners or captains were seeing to provisions. After talking with each and passing several coins their way, he felt fairly confident that if Domitus tried to book passage before the end of the week, he would be notified.

Gallius stopped for a moment, looking out over the beautiful, gleaming harbor. It truly was a remarkable feat of engineering, the manmade white walls glistening in the sun. In the distance, two giant towers marked the harbor's entrance. Even as he watched, one ship entered the tranquil waters, while another departed. He breathed deeply of the fresh, clean smell of the Mediterranean.

Barely avoiding a stevedore loading a basket of wool, he quickly moved out of the way of other workers moving large loads. He noticed a perfume merchant unloading supplies from the East, exotic spices to be made into expensive fragrances. What would it be like to have Tirzah at his side, wafting in a tide of spicy fragrance? Though the image left him breathing harder than normal, he still thought he much preferred her own natural, musky fragrance. She needed no artifice to stir his blood, especially after that kiss a few nights ago. Just the thought of her soft skin and luminous eyes made him warm all over.

Aggravated that he should have the woman so constantly on his mind, he withdrew from the quay. Feeling hungry, he decided to find a tavern and get himself a meal. Servants hustled about, serving the growing crowd of customers. Gallius found himself a seat at an empty table, but with the room growing more crowded, he soon had to share it with others.

A legionnaire chatted on about his assignment in the city, but Gallius barely heard him. His mind was on other things. He was still grappling with how he was going to be able to gloss over Rebekah's disappearance from Jerusalem without making her a target of Jewish religious zeal. Before Judea had come under direct Roman control, Jewish laws had been upheld even to the point of allowing executions for religious purposes. Though such executions were now forbidden by Roman law, sometimes zealous Jews overlooked the law for their own purposes. It was extremely hard to find the perpetrators in such instances—not that Roman authority particularly cared what happened to the Jews.

Still, Rebekah was Tirzah's sister and the object of his own brother's affection, and for those two very good reasons, he couldn't just stand by and watch her be murdered for the sake of purity.

His look wandered around the room and settled on a young slave girl, her Hebrew heritage apparent by her striped belt. He could have been looking at a younger version of Tirzah, and he found his mind wandering, filled with thoughts of the last time he had seen her.

Gallius barely touched the meal set before him, his appetite quickly diminishing. He suddenly wanted nothing more than to return to the wretched city of Jerusalem. He laughed harshly at the thought, causing the others around him to stare at him with open curiosity and some disquiet.

It didn't take much thought to realize what drew him back to that accursed city, and that knowledge didn't please him at all. He suddenly felt as though he no longer had control of his life. Angrily throwing a coin on the table, he got up and left.

When he entered the courtyard of the garrison, a soldier at the gate told him he was wanted by the garrison commander. Surprised, Gallius nodded and hastened to find the man.

He found the commander in the peristyle of the fortress, the coolness of the garden surrounding him as he made his way forward. The commander was reclining on a couch next to a marble fountain, his eyes closed. At Gallius's entrance, he lazily lifted his lids.

"Centurion Gallius," he greeted cordially.

Gallius slammed a fist against the left side of his chest in salute. "Commander."

The commander motioned for Gallius to have a seat beside him. "I understand you are returning to Jerusalem." At Gallius's confirmation of that fact, he continued. "I have a missive for you to deliver to the commander of the garrison in Jerusalem. It has to do with a certain group in that city that Emperor Nero has heard are plotting against his life."

Gallius almost snorted in disbelief but checked himself in time. The emperor Nero thought everyone was out to take his life. His paranoia would one day be his downfall. Already the people of Rome were beginning to grumble in protest of his blatant atrocities against those he suspected.

Pulling a scroll from his belt, the commander handed Gallius the message. "Give this to Commander Claudius Lysias. Tell him the emperor wants him to investigate, and if he finds it to be true, he wants these Christians eradicated. The commander will know best how to go about it."

At the word Christian, a cold vise seemed to clutch at Gallius's heart. His warm skin tingled as though it were being pelted by tiny crystals of ice. He opened his mouth to speak, but no words came forth. The commander continued.

"These Jews! Even here in the Roman capital of Judea where they are a minority, they are a nuisance. They are forever causing problems in the city with their confounded religious views."

He looked at Gallius, his expression puzzled. "Is something wrong, Centurion?"

Gallius shook his head. "No." He swallowed hard, staring at the scroll as though it were an asp about to strike. Forcing himself to take it, he placed it in his own belt. "When am I to leave?"

The commander waved his hand airily. "Take a day or two," he suggested magnanimously. "It's been a hard trek from Jerusalem, and I know how little that city offers in the way of entertainment." He lifted one eyebrow slightly, grinning slyly. "Enjoy yourself for a short time. I'm certain the Christian miscreants will do nothing and that it is just a rumor, but we must humor our emperor, mustn't we?"

Gallius forced himself to hide his feelings behind a bland mask. If this attitude was typical of feelings held by other leaders in Rome's army, what would happen to the great Roman Empire?

Two days later a young boy brought news that sent Gallius to the wharf. Although the quay was crowded, he had no trouble spotting Domitus arguing with a ship's captain. He crossed quickly to them.

Domitus glanced up impatiently, the expression on his face changing so quickly to consternation that it almost made Gallius laugh. Almost. The rage he was feeling, however, held supremacy.

"Come with me," he commanded, including Rebekah in his look. His voice held a note of authority that Domitus was quick to respond to, however reluctant he might feel. The ship's captain stared at them curiously as they walked away.

Silently, the two followed Gallius as he led them to the tavern he had visited previously. The young slave girl was there, moving quietly around the room, and Gallius found himself once again struck by her resemblance to Tirzah. The place was almost empty due to the early hour. Gallius seated himself at a table and motioned for Domitus and Rebekah to join him. He fixed his intense gaze on Domitus, and his silence spoke more eloquently than words.

Rebekah sat with bowed head while Domitus swallowed several times before speaking. "How did you know where to find us?" he finally managed.

Gallius glared at him several seconds before he answered. "Is that all you have to say?"

"Gallius, I—"

Slamming his fist on the table, Gallius exploded with anger. "You have done some foolish things in your time, but this borders on sheer lunacy! What? How?" He flung his hands in the air, suddenly bereft of words.

"We wanted to get married, and Rebekah's mother was going to make her marry another. I couldn't stand by and let that happen!" Domitus argued belligerently.

In a towering rage, Gallius bit out at him, "She is already betrothed, you fool. You have caused her to commit adultery. Do you have any idea what they will do to her for that? You call that love?"

Rebekah lifted a pale face, her eyes dark with despair and fear. "We did nothing wrong."

Gallius fixed his glare on her. "And do you think anyone will believe that?"

Rebekah flinched as though she had been struck. Domitus glared at his brother. "It's the truth!"

"I repeat," Gallius gritted. "Who do you think will believe such a thing? Would you?" Seeing the confusion on Rebekah's face, Gallius pressed his advantage. Holding her gaze, he asked, "You are willing to leave your mother, sister, faith, and home for a life of hardship?"

Domitus interrupted. "She will have everything I can give her. We aren't a poor people, Gallius, you know that. We can live in our villa in Rome. No one can touch her there."

Nostrils flaring, Gallius scowled at his brother. "Our villa? You will have nothing! The best that could happen to you for deserting your post would be receiving a dishonorable discharge and being expelled from Rome. The worst that could happen is that you would be executed. What will happen to Rebekah then?"

Domitus opened his mouth, then snapped it shut. He glanced at Rebekah, her white face partially hidden from view. Her hands, though clutched together in her lap, shook violently. He looked back at Gallius helplessly.

"To protect someone he loves, sometimes a man has to act without thinking," he said softly. "I hoped that you would speak to the general on my behalf. Fix things with him."

Not for the first time, Gallius had the urge to grab his brother and hurl him against a wall. How many times had he gotten Domitus out of trouble due to his impetuous ways? But this? This was well beyond anything his brother had done before.

Gallius's face felt set in stone as he replied, "I will do nothing of the sort. I don't intend to ruin my career because of my brother's stupidity. If you want to talk to General Galba, do so on your own. And you had better leave me out of it!" He glanced once more at Rebekah. "Your sister is very anxious about you. So is your mother."

She chewed on her bottom lip, then looked at him with huge, haunted eyes, her face a picture of remorse. She looked no more than a child, and Gallius had to pull on reserves of strength he didn't know he possessed to refuse the plea in her eyes.

"I'm taking you both back," he told them inflexibly.

Domitus came to his feet. "You can't! Do you know what they will do to Rebekah? They'll stone her to death!"

Gallius stared back at him impassively, though his stomach tightened within him. "It is against the law to kill someone without a trial. Roman law does not forbid adultery, and that is the law Judea is under. Desertion, on the other hand, is punishable by death. Does Rebekah wish that for you?"

In the end, there was no other option, and they all knew it. Traveling back to Jerusalem the next day, Gallius only hoped that this Judean God was a little more tolerant than His ardent people.

Chapter 7

Rebekah and Jacob stood before the priest, Rebekah's head bowed with respect. Jacob's face seemed etched in granite, and never had Tirzah seen anyone look so betrayed.

The priest addressed Jacob. "And you, Jacob. What do you wish to do?"

Tirzah held her breath, praying that Jacob wouldn't suggest the trial of bitter herbs, which was completely within his rights. It was rare for a woman accused of adultery not to become sick after drinking the brew, and if she became sick, she was considered guilty of adultery and stoned to death.

Jacob glanced at Rebekah's bowed head. Pain filled his eyes, as well as resignation. He turned back to the priest. "Rebekah is free if she so wishes it."

Rebekah jerked her head up and stared at him in surprise. The pain Jacob must have been feeling made his mercy all the more poignant.

Rebekah hesitated, studying Jacob's averted face. Her eyes filled with tears, and she turned back to the priest. "I do so wish."

The priest nodded, indicating that with the consent of both parties, the betrothal was dissolved as though it had never been. Jacob strode out of the room without looking back, and Tirzah's heart went out to him.

The two sisters made their way back to their home in a profound silence. The crowds jostling around them went unnoticed, as did the merchants hawking their wares. Their mother met them at the door, her face a study in emotions. Neither girl could meet her eyes. "It's done?" she queried.

Tirzah nodded, watching Rebekah pass her mother and enter the home. The older woman sighed, frowning at Tirzah. "I should have waited and asked Rebekah before committing her to Jacob. I'm afraid we've lost not only a good husband but also a true friend."

Tirzah had to agree. She doubted if Jacob would be at the gathering of believers that night. Probably he would go to one of the other house churches farther away. She would truly miss him.

She followed her mother inside, wondering if things had turned out as favorably for Domitus.

Gallius stood before Commander Claudius Lysias, thankful that the note he had handed him had taken his interest from inquiring any further into legionnaire assignments. If he wasn't asked, Gallius had no intention of mentioning Domitus's temporary defection.

Dismissed, Gallius exited the room only to come face to face with his brother. Domitus stood in his way, forcing Gallius to stop.

Gallius wasn't in a particularly forthcoming mood. "What do you want?"

"I need to see Rebekah."

Teeth clenched, Gallius took his brother by the forearm and moved him away to afford them some privacy. Soldiers came and went along the passageway, and Gallius lowered his voice to keep from being overheard. There was no denying the command behind his words. "Stay away from Rebekah. You've caused enough trouble, and I won't intercede on your behalf again. Do you understand me? That is a direct order, Soldier."

Though Domitus's eyes flickered with uncertainty, he stood his ground. "I need to know that she is all right. She was to go before their priest today with. . .with her betrothed." His lips thinned. "I must know if she is all right."

Feeling some of his earlier irritation ebb, Gallius sighed. "You stay away from her, do you hear me? I will find out what has happened."

Gallius could see the arguments forming in Domitus's eyes, but one look at Gallius's set face and Domitus subsided. He gave a jerk of the head in acceptance and swiftly walked away.

Having been released from duty for the day, Gallius reluctantly made his way to the lower section of the city where Tirzah lived. His thoughts were a muddled mess. How could he command his brother to stay away from Rebekah when he found himself looking for excuses to seek out Tirzah?

Finding the home empty, he settled himself in the shade of the house, pulling a small stalk of dried grass from a tuft beside him. He chewed on the piece of grass while he pondered the problem of his brother and Rebekah.

Domitus still had twenty years of service left in the legion unless they were demobilized. With tensions escalating here in Judea as well as in the outermost frontiers of the empire, he didn't see how that was going to happen.

He sighed. Although he had gone to Tirzah's home with the

intent of finding out for his brother how Rebekah had fared, he would have made his way here eventually anyway. He might as well face the truth. Tirzah drew him back whether he willed it or not. He wanted her. He also wanted the peace that she had. Could he have both, or would her faith take her away from him?

He leaned his head against the home, closing his eyes. For some reason, she had grown more attractive to him every time he had seen her. It was not due to lack of female company, for Gallius had had many opportunities, but no woman had interested him since he had first set eyes on Tirzah in the glade. Her face had ever been before him. She haunted him day and night. He wondered if she even thought of him. He remembered her reaction to his nearness, but all he had seen in her lovely eyes was fear. Was that fear of him or fear of what she felt?

He heard a scuffling and got quickly to his feet. Peeking his head around the corner, he saw Tirzah coming toward him, her feet moving heavily as though bogged down by some great worry.

He stepped out, and she froze. Panic filled her eyes at the sight of him.

"I wanted to find out how Rebekah fared with the priest today," he said, trying to reassure her.

She took a deep breath and looked away. "Do you really care?" she asked bitterly.

He came closer. "I care," he told her softly.

Tirzah's eyes met his and stayed. "The betrothal was dissolved."

He was surprised. "That's all?"

Her eyes darkened with anger. "If two people agree, a marriage or betrothal can be dissolved as though it had never existed. Jacob is too honorable a man to insist on subjecting Rachel to a trial for suspected adultery."

"This Jacob must be a fine man," he told her, his voice holding an edge.

Her eyes widened slightly at his words, recognizing in his voice the sound of jealousy and just as quickly dismissing the notion. Her lips parted slightly. "He is," she agreed quietly.

As she saw him move even closer, Tirzah felt alarm seize her. For each step he took forward, she took one in retreat until she found herself backed against her house. Gallius stood before her, so close she could feel the heat emanate from his leather chest piece. His gaze roved her face in an unhurried inspection, and Tirzah had difficulty swallowing, much less breathing. The last time they had seen each other, his kiss had sealed her doom where he was concerned. She loved him, but she was also afraid of him. Or was she afraid of herself?

"I have told my brother to stay away from Rebekah." He smiled wryly, leaning one hand on the wall behind her head and drawing closer. "But I doubt if he will listen."

Tirzah tried to will herself to calmness. Every time Gallius was near her, she lost the ability to think clearly. "I thought Roman soldiers were trained to obey without question," she told him hoarsely.

His gaze fastened on her lips before moving back to her eyes. "In matters of the heart, many have forgotten who their master is," he replied softly. "It won't be the first time, and I sincerely doubt if it will be the last."

His words brought her back to her senses. She would not tread the path that her sister had so recently trod. She would be lying if she said that she didn't want to, but her commitment to her Lord helped her to overcome her confused senses.

He moved his head down slowly, his breathing quickening. "I want to get to know you," he said quietly.

Suddenly frightened, she pushed away from him, moving herself to a safe distance. She shook her head vehemently. "No!"

His eyes narrowed. "I won't hurt you," he said. "I only want to know you better. To find out what makes you so different from other women."

Tirzah thought of a cross on a hill not so far away, not so long ago. She shook her head at Gallius. "I don't think you truly want to know," she told him firmly.

He stepped away from the house and closed the distance between them. Folding his arms over his chest, he lifted one dark brow. "I already know that you are a Christian. Is that what you are referring to?"

Surprised, Tirzah could only stare. She was filled with sudden trepidation. "Your brother told you?"

He relaxed his arms. "No, though I suppose I should have figured it out sooner. Actually, it was something the prisoner Paul said."

Tirzah's heart accelerated at this declaration. Without thought, she moved closer, resting a small hand on his sun-darkened arm. He glanced down at it before meeting her look.

"Paul. What happened to him?"

"He is still in Caesarea, as far as I know." Gallius's look darkened. "I thought you didn't know this Paul."

She turned away. "I told you. I know of him."

He took her by the shoulders and turned her to face him. His look was so intent, Tirzah blinked back at him, disconcerted.

"There is something I would like to know about Paul. How could a man who so despised and persecuted Christians change so much in such a short time? I have heard the stories of how he stood by while others stoned a man to death for his Christian beliefs."

Tirzah was afraid, but she couldn't let that fear cause her to miss this opportunity to share the good news with Gallius. Even now Paul was in prison for doing the same. Could she do any less?

Taking her courage in hand, she told Gallius about Christ, His death, and His resurrection. She forgot who Gallius was. Who she was. She forgot everything but the words of the Lord.

Gallius listened to her for some time before he finally interrupted. "Paul told us this on the way to Caesarea." His gaze searched her face. "And you believe all of this?"

"Yes."

The one word resonated in the hot air around them. Gallius sighed. Whenever an emperor died, the Roman Senate proclaimed him a god, yet he remained just that: dead. Statues of Greek gods had infiltrated the temples of Rome until it was hard to know where one religion began and another ended. Toppled temples of so many gods. It made sense, in a way, that a god would live in the hearts and minds of his people rather than in a stone temple that could be destroyed on a whim. No one had been able to eradicate the Jewish God, and not for lack of trying. After millennia, their God still existed. Lately Gallius found himself wondering if it was that permanency that caused these Christians such peace.

"Paul said that even Gentiles are welcomed by your Lord. Is this true?"

Tirzah smiled. "Yes, Paul is a missionary to the Gentiles. Many have believed because of him."

Gallius looked thoughtful. He allowed his hands to slide from her shoulders to her hands, gripping them lightly. "I would like to know more."

Tirzah's heart leaped at the softly spoken words. She opened her mouth to speak but wasn't certain what to say.

"Would you walk with me?" he asked quietly. "I would like you to answer some questions."

Tirzah was afraid. Not of Gallius, but of her escalating feelings for him. Even if he were to become a believer, there were too many differences to overcome for her to believe anything could develop between them. She recognized the interest in her that she saw in his eyes, but how far did that interest extend? Her uncertainty left her vulnerable.

Nodding without speaking, she pulled her hands from his. They walked through the less crowded streets, yet wherever they went, people eyed Gallius with open hostility, Tirzah with disdain. She flushed under their regard, but Gallius seemed oblivious.

"How do you get such faith?" he asked quietly. "How can you be so certain there is only one God? And if He exists, why has He allowed His people to suffer so much?"

Tirzah laughed lightly, self-consciously. "I am not certain that I can explain things adequately." In truth, she felt very inadequate.

He looked at her. "Tell me what you believe." He stopped her and had her sit on a low stone wall. When he leaned next to her, she had to look away to still the fast pace of her heart.

"The apostles have taught us that having faith means being sure of what we hope for but do not yet see," she told him quietly.

He frowned. "That makes no sense."

"They also say that when faith is limited to only what we can see, it is no faith at all."

His frown deepened. "You speak in riddles, like the oracles at Delphi."

She smiled slightly. "Not really. You have faith that the sun will come up tomorrow, but you haven't seen it happen yet. You hope that it will, but until it does, you cannot be certain that it will. In spite of this, you remain convinced that the sun will rise."

Gallius wasn't sure about anything anymore. He stared at Tirzah, wanting to understand. He believed that she held the key to the peace he sought. He was also beginning to believe that she held the key to his heart.

He reached over and took her hand, holding fast when she would have pulled away. She stared into his eyes, and for the first time he read past the fear to her matching desire. His heart rate accelerated.

"And why have your people been made to suffer so much if what you say is true? Why does your God allow it?"

"Even the Christ learned obedience through suffering," she explained softly. "Our suffering is for just a short time. In the end, there will be no more suffering. The prophet Isaiah said that the punishment that brought us peace was upon Him. It's in His death that we find peace because we know that He has removed the barriers that kept us from the one true God."

Peace. The thing Gallius hungered for most. He was tired of slaying women and children and of executing men who wanted only to defend their families from the invading armies of Rome. He wanted most to settle down and have a family, a place where he could call home. For years he had been serving in the outermost fringes of the empire, and he was tired. So very tired.

He looked at Tirzah sitting quietly beside him and realized that he wanted her to be a part of his dream. The question remained, how to overcome their differences.

When they returned to her home, Gallius stared at Tirzah reflectively. "You have given me much to think about," he told her softly. Tirzah said nothing. Bending, Gallius quickly placed a kiss on her unsuspecting lips. When she didn't resist, he allowed the kiss to deepen until finally, at a slight movement from Tirzah, he pulled away. He looked into her eyes and read her feelings accurately. With great determination, he forced himself to leave and hurriedly made his way back to the fortress.

Chapter 8

The silence in the room was oppressive. Ephraim sat with his white, strained face regarding the group of believers solemnly. He had just informed them that Demas had been murdered and found only that morning outside the walls of Jerusalem.

Tirzah felt his sorrow as her own. Over the past weeks, most of their group had come to know and love the gentle Greek. Only the Zealots could have done such a deed, their fiery defense of the Jewish homeland knowing no bounds.

Ephraim cleared his throat and asked those present to join him in prayer. Tirzah bowed her head, feeling the healing balm of his petition flow over her. She frowned when he asked forgiveness for the ones who murdered Demas, but the frown quickly fled when she was reminded of the Lord's own words of forgiveness from the cross.

As they partook of the Lord's Supper, a thunderous banging sounded at the door. Startled, many in the room jumped to their feet, their anxious gazes searching for a means of escape, but there was nowhere to flee.

Silently motioning them back to their seats, Ephraim made his way to the door. As he opened it, he was unceremoniously thrust back into the room by a group of Roman soldiers barging their way into the room. Gallius was among them. His eyes widened at the sight of Tirzah.

Commander Claudius Lysias glared at Ephraim. "Are you the one called Ephraim, and is this your house?"

Ephraim stared back steadily. "I am, and it is."

The commander snapped his fingers. "Take him."

Everyone in the room came to their feet, an angry protest rising until it threatened to become a full-scale riot.

The commander's icy look went swiftly around the room. "Silence! All of you!"

Though his words brought the room to instant quiet, the tension in the air spoke of tempers that could erupt at any moment.

"What has he done?" one angry young man inquired.

Commander Claudius Lysias fixed him with a steely eye. "I am not in the habit of giving an accounting of my actions to upstart youths, but so that you may know that your own lives will be held under suspicion, I will tell you that this Jew is accused of murdering a Greek by the name of Demas."

Several of the men started speaking at the same time.

"Lies!"

"It's not true."

"He was Ephraim's house guest."

The commander glanced warily around the room. Though he had several troops with him, these Jews looked capable of murder. He could only be aware that the slightest wrong move on his part could result in serious injury, if not death, to many people. He tried to reason them into submission.

"There are witnesses," he told them loudly, trying to lift his voice above the babble of angry speakers.

Several men moved forward as one. "Liars! If they did it to our Lord, they would do it to anyone!" At the Jews' threatening posture, the soldiers lifted their spears high in warning.

Ephraim held up his hands. "Brethren! Enough! In the end I will be justified. If not, then I will be with our Lord. Don't be foolish enough to join in my misfortune. Be calm." He glanced at each one in turn. "Pray for me."

Some of the soldiers took him away, but other troops remained behind. Anger was quickly being replaced by fear among those present.

Tirzah met Gallius's gaze but couldn't understand the message that flashed from them. Fear radiated from his own dark eyes, and she knew that it was fear for her.

"Line them up," the commander ordered.

The soldiers moved forward, their swords drawn from their scabbards. Several people tried to rush from the room but were halted by the slamming of sword hilts against their skulls. Pandemonium reigned for several long minutes.

When everyone was grouped to the commander's satisfaction, he walked down the line, studying each person in turn. He glanced around the room, his look resting on the table that held the silver chalice. Striding over, he jerked it from the table. Wine sloshed over its sides and onto his fingers. He sniffed at it suspiciously, his face clearing as he turned to Gallius.

"Portius was wrong. It's wine, not blood." He motioned with his fingers to Gallius. "Hand me the vial."

With his attention on Tirzah, Gallius pulled a vial from his belt and obeyed. Commander Claudius Lysias then poured the contents into the cup with the wine, swishing it around to stir it in. His look was forbidding as he faced the assembled crowd. "Since all of you are assembled here in Ephraim's house, I am assuming you are all accomplices in his act of murder. Therefore, you are all guilty."

He moved to Abinidab, the first person in line, standing to Tirzah's right. The commander lifted the cup toward him. "Drink it," he commanded.

Tirzah recognized this form of Roman punishment. Usually it was used for Roman troops convicted of murder or to restore discipline where it had been lacking in battle. Poison was given to the first person in line, and if that person had the compassion, fortitude, and heart, he could drink the whole cup and thereby save the others from the poison's bitter agony. Each man was offered the same option: he could drink only a portion and possibly save himself, or he could take the full measure of the cup for himself, drinking it to its bitter dregs.

Abinidab's face turned deathly white. He took the cup slowly, his agonized glance flickering around the room at the others present. Tirzah said a quick prayer for him. Abinidab had a sick wife at home and three children whom he needed to support.

After taking a sip, Abinidab quickly handed the cup to Tirzah without looking at her. Reaching out, she squeezed his hand reassuringly to let him know that she understood, and she saw his shoulders sag. Out of the corner of her eye she saw Gallius move forward.

She noted the curling thorn vines and the river of blood, and she finally understood what it meant to give her blood for someone else. Praying for strength, she took the cup and lifted it to her lips, drinking heavily until the goblet was empty. Gasps echoed around the room, and glancing at Gallius, Tirzah noticed that his eyes were closed, his face wreathed with distress. Appalled, the commander was looking at her as though she had suddenly sprouted two heads.

The last thing she saw was Gallius rushing forward as she tumbled toward the floor.

Gallius sat in his quarters with his elbows resting on his knees, his head clutched between his hands. His thoughts were in turmoil, his emotions in chaos.

Tirzah.

If he lived to be a hundred, he would never forget that awful moment when Tirzah had chosen to give her life to save others. But then, wasn't that what she had tried to tell him before? Wasn't that what she had said this Jesus of hers had done for everyone, even him?

A door slammed in the distance. Slow, unhurried footsteps grew louder. Gallius got quickly to his feet as a tall, thin man entered the room, his purple-trimmed toga marking him as a member of the Roman aristocracy.

"Well?" Gallius questioned impatiently when the silence lengthened between them.

The older gentleman sighed, his white head shaking from side to side. "She is as well as can be expected after taking such a massive dose of mandragora. If she survives the night, she should live." He tilted his head inquisitively. "It was my understanding that she consumed hemlock."

Gallius looked away. "No. It was only meant that they think it was. Commander Claudius Lysias was trying to trick them into an admission of guilt." He said no more, and after a moment the physician took his leave. Physician to the troops garrisoned in Jerusalem, the man was conditioned to obey, and he had unquestioningly followed Gallius's command to care for Tirzah, for which Gallius was most thankful.

Gallius lifted a goblet of wine with shaking hands, then flinched as though he had been struck. Quickly he returned it to the table. He needed no further reminders of the day's horrors.

Two days later, Tirzah awakened to find her mother and sister bending over her. She didn't recognize the room, nor could she remember what had transpired. Her mother recounted what had happened, then the two women helped Tirzah to a sitting couch next to a window where the hot summer sun was able to warm her chilled body. It was good to see them both well, but she knew that her brush with death had caused the shadows under their eyes.

"Mother has consented to marriage between me and Domitus," Rebekah announced.

Tirzah lifted startled eyes to their faces.

Rebekah continued, "Ephraim has been studying with Domitus over the last several weeks, and Domitus has confessed his faith in Jesus and was baptized."

Tirzah wasn't certain whether to be happy or not. She glanced at her mother's closed expression. Although she didn't seem happy, the look in her eyes was one of resignation.

"Gallius can explain things to you," her mother said, and for the first time, Tirzah noticed Gallius standing in the doorway. Rebekah rose to her feet, squeezing Tirzah's shoulder as she passed by on her way to the door. "We must leave. We need to make some preparations."

Tirzah wondered just what preparations but didn't ask. When the two women left, Gallius entered the room. Tirzah thought he looked tired, his normally clean-shaven face tinted with several days growth of whiskers.

"How are you feeling?" he inquired softly, seating himself beside her.

She smiled slightly. "I am well."

He took her hand in his, entwining their fingers. When his gaze met hers, Tirzah caught her breath at the force of the emotions his look revealed.

"I asked your Jesus to spare your life," he told her huskily. "I promised Him my life if He would only let you live."

Humbled by his confession, she nonetheless told him, "You cannot bargain with God. You must serve Him with your heart, not because He fulfills your wishes. He is not some merchant with whom you can haggle."

He sighed, taking her other hand into his. He pulled them both to his lips, pressing a kiss firmly on her cold knuckles and bringing more warmth to her than had the hot sunshine. "I know. I soon realized that. He is much more than I can ever hope to understand."

Tirzah agreed. Although her people had had the Lord's Word for many years, they were no closer to understanding His infinite majesty. Still, there was hope. "If you seek Him with all your heart, you will find Him. That is a promise He has given us," she stressed, and Gallius looked deeply into her eyes. Searching.

"Then let us seek Him together. Marry me, and we will spend our lives learning what we can about Him. You and I."

Surprised, she studied his face.

"Our unit has been recalled to Rome. We are being demobilized. If we wish, Domitus and I can resign."

"Oh, Gallius." Tirzah didn't know what to say.

He stared intently into her eyes. "This does not mean

anything good for your people here, Tirzah. Commander Claudius Lysias is being replaced with another commander who is far more ruthless and a devout hater of Jews. There will be much trouble in the future, especially with the Jews' hatred of Rome being inflamed daily by Roman leaders trampling on their beliefs."

Tirzah remained silent, trying to digest what he was saying. He was trying to protect her, that much was very clear to her.

"Do you love me, Tirzah?"

After such a long time of being afraid, her brush with death had given her new freedom. Now was the time to speak honestly, but the words wouldn't come. She nodded.

Smiling, Gallius gathered her into his arms, holding her close. She could barely hear the words he whispered against her neck. "I almost lost you."

Tirzah pushed back and looked at him tenderly. "But God didn't lose you. Oh, Gallius, God is good!"

"Domitus and Rebekah have decided to marry quickly. They are preparing to take your mother and move to our villa outside Rome. We will join them there later."

At her startled look, he told her, "It will be best, at least until the famine here corrects itself and the trouble settles down."

Tirzah wasn't certain just what she thought of such an arrangement but decided that as long as she was with Gallius, she could live anywhere. Demas had taught her that. Reminded of the Greek, she tilted her head slightly. "What happened to Ephraim?"

Gallius laughed. "The soldiers found the ones who murdered Demas. They were to be executed, but hundreds of Christians petitioned the commander to spare their lives. Poor Commander Claudius Lysias doesn't know what to think. First you, now them. He doesn't understand such love. Neither did I. Before."

He pulled her more snugly into his arms, nuzzling her neck. "Ephraim is free. He said something about the beginnings of distress and that it was time to start leaving Jerusalem. Do you know what he was talking about, Beloved?"

Tirzah settled into his arms. Yes, she knew. The Lord had warned them to watch for the signs. Suddenly, leaving Jerusalem didn't seem such a hard thing after all. The Lord had said the temple would be destroyed, and He had also warned of severe distress. A chill of dread passed over her. She explained Ephraim's words to Gallius, and he frowned.

"We must leave quickly," he told her firmly.

Tirzah looked him in the eyes, knowing her love shone forth. "Whither thou goest, I will go."

She didn't need to finish the statement Ruth had made so many years before, for Gallius's God was her God.

"Ephraim asked me to give you this to take with you," Gallius told her, reaching behind her and lifting a silver goblet from the windowsill. "He said that the cup was meant for someone like you."

Tirzah recognized the vessel at once, its thorns twining around a river of blood. She was touched by Ephraim's belief in her.

"What do the words say?" Gallius asked. "I can't read Hebrew, only Aramaic."

Tirzah let her fingers slide over the letters. "I will pour out my blood for you," she murmured softly, her smile sad.

Gallius took the cup from her and set it aside. "Never again," he promised hoarsely, fear curling his insides at the thought of what she had been through and what he had almost lost. "If anyone is going to give their blood, it will be me."

When Gallius saw the love shining in her eyes, he did the only thing humanly possible. He kissed her thoroughly, promising her his love for all eternity. The words she had spoken echoed through his mind, the words that spoke of Jesus' love for everyone: *"I will pour out my blood for you."* With the help of God, Gallius promised himself he would spend a lifetime trying to show that love to others, beginning with his future wife.

DARLENE MINDRUP

Darlene is a full-time homemaker and home-school teacher. A "radical feminist" turned "radical Christian," she lives in Arizona with her husband and two children. Darlene has written several novels for Barbour Publishing's **Heartsong Presents** line. She has a talent for bringing ancient settings like the early Church in the Roman Empire and medieval to life with clarity. Darlene believes "romance is for everyone, not just the young and beautiful."

Cup of Hope

by Susannah Hayden

Chapter 1

A.D. 1187

Christina's heart beat nearly as wildly as the horses' hooves she heard pounding down David Street. Letting her washing slide back into the lukewarm tub, she whirled around and spurted across the stone courtyard.

"I'm scared! I'm scared!" cried a little voice behind her.

Christina halted. Stephen, the dark-haired three year old, had been playing quietly with a handful of pebbles—until a moment ago. Now he pumped his chubby legs to keep up with Christina's stride. She made herself kneel down to face him, brushing black curls away from her green eyes.

"The noise! I'm scared!" he cried, tears welling in his eyes. Stephen had come to the Children's House after his parents were killed when the horse pulling their cart had been spooked, then careened off the road and rolled down the hillside, pulling the young couple with it. The little boy was loved and cared for at the house, but every little commotion stirred his fear. However this time, Christina thought Stephen might be right to be frightened.

"I'm going to find out what the noise is," Christina told

the child. She squeezed his shoulder reassuringly. "You must wait here."

"It's bad! It's bad!"

"We don't know that, Stephen," Christina said with more assurance than she felt. "You go find Sister Angelica. I'm sure she needs help getting the table ready for supper."

Reluctantly, Stephen turned and shuffled toward the dining room of the Children's House. Christina quickened her pace across the courtyard, through the alley, and into the main street. The Children's House where she lived and labored had a prime location on the western side of Jerusalem, convenient to such sites as the Church of the Holy Sepulchre and the market streets, but far enough out to be a refuge from the busiest sectors of the city. They were also close enough to the David Gate to hear the unexpected roar of war horses pounding past. The dust stirred up by the great beasts swirled in gray-brown patterns. Christina reached the David Gate just as a knight reined in his horse. From his clothing, she could tell he was one of the Hospitalers, the warrior knights who guided Christian pilgrims to the Holy City and offered lodging in their expansive hospice on the eastern side of the city.

Christina joined the burgeoning crowd, nudging her way to the front where she could hear what the warrior had to say. The knight snapped open his helmet with one hand while he kept his restless animal under control with the other.

"Tiberias has fallen," he said simply. "The Saracens have taken Tiberias."

"But we have peace with Saladin," a man's voice protested. "Why should he now attack Tiberias?"

The newsbearer shook his head. "Reynald of Chatillon broke the peace. He attacked a group of Turkish pilgrims. There is a report that Saladin's sister was among the pilgrims, so he has retaliated."

"Reynald of Chatillon again! Didn't he learn his lesson five years ago?"

"The Muslims are gaining strength," another man called out. "If men like Reynald of Chatillon are not more careful, the Saracens will have Jerusalem again."

"Not without a battle!" the knight said fiercely. "Jerusalem has belonged to the Christians for nearly ninety years. It is our holy city. We will not let it go easily." He turned his horse and resumed his gallop to catch up with his fellow soldiers.

"There will surely be a battle," a woman said mournfully, so quietly that perhaps Christina was the only one to hear her. *Lukas,* Christina thought. *I must find Lukas.* She glanced back at the Children's House. She would quickly explain to Sister Angelica what she had learned, then she would search for Lukas.

Christina found Lukas's grandmother, shriveled and frail, sitting at her table, mopping her plate with a chunk of bread. Christina paused briefly before knocking on the open door, studying the familiar features that had passed from Devorah to her grandson Lukas. They shared a strong jaw line and determined black eyes set close together. But Lukas also bore evidence of his Greek heritage. Devorah, the daughter of displaced Jews, had married a Greek Christian, to the dismay of her family, and had returned to the city of her ancestors under his protection. Now he was gone, and Lukas looked after Devorah.

Since the earliest days of her childhood, Christina had known Devorah, and her family had been friends with Lukas's family. Devorah had always seemed old to Christina, but under the weight of the latest news, Christina thought she looked ancient. And alone.

When the old woman saw Christina at the door, she stood to push her chair back and welcome the girl properly. Her movements were painful and slow, determined and steady. Normally Christina's deep compassion for Devorah fueled her patience for the almost imperceptible pace at which the old woman moved. At this moment, though, Christina wished Devorah's troublesome hip would be more accommodating.

"Come in, Girl," Devorah said, gesturing her welcome as she continued her slow progress toward the door. "Have you had your supper? No, of course not. It's too early. I suppose you'll be eating with the children later."

"Yes," Christina said patiently. "Sister Angelica is expecting me. I thought perhaps Lukas was here."

Devorah shook her head. "Lukas has not been to visit me for days. Sit down, Girl. I'll bring you something to drink."

Christina shook her head. "I'm sorry, I can't stay. I must find Lukas."

Devorah looked up, alarmed at the urgency in Christina's voice. "What's happened?" she asked sharply.

"Tiberias has fallen to Saladin and the Turks."

"Tiberias? But that's—"

"Too near." Christina finished the thought.

"Lukas has his grandfather's soldiering blood in him," Devorah said softly.

"If there is a battle, he will be there, knight or not," Christina responded. "I must find him."

She did find him, at last, in the throng outside the palace of

King Guy. His grim expression told her there would indeed be another battle. Lukas took her elbow and steered her out of the crowd so they could talk without having to shout above the din.

"King Guy is furious," he explained. "He is determined to recapture Tiberias."

"And will he?" Christina asked fretfully.

Lukas shrugged. "We are told that Saladin had eight thousand men when he attacked Tiberias. If he attacks Jerusalem, it would be difficult to defend ourselves against such a force. King Guy does not want to wait for that to happen. He is anxious that we reclaim Tiberias and send a clear message to the Turks that they must come no closer. He is calling for volunteers."

Christina sighed and leaned her dark forehead on Lukas's shoulder, an old habit from their childhood. Sister Angelica habitually warned her that she ought not to be so forward with Lukas, especially when they were not officially betrothed. But Christina didn't care. She and Lukas had consoled each other through greater tragedies than this all through their childhoods—the loss of his parents when they were small, the accident that took his grandfather, the illness that brought death to her parents and brother two years ago, the loss of friends who set out for Europe to plead for more help for the Christians in Jerusalem and never returned.

"Will you go?" she asked, her voice barely audible.

"I must. It is my duty." His dark eyes flashed with sincerity.

"You are not actually one of the warrior knights," Christina said softly. "They will still need men to work at the hospice as you have been."

"It is my Christian duty," he responded emphatically. "When your great-grandparents came from France almost a hundred years ago, they did not consider their welfare. They came to reclaim Jerusalem for the Christians. They settled here to live in this holy place. You have known no other home. I am a Greek Christian, and Jewish blood runs through my veins as well. I have double reason for defending the Holy City from the Saracens. I could never stand by and watch the evil Turks inhabit this city again."

"I have loved you since I was a little girl," Christina said. "But I don't always love that you are inclined to be a warrior. There is too much danger."

"God protects."

"Then why are your parents dead—and mine and my little brother!" Christina pulled herself away from Lukas.

"Our families are with God. What better protection is there?"

Christina sighed. "I love God, Lukas. But we're young. I want to be betrothed. I want to marry you. I want to share my life with you. If you go to Tiberias. . ." Her words trailed away.

"We will win Tiberias, and I will return!"

Christina shook her head. "Do they teach you to talk that way in soldier school?"

Lukas laughed lightly and stroked her hair. "You should go back to Sister Angelica and the children. They will hear rumors in the streets and be frightened."

"There is good reason to be frightened."

"But more reason to be hopeful."

Christina raised her eyebrows in question.

"Did Gideon have hope with his little band of three hundred men? Or David with his five smooth stones?" Lukas asked. "I do not go without God's strength. You know that."

She nodded as a tear slid down her cheek. "Your grandmother is waiting for word from you. She says you haven't been to see her for days."

"I will see her before I go. And while I am gone, she will have you to look after her."

They parted soon after that. As she walked down the street away from Lukas, Christina refused to turn and gaze on him. Tiberias was not far, but the danger was great.

The rapid beating of her heart did not stop all evening.

Chapter 2

Christina heard the sobbing and knew, of course, that it was Stephen, once again frightened by a sudden noise. She did not see him at first but kept listening. With a damp rag, she wiped off tables and chairs as she moved about the dining room of the Children's House. Many of the children had barely touched the meal set in front of them that night. Their brooding gazes, set in wan faces, followed Christina around the table as she served a simple meal of flat bread, cheese, and soup. Sister Angelica muttered about the waste as she carried untouched plates out to the courtyard to be cleaned and put away. That was her way, and Christina had long ago given up hoping to change her. Sister Angelica dealt with crisis by focusing on insignificant details.

Christina's way was different, especially with the children. The older ones knew what had happened in Tiberias; it was impossible to shield them from the truth. And they knew that, if King Guy's armies did not defeat Saladin's forces, their lives would once again be turned inside out. In Christina's mind, most of them were far too young to have to worry about such things.

She had been seventeen years old when she'd lost her family; she understood the raging disease that had taken her parents and little brother. She knew that they had been three among hundreds, perhaps thousands, to succumb to illness that wretched winter. Christina had known and loved them well. But the children at the Children's House suffered far greater pain. Most of them were very little when they came to the house. One day their worlds were secure; the next day, everything they knew was wrenched apart—parents dead or disappeared, homes gone, meals uncertain, no one to kiss their faces and let them know they were loved.

Not a night of Christina's childhood had passed without her father's kiss on her forehead and the exhortation to "Go with God and serve Him well." So Christina had come to the Children's House, not because she was a needy orphan, though she was in many ways, but out of determination that the children behind those stone walls would know they were loved. Even now she yearned to protect them all from the violence that was sure to break out around them. But could she?

She found Stephen huddled beneath Sister Angelica's mahogany carved chair at the head of the table. Stooping, she watched his little shoulders rise and fall with his sobs, then reached for him.

"Come, Stephen," she said, "let's say our prayers and get you into bed. You'll feel better in the morning."

Stephen squeezed her neck as she carried him to the boys' bedroom. Gregory, Daniel, and Charles were already in bed. After settling Stephen, she made the rounds and checked on all the children. Judith, Elizabet, and Marie were in the older girls' room, while Rebekah, Leah, and Louisa were in the little girls' room across the hall. Baby John, the newest resident of the house, slept peacefully in a curtained alcove at the end of the hall. Many of the children were awake to receive the kisses Christina left on their foreheads. After the nightly ritual, they snuggled under their bedding and soon fell into an even rhythm of quiet breathing.

Christina left the side of the last child, sighed deeply, and padded down the stairs and through the hallway to the door that would take her out into the courtyard. Since the fall of Tiberias, Sister Angelica had decreed that the children must not go outside except for thirty minutes of fresh air each afternoon. The rest of the time, for their own safety, Sister Angelica wanted the children to remain within the confines of the stone walls that made up the Children's House. Christina ventured out for marketing, washing, and errands, but she kept her absences to a minimum to keep the children at ease.

The Jerusalem armies had left for Tiberias quickly, just as Lukas had said they would. She had heard nothing of the battle since the day the horses had thundered through the city gates headed for Tiberias and the Muslim leader Saladin. Anxiety gripped all of Jerusalem as the inhabitants waited for confirmation that King Guy's decision was the right one.

Enjoying the breeze blowing across her face and fluttering the loose curls at her neck, Christina lifted her gaze to the night sky and prayed—for Lukas and all the soldiers facing Saladin, and for Stephen, the other children, and all those wondering how word from the battlefront would rock their lives.

The next morning Sister Angelica brushed past Christina in the kitchen, nearly knocking a bowl of eggs from her hands.

"When Jacob comes, I want to talk to him," Angelica said curtly.

"Of course, Sister," Christina replied as she cracked an egg into a sizzling pan. "Has he not been bringing enough goat milk?"

"He will have word."

Christina understood Angelica's logic. Jacob, a shepherd of vague Jewish ancestry, had tended sheep and goats in the hills outside Jerusalem for decades reaching back into his own boyhood. Three days a week he brought fresh goat milk, often "forgetting" to pick up the coins that Angelica left as payment. He might very well have word from Tiberias.

"I want to talk to him before the children come for breakfast," Angelica said, standing anxiously in the doorway. "There he is!" She stepped into the courtyard and grabbed the gray woolen covering over the old man's arm. Jacob stumbled into the cooking hall, setting three clay jars on the rough-hewn table.

"What do you have to say, Jacob?" Angelica demanded. "I know you have friends who travel the road to Tiberias. Surely there is some word from the battle."

Jacob sighed and wiped his forehead with a dingy rag.

"What is it? Speak, Man!" Angelica demanded.

"I have indeed heard news," Jacob began, his voice barely audible.

Christina gulped. His tone conveyed the news was not good. "Is Lukas. . .are the soldiers. . . ?"

Jacob shook his head. "They battled at Hattin, outside Tiberias. The Turks are very well supplied," he said dryly, "and our men have too little. Saladin retreated to the edge of the lake, blocking it completely."

"Our men have no water?" Christina asked.

Jacob nodded. "That is the word I've heard. They are weak from lack of water, and Saladin's army attacked them even as they marched. They've had no opportunity to eat properly. The cavalry has been very brave. They've made several charges, but I'm afraid. . ."

"Is there no hope of victory?" Angelica asked.

Jacob shook his head. "Very little. The Christian soldiers have no food, no supplies, no troops to relieve them, while the Turks have everything they need."

Angelica brusquely and needlessly moved a jar of milk from one end of the table to the other. "I suppose you Jews wish Christians and Turks alike would go home and leave your land alone."

Jacob did not answer.

"It's our Holy City!" Angelica cried.

"It's our Holy City too," Jacob reminded her. "Christians and Jews have shared it for a hundred years. And before that we shared it with the Muslims for hundreds of years. Why must we all fight in the name of peace? Is there not enough holiness in this place for everyone?"

"Is there nothing more to say, Jacob?" Christina asked.

"My friend says that King Guy and Reynald of Chatillon were both taken prisoner. I cannot believe that Saladin will let them live."

"King Guy?"

"I'm afraid there will be very few survivors," Jacob said.

"What will happen next?" Angelica asked.

"Saladin will march toward Jerusalem."

"When will he get here?"

Jacob shrugged. "That depends on how much resistance he meets on the way. If no one puts up a fight, he could be here quite soon. A few weeks, a few months at most." He turned toward the doorway. "I will bring milk as long as I can. None of this is the fault of the children. They should not suffer."

The first of the children slid into a chair at the table just as Jacob left.

In the days that followed, Christina longed for word from Lukas. Defying Angelica's fears, she used every excuse she could think of for errands that would take her into parts of Jerusalem where people gathered.

Gradually the few surviving Christian soldiers straggled back to Jerusalem. When she saw them in the market, Christina was horrified at how they looked—thin, weak, yellow. Any vision of a robust army to resist Saladin's advances evaporated. Far more women and children inhabited Jerusalem than men, and many of the men who remained were not soldiers.

In the Street of the Vegetables, under the vaulted covering that protected wares from the hot sun, Christina pulled Claude, a favorite vendor, aside. Somehow he seemed to get word of important events before the rest of the city.

"Have you heard about Lukas?" she asked him.

The man's face softened. "Ah, Christina. He will be glad to see you."

"Then he's alive!"

"Yes, he's alive. Or he was when I saw him last. He's badly wounded. They have carried him to the hospice with the few warriors who are left."

Christina's heart thumped. "How badly?"

"He will need your care for a long time."

"Will I have time to care for Lukas?" Christina asked anxiously. "How far behind is Saladin?"

Claude shook his head. "Saladin will have no trouble between Tiberias and here. He was so angry with Reynald for attacking his sister's pilgrimage that he personally cut off Reynald's head."

"I must find Lukas," Christina said urgently.

Ignoring the errand that had taken her to the market in the first place and pushing out of her mind the thought that she ought to be helping Angelica with the evening meal, Christina hurried through the streets until she came to the entrance to the Hospitalers' lodging. "God in heaven, help me find Lukas before it's too late," she murmured as she ran.

A small band of weary soldiers approached. Several of them were on foot, carrying a pallet. Christina instantly recognized the shock of dark hair that she saw at one end of the makeshift bed.

"Lukas!" She flew toward him and made the soldiers put the pallet down. "You're alive! You're here!"

He turned his head slowly toward her. "God has been good to me. But many of my friends. . ."

"I know, I know, Lukas." Christina buried her face against his chest. "I'm sorry for your friends, for all the soldiers who lost their lives. But I am so glad you came back. Let me be grateful for that."

"Saladin. . ." Lukas's voice was weak. "There is no. . .stopping him. . .now. . ."

"Lukas!"

But he had lost consciousness.

Chapter 3

Her sandals clicked against the stone-laid street as Christina made her way past the familiar merchants. She nodded politely without breaking her pace. She would stop and look at vegetables on the way back to the Children's House. Right now she wanted only to see Lukas.

A few blocks later, Christina knocked on Devorah's door and pushed it open without waiting for the frail woman to make her way across the main room. Christina knew Devorah was expecting her; she had hurried over every morning that week as soon as her breakfast duties were fulfilled.

Lukas, while getting better every day, was quite weak. The children needed Christina. Lukas needed Christina. There was never enough of her to go around. Morning and evening, she visited Lukas and, for a few minutes at a time, imagined that their comfortable life in Jerusalem was not going to change.

Hearing Christina come in, Devorah stuck her head out of the small room where she sheltered and nursed her only grandson.

"Ah, so you're here now," Devorah murmured.

Christina stepped across the room and kissed the old woman's cheek. "I didn't stop in the market today. I thought you might like to go yourself and get some fresh air."

Devorah snorted. "I suppose you've decided I'm too particular about my vegetables."

"You should have the chance to choose what you want," Christina responded smoothly.

Devorah wrapped a light shawl around her shoulders. "He's just woken up." She turned to the door, while Christina peeked into Lukas's room.

"Good morning," Christina said gently.

He smiled and sighed. His wound, a gash in his side, had taken his strength with the pulsing blood. The injury was healing reasonably well, as long as he restrained his movements. At times Lukas's gaze would drift off, and Christina knew he was thinking of the soldiers who had fallen at Hattin, whipped back by thirst and heat.

"Are you going to tell me today?" Lukas asked.

"Tell you what?" Christina perched on the end of his bed where he could see her without having to move.

"Tell me the truth."

Christina shifted uncomfortably. "I always tell you the truth, Lukas."

He fixed his gaze on her. "Lately you tell me the parts of the truth that you want me to hear."

"Why do you say that, Lukas?"

"I've come home from a battle where we were nearly completely destroyed. Yet you come each day with a new story about Stephen or Louisa or one of the other children. You give me no news of war."

"Perhaps that's because there isn't a war, Lukas."

"Christina. . .please." His eyes brooded with pleading. "I must know. Is anyone planning retaliation?"

Christina let her shoulders droop. “I can’t see how speaking of such things is going to help you get better.”

“I lie here all day wondering what is really happening. Grandmother fusses about, but she doesn’t talk to people, not even when she’s in the market. When she’s out, she just wants the best buy on her vegetables or a new basket. You are the only one who comes to see me. You must tell me what’s going on.”

“I don’t know very much.”

“But you know more than I do.”

“I do hear things in the market or from Jacob when he brings the goat milk. But how do I know what is true? I don’t want to upset you with stories that may come to nothing.”

“Christina, I was at Hattin!” Lukas was becoming uncharacteristically impatient. “Tell me the truth. Is Jerusalem going to be attacked?”

Christina bit her lower lip and looked at her hands twisting against each other in her lap. “They say Saladin is approaching.”

“And?”

“There is very little resistance. He is taking castles, even whole cities, simply by appearing over the crest of a hill. No one wants to stand up to him.”

Lukas sighed. “Thank you for the truth. And what about our own city?”

Christina rose to her feet and began to pace slowly around the room. “He is not here.”

“But he is on his way here?”

“Some think so. Some are hopeful otherwise.”

“Why would he not come here, to the Holy City?”

“Perhaps the battle over Tiberias was enough for him. Perhaps he is satisfied to be the powerful threat that he is. No one would dare to make him angry again. He was angry that Reynald attacked his sister's pilgrimage, and now he has killed Reynald with his own hand. Isn't that enough?"

Lukas shook his head. "No. He also took King Guy. And he massacred hundreds of soldiers. He knows Jerusalem is weak. The years of peace are over, Christina."

Christina wrapped her arms around herself and clutched her elbows. "Perhaps not. I have heard that Saladin can be very kind. Why must he punish all of Jerusalem for the thoughtless act of Reynald and his men?"

"Reynald attacked that pilgrimage in the name of Christ," Lukas responded. "Saladin will want to hold all Christians accountable for the attack that killed his sister."

Christina sighed. "I love Jerusalem. I know nothing of France, where my ancestors came from. And your family, Lukas—you trace your lineage back hundreds of years when both Greeks and Jews lived here. Why must there be further bloodshed in the name of Christ?"

Lukas's eyes grew dark and brooding. "Jerusalem cannot defend itself," he said bluntly. "Too many men have been lost."

Christina nodded. "You're right. When I walk through the streets, the only men I see are the ancient vendors in their stalls or little boys like Stephen and the others at the house."

"Christina, Saladin will come."

"Oh, Lukas. . ." She turned to stare emptily out the window.

"I must get well so I can help defend our city."

Christina whirled around and faced him once more. "If only the kings of Europe would respond to our pleas for help! Why haven't they sent more troops? If the Holy City is as dear to them as they say, why do they not help us?"

"Because they know there is so little hope," Lukas said softly. "The Saracen are mightier than a hundred years ago when the Christians took Jerusalem. They are fiercer, more determined. And don't forget, barely forty years ago King Conrad III and King Louis VII from France were defeated by the Saracens and returned to Europe without the victory that your great-grandparents had in the 1099 Crusade."

"And no one dares try again?" Christina cried out. "Do they really expect that we can defend the Holy City without more help?"

"Perhaps the excitement and adventure has worn off. Europe is no doubt a very comfortable place to live."

"Europe is nothing to me," Christina retorted. "I live here. Jerusalem is my city, our city. The Holy City."

"Holy to the Muslims as well," Lukas reminded her. "And to the Jews."

"How can God be pleased by any of this?" Christina agonized. "Did our Lord Jesus Christ give His life so that men would fight over this city for hundreds of years, shedding blood needlessly?"

"You ask very deep questions. I only wish I had answers."

"What about the children, Lukas? If there should be a siege against Jerusalem. . .how would we feed them? How would we take care of them? I can't imagine that Sister Angelica has a plan for what we will do."

"God has a plan, Christina, even if Sister Angelica does not."

"I do not believe it is God's plan for people to be slaughtered, Christian, Jew, or Muslim."

"Christina, come sit with me again." Lukas weakly reached out toward Christina. "You're upset. I want to comfort you."

"Look at me, falling to pieces," Christina said, tears welling up in her eyes. "I came to care for you. I promised your grandmother I would look after you, and look at me!" She moved toward him, sitting on the edge of his bed and taking his outstretched hand.

"Many men would think that you ask far too many questions for a woman," Lukas said. "But I believe you ask your deep questions because you want to know the truth."

"Am I not right to want to know the truth?"

"Perhaps God does not mean for you to know all the truth at one time. I will defend Jerusalem because I believe in the truth of the Christian faith, even though Jewish blood runs in my veins as well. But I do not claim to understand God's plan for this special city. I only mean to say that God has a plan for you, Christina. If the city does fall under siege and if Saladin triumphs, God has a plan."

"Does he have a plan for us, Lukas? I want us to be together in God's plan. I want to grow old with you at my side, surrounded by the children God gives to us."

"I love you. I want you for my wife," Lukas said calmly. "The next few weeks will help us know if that is also God's plan."

"When do you think Saladin will arrive?" Christina asked hoarsely.

"It could be a few months or a few weeks. But I do believe he is coming."

"Lukas, I'm not sure I can bear what these next weeks will bring." She laid her head on his chest, looking for comfort in his heartbeat.

Lukas stroked her dark curls. "Christina, have you ever noticed the silver cup on my grandmother's mantel?"

Christina raised her head and shook it slowly, confused.

"Go find it and bring it here."

Christina quickly found it. How had she never noticed the silver chalice before? It badly needed polishing, but even so, it was beautiful. She handed it to Lukas.

Lukas turned the cup in his hands with honor. "This cup has been in my family for generations," he explained. "Do you see the writing here?"

Christina squinted at the edge of the cup as Lukas rubbed at it.

"It's very hard to read," he said. "And it's not French, which is the only language I learned to read. Grandmother tells me it's Hebrew. The words are from the psalms of David. It says, 'I will pour out my blood for you.' "

"I've heard the priest say those words at church. It's a Christian cup!" Christina exclaimed. "How did your Jewish grandmother come to have a Christian cup?"

Lukas shook his head. "I don't know. Grandmother doesn't know either. But here it is, and the words are as timely now as when this cup was forged. Whatever happens, we must remember the sacrifice of our Lord."

"It's a beautiful reminder, Lukas. Thank you for showing it to me."

They heard the door open and close as Devorah returned.

Chapter 4

"Hai! hai!"

A shrill trumpet followed the Turkish shout, blasting open the early morning gray.

"Hai! Hai!"

Christina lurched up in her bed before the last blare faded, her heart racing. The shouts were so close! Surely the enemy was just beyond the Gate of David. How had they come so quietly in the night?

The door to her bedroom burst open, and Stephen hurled himself at her. Christina caught him and squeezed him against her trembling chest. The boy sobbed in her embrace. "It's bad, it's bad," he said between sobs.

Christina did not contradict Stephen. Weeks had passed since Lukas had warned her that it was only a matter of time before Saladin would arrive at Jerusalem. Jerusalem was bursting at the seams with the tens of thousands of people from the surrounding countryside seeking refuge within the city walls as Saladin marched toward them.

"Hai! Hai!"

Where was Sister Angelica? Christina wondered. "Stephen, are the others awake?"

The little boy nodded his dark head. "Rebekah and Louisa and Leah and Gregory. Everybody's awake." They were just children, and they'd already known enough tragedy for a lifetime. Urgently Christina wanted to keep the children safe.

"Let's go find the others," Christina told Stephen in as soothing a tone as she could muster. "Perhaps Sister Angelica is already with them."

Stephen would hardly loosen his grip enough for Christina to stand up. She held him against herself with one arm while she snatched up the shawl from the end of her bed with the other. Christina walked down the hall to the little girls' room and saw that Angelica indeed was there and had already gathered the older children as well: Marie, Daniel, Charles, Judith, and Elizabet. Rapidly Christina ran through the ages of the children. The oldest was fourteen-year-old Daniel, nearly a man, and the youngest, baby John.

Sister Angelica, holding John, raised her gaze as Christina entered the room. "And so the day has come," she said quietly.

Christina only nodded.

"What will we do?" eleven-year-old Marie asked.

"We will trust God," Angelica responded resolutely. "We have a home built of stone, and the city wall is still between us and the enemy."

Clearly Angelica intended to stay put, despite the house's proximity to the David Gate, beyond which Saladin was even now lining up his forces. Perhaps Angelica was right to stay, Christina told herself. If the city were to fall, there would be no safe corner. But Christina's own instinct told her that the children should be moved.

"Let's go have breakfast," Sister Angelica pronounced. "We will eat heartily for the days ahead."

Christina had to admit there was some practicality in breakfast. Stephen seemed to relax a bit in her arms at the mention of food. She set him down and turned and led the way downstairs.

"Daniel and Charles," Angelica directed, "go gather the eggs. Today we will eat all that you can find."

"Won't we save any for the market?" Leah asked Christina.

Christina shook her head. "I don't think we'll be going to the market today," she told the seven year old.

The boys returned with the eggs, and Sister Angelica fried them while Christina sliced bread and poured the last of the goat milk into earthen mugs. It was unlikely that they would see Jacob again, she knew. The children ate in hushed solemnity. Elizabet pushed away her own plate and turned to feed John, who was anxious to explore the food she rejected. For a long time it seemed that the children were not eating, but at last Christina scraped the last of the eggs onto Daniel's plate to finish up. Angelica informed the children that they would have prayers in the chapel immediately after breakfast and instructed them not to dawdle.

Christina stayed behind to clean up. She could appreciate that Angelica was trying to maintain normalcy, and perhaps that was what the children needed in the face of the unknown days ahead. But Christina knew that nothing would be normal again. If Lukas was right—and she was sure he was—Saladin would soon have his Jerusalem prize.

As she stepped out into the courtyard to fetch water, Christina heard the voices crying in the streets.

"True and Holy Cross!"

"Sepulchre of Jesus Christ's resurrection!"

"Save the city of Jerusalem and its dwellers!"

The thin cries came from women and older men. Jerusalem did not have enough healthy young men to defend itself. Lukas was one of a small contingent of men of fighting age left. Christina squelched the urge to leave her water bucket and instead wrap her shawl around herself snugly to run to Lukas. But she heard little John's cry and Stephen's footsteps and knew she could not leave the children.

The siege continued for days. The Turks had cut off any traffic in or out of the David Gate, for it would have been suicidal to open the gate. The market in David Street, just inside the gate, dwindled as vendors ran out of wares and people grew too fearful to leave their homes. The city had four gates and two main streets that formed a cross. No one could be sure that Saladin had not stationed part of his forces outside those gates as well, for arrows seemed to fly over the wall in every part of the city. Arrows arced randomly over the wall, missing one person and striking another. So many people were hit that the hospitals and physicians in the city worked around the clock, pulling arrows out.

The few soldiers left in Jerusalem fought valiantly, aided by others of any age and gender who dared to take up arms. Christina dared not leave the house. Even going outside to fetch eggs or water was dangerous, and Sister Angelica refused to let any of the children do outdoor chores. They herded the chickens into the cooking hall and prayed that they would continue to lay eggs. Christina, keeping herself pressed against the house's walls as much as possible, carried water and pulled the remaining vegetables in their garden.

On the fifth night, as she quietly crossed the courtyard in

the late evening shadows, Christina gasped at an approaching shadow.

"Shhh. It's me."

"Lukas!" She threw herself into his arms. "I've been so worried. So many people are hurt. . . ." Lukas held her against his chest. She could feel his heart beating.

"The arrows are like raindrops," he said. "We don't dare show a finger above the ramparts without being hit."

Christina lifted her gaze to his face. "You were hit, weren't you? There, in your cheek."

Lukas nodded. "Yes, I was hit three days ago. But the arrow barely penetrated my skin. So many are fighting courageously, and so many are hurt much worse."

"How much longer can the city hold out?" she asked anxiously.

Lukas shook his head. "Only a few days, at best."

"Is there any talk of surrender?" Christina asked. "If we are going to lose anyway. . ."

"The knights will want to fight to the end. It is a matter of honor."

"But if lives can be saved by surrendering, perhaps that is the greater honor."

"How are the children?" Lukas asked, changing the subject.

Christina stepped back from him and sighed. "Frightened, of course, and we are running out of food."

"What does Sister Angelica say?"

"All Sister Angelica does is pray," Christina said with an unexpected edge. "She insists the children pray with her for hours at a time, but she prays only in Latin, and the children speak only French. I don't understand what she is doing."

"Do you not believe in prayer?" Lukas challenged her.

She softened. "Sister Angelica is praying with all her heart, and I don't doubt her sincerity. But I would feel comforted if she were thinking with all her mind as well. If we truly have only a few days left, we must do something to be sure the children are safe."

"I have always teased you about your sharp mind, Christina," Lukas said with a soft smile forming on his lips. "Perhaps now is the time that God will use your mind. Perhaps you will be the one to decide what to do for the children."

"Oh, Lukas, I'm not sure I want that responsibility. What if I choose wrongly?"

"You will do what God puts in your heart to do. I am sure of that." He glanced across the courtyard into the darkness. "I must go before I am missed at the hospice."

"But there are no pilgrims to entertain now."

"I must be prepared to fight."

"When will I see you again?"

But he had already turned away from her and slipped into the darkness.

Chapter 5

Miss Christina?"

Christina smiled at the soft voice as a pleasant warmth oozed through her dream. Just under the edge of consciousness, she responded to the light filtering through her window.

"Miss Christina?"

Now she opened her eyes, realizing the voice was not in a dream. Judith stood timidly in her doorway, framed by the gray light of the hallway.

"Judith! What is it?" Christina roused and propped herself up on one elbow.

"Sister Angelica wants to know why you are not in the cooking hall. She sent me to call you."

Christina gasped and glanced at the window. The sun was well beyond the horizon—and it was well past time to begin breakfast.

"Oh my, I overslept." Christina slung her feet over the side of her bed. "Please, tell Sister Angelica I'll be right there."

Judith scurried away while Christina rapidly dressed. Despite the abrupt awakening, Christina felt refreshed from the deepest sleep she had fallen into in the last six nights. The early morning hours had been silent, rather than ravaged with the cries of the Turks and the sounds of whizzing arrows and their victims. In the hours after midnight, Christina had sunk into the blackness of an unconsciousness not penetrated even by the rising sun.

As Christina made her way toward the cooking hall, she listened for the sounds of the children. In the last several mornings, they had learned to temper their rambunctiousness, not only to please Sister Angelica but out of their own uncertainty of what the day would bring. Sister Angelica had launched an intense regimen of lessons even for the youngest children to keep them occupied from early morning until bedtime, subdued and indoors.

This morning Christina could hear the sounds from the cooking hall waft through the house, the clink of spoons against bowls, the scrape of chairs, John's giggle as Elizabet or one of the other children tried to feed him. This morning Christina heard every creak on the stairs, every dragging footstep, because outside the house the air was silent. No arrows flew, no Turks cried out, no Christians shouted the glories of the resurrection in response to enemy taunts. What had happened? Where was Saladin?

Christina entered the cooking hall just as Stephen stood on his tiptoes and put his gruel bowl on the sidebar. No doubt Sister Angelica had thinned the gruel even more than the morning before. The cupboards grew increasingly bare each day.

Sister Angelica stood with her back to Christina, nervously rattling dishes and accomplishing very little with them. Christina stepped forward to help.

"I'm sorry, Sister Angelica. I overslept. It's been so many nights since I've slept soundly, I—"

"There is no need to explain, Christina," Angelica said. "We are all weary. And today there was nothing to wake you early."

Christina stacked bowls, preparing to wash them. "What does the silence mean?"

"Perhaps Saladin has turned away," Angelica said with a thin hopefulness. "He has been attacking Jerusalem for six days and has not gotten through the gate."

"But a siege could go on for weeks, even months," Christina countered. "I can't believe that Saladin would give up so quickly."

"I would like to think our prayers have been answered," Angelica retorted. "Have we not been praying day and night for deliverance from the enemy?"

"Yes, of course." Christina wasn't sure how to respond. She stacked the bowls more slowly.

A soft knock at the door startled them both. Christina recovered and moved across the room to open the door from the courtyard.

"Jacob!" Christina exclaimed.

Jacob pushed into the hall and set two jars of milk on the table. "I came as soon as it was safe."

"Jacob, we didn't expect you," Angelica said, peeking in the jars.

"It's fresh," Jacob assured her. "Probably still warm."

"You've come just in time," Christina said. "We've had no milk since day before yesterday. Baby John will be happy."

"How did you get through the city gate?" Angelica asked. "Surely it's shut tight."

"The gate was not so heavily guarded today. I have my ways. But I don't know when I will be able to come again," Jacob said mournfully.

Christina and Angelica looked at him expectantly, waiting

for him to say more.

"Saladin has left the David Gate," he explained. "I've been hiding in the hills, keeping the herd in caves." He chuckled. "Have you any idea how difficult it is to hide a hundred sheep? And those goats! They get noisy when they don't get their way."

Christina smiled. Hearing Jacob talk about sheep and goats was somehow relieving. But Sister Angelica pressed him.

"Where has he gone?" Angelica asked. "If we have been delivered, why are you uncertain about coming again?"

Jacob shook his shaggy head. "No one has been delivered, Sister."

"But Saladin is gone!" Angelica insisted.

"And we don't know where he has gone. Don't be fooled by the silence of this morning."

"But, Jacob, surely—"

"I must go. If I can come again, I will." Jacob left.

Christina pressed her lips together. Dared she ask Angelica for permission to leave? She caught Angelica's gaze but did not speak.

"Go," Angelica said softly. "Find him during this day of silence."

Christina hurried out into the still morning. Even in the absence of arrows, few people ventured out. She kept close to the stone buildings around her, always alert for an open doorway she could duck into. Her own footsteps were the only sound she heard, the eerie slapping of sandal against stone. Soon her ankles stiffened from the effort of making less noise as she made her way to Devorah's house. She slowly pushed the door open to find Devorah huddled in the corner near the oven, as if she could will her bread to bake more quickly.

"Devorah," Christina called softly as she entered.

The old woman shook her head. “He is not here.”

“No, of course not,” Christina responded. “He is with the other soldiers. I came to see how you are.”

“I am baking bread. Will you have some?”

Christina shook her head. “I can’t stay long.” Try as she might, she couldn’t get Devorah to look at her. “Devorah, are you unwell?”

“I have not been sleeping.”

“Have you been eating?”

“Just bread. I have no meat or vegetables, but I have plenty of flour.”

“Devorah, why don’t you come home with me? It’s not good for you to be alone here.”

Devorah shook her head. “No. You have your hands full with all those children. You don’t need an old woman to look after.”

“But, Devorah, I want to be sure you are safe.”

“Can you promise I will be safe at the Children’s House?”

Christina sighed. “No, of course not.”

“I am in God’s hands, whether I am here or there. I will stay here.”

“I will come again when I can.”

“Go find Lukas. I want to know that he is safe.”

Christina swallowed the lump in her throat. “I will try to bring you word.”

Lukas was at the hospice. Christina found him after only two inquiries. When she touched his elbow, he looked up, momentarily startled.

“Christina! You must stay safe.”

“Lukas, tell me what is happening! Sister Angelica believes

that God has answered our prayers and delivered Jerusalem."

Lukas shook his head. "If she believes Saladin is gone, she is wrong."

"But Jacob says Saladin is no longer at the David Gate. Where has he gone?"

"It's a ploy," Lukas responded. "He has a new strategy."

"But what is it?" Christina demanded.

"If I knew, I would tell you!" Lukas answered. "But I am certain Saladin would not retreat after a mere six days of siege. He is simply moving his army. Perhaps his spies have found a weakness in the wall."

"Is there a weakness to be found?"

He shook his head. "I don't know. There are so few of us left to defend Jerusalem. He must know that it is only a matter of time before he wears us down."

"Is there truly no escape for us, Lukas?" Christina's face filled with fear.

"You must be prepared to move quickly now," Lukas said. "Be alert. Never forsake your vigil. Be ready, for the sake of the children."

"How will I know what to do, Lukas? I never know when I will see you, and I know no one else I can trust as I trust you."

"Trust God, Christina," Lukas said firmly. His brooding eyes locked onto her gaze. "Christina, when Saladin comes through the wall—and I'm certain he will—I may not be able to get to my grandmother."

Christina nodded. "I asked her to come home with me. But she doesn't want to."

"Promise me," Lukas insisted, "that you will help me look after her."

Tears welled up in Christina's eyes. "Lukas, I'm frightened."

He took her in his arms. "Of course, you are. We all are. But God is with us." He squeezed her, then pushed her away gently. "Now go home to the children. Sister Angelica needs your level head."

She stepped away but turned her head to watch him, wanting him so badly to stay with her—to want to stay. But she saw no change in expression.

"Go," he said. "I will find you."

Chapter 6

The gray morning sky oozed into the sunny warmth of a late September day. While the arrow attacks had stopped for the time being, Lukas was convinced they would revive without notice. Only the most naive of the citizens of Jerusalem believed that Saladin had given up his siege and withdrawn his troops. Lukas was not among them. Unfortunately, some of the handful of Hospitaler knights who remained in the city were. God had heard their cries to protect His holy land, they asserted. Lukas had shaken his head and gone his own way from the hospice.

Now he moved irritably through a narrow street near the city wall, close to the Gate of Jehosaphat on the northeast side. He was not of pure European descent and would never be a true Crusader knight. Sometimes he asked himself why he cared so much about their cause. His family had been in Jerusalem for generations, since the height of the Greek empire on his father's side and thousands of years on his mother's side. Devorah, his grandmother, had held strictly to Jewish tradition even when surrounded by Christian culture and family. If anyone had cause to defend Jerusalem, it was Lukas.

The Europeans had been in the city scarcely a hundred

years, and their hold had been tenuous at best. Lukas often thought that he understood the significance of this holy place far better than the Europeans. True, many had adopted the loose dress of the desert climate, and many cultures had mingled in the last hundred years. But Lukas never forgot that the European Christians who conquered Jerusalem in 1099 had slaughtered Jews as well as Turks. Somehow his grandmother's family had escaped. Christians ruled the city. A few Jews with Christian connections, such as Devorah, were tucked in corners of the city.

Lukas thought of himself as a Christian with a firm faith. At the same time, he felt his Jewish lineage keenly. Perhaps it was this constant conflict that kept him alert to the dangers threatening Jerusalem even now. Knight or not, he was determined to do everything possible for this city, his city.

Christina pushed her chair under the table as quietly as she could and turned to listen to Sister Angelica. The children had awakened early, and Christina had risen with them, rather than force them to go back to sleep when she knew they could not. Even now, with breakfast cleared up, it was barely dawn. All except baby John had finished breakfast and helped with the clean-up chores. John napped on a mat in a corner of the cooking hall. Christina had insisted on it. His upstairs alcove was too far away in the sprawling house. If they should have to leave on short notice, the moments consumed by fetching napping children would be precious. Christina had pressed Angelica until she agreed that the younger children could nap downstairs in the daytime, but they would sleep in their beds at night.

"You will accompany me to the chapel," Sister Angelica said to the children around her. "We will pray for deliverance from the infidel."

None of the children dared contradict Angelica, but Christina could see the frustration and anxiety in their eyes as they murmured, "Yes, Sister Angelica."

Angelica turned sharply and began to lead the entourage to the room she had carefully furnished as a chapel. Reluctant children shuffled after her. Christina could bear it no more. She knew the little ones would not be able to sit still for the lengthy prayer session Angelica had in mind. They would come to the supper table cranky, their anxiety only heightened by the restricted activity of the day.

"Sister Angelica," Christina said cheerfully, "I wonder if the children might stay with me this morning."

Angelica turned and raised an eyebrow. "Why should they not pray? Indeed, why should you not pray?"

"Oh, we will pray, of course," Christina quickly assured her superior. "I thought perhaps the children would like to hear some stories from the Bible so they learn what God can do. That will only help them to pray more fervently." Her heart thumped rapidly as she waited for Angelica's response.

Lukas checked his foothold and continued his ascent of the wall by the Mount of Olives Gate. The air around him was thick with expectation. The knights ought to have sent scouts to look over the wall on all sides of the city. How had Saladin managed to move the masses of Turkish soldiers undetected? But there were so few knights left. Even if they weren't deluding themselves about their victory, Lukas doubted that they could do anything to stop Saladin, no matter what part of the city he attacked.

With one final push, Lukas was able to see over the top of the wall. He gasped at the vision. Had no one else seen this yet? Had ignorance led to complacency? Outside the northeast side of Jerusalem stood rank upon rank of Turkish troops. How they had managed to move so stealthily flabbergasted Lukas. Thousands of men were assembled, their tents pitched in the Valley of Jehosaphat, on the Mount of Olives. Lukas quickly estimated that there were at least twenty thousand Turkish troops. Jerusalem could muster only a few dozen men. If the attack from this side of the city was successful and the Turks broke through the wall, the few men left in Jerusalem could never be able to defend the women and children.

Between the Turkish troops and the city wall was an enormous and still growing pile of olive branches and felled trees. Lukas knew that soon thousands of Turkish soldiers would take cover behind the heaps of trees as they shot their arrows over the city wall. Behind the trees, Saladin had kept his troops up all night assembling their battle formations. The battle engines would soon fire rocks to break down the wall.

Lukas scrambled off the wall. He would tell the knights, then he would find Christina.

Christina gathered the children around her at the far end of the hall from where John still slept.

"Why does Sister Angelica always want to pray?" Stephen asked.

"Because she knows only God can help us," Christina answered, hoping she sounded confident.

"He didn't help my parents. They died."

"Yes, I know," Christina said, reaching out to touch his shoulder. "But they are with God now, and you are with us, so you see, God has taken care of all of you."

"Are you really going to tell us a story?" Gregory asked.

"Of course, I am," Christina answered, gesturing that they should scoot in closer and be ready to listen. She glanced over at John, whose even breathing told her he was sleeping deeply. "Do you know the story about Daniel?"

"Our Daniel?" Leah asked.

"Daniel in the Scriptures!" Christina said. "Daniel believed in the one true God, but many people around him didn't," she began. "One day some of the king's advisors tricked him into making a law that everyone had to worship the king. Anyone who didn't worship the king would be thrown into the lions' den. But Daniel didn't care about the law. He wanted to worship the one true God, and that's exactly what he did. In the morning and in the evening, he went to his room to pray. Daniel didn't try to keep his prayers secret, so the king's advisors soon found out. They went to the king and said, 'Daniel isn't obeying the law to worship you. You have to throw him into the lions' den.'

"Now the king liked Daniel. He didn't want to hurt his friend. But a law was a law. So the king ordered Daniel to be thrown in with the hungry lions. All night long the king worried about Daniel. Then when morning came, the king ran to the lions' den and called out for Daniel. And do you know what? Daniel answered! Daniel was fine! The hungry lions hadn't hurt him one bit. God had sent an angel to close the mouths of the lions. Now the king made a new law. No one could hurt anyone who wanted to worship the one true God."

"Miss Christina," said eight-year-old Rebekah, "if there is

only one true God, then why is everybody fighting over Jerusalem?"

Christina let her shoulders sag ever so slightly. "I wish I knew the answer to that question," she said. "I suppose everyone has a little bit different idea about the one true God, and that's what they're really fighting over."

"Will Sister Angelica's prayers help?"

Christina nodded. "I believe so. Do you remember the story of Peter? He was put into prison for telling people about Jesus. But his friends were in a house praying. And an angel came to Peter in prison and led him out into the street. Peter went to tell his praying friends all about it."

The door to the courtyard creaked, and Christina started. Immediately she calmed herself, but she kept her gaze riveted on the door. Instinctively she moved swiftly across the room and scooped up John. The door opened widely.

Lukas stepped into the kitchen.

"Lukas!" Christina cried. "You gave me a fright."

"I'm sorry. But time is short, Christina." He glanced toward the wide-eyed children still sitting on the floor across the room.

"What do you mean?" She asked as John stirred in Christina's arms.

"I've just come from the wall near the Mount of Olives," Lukas explained as quietly as he could. "Saladin has moved over there. They are getting ready to begin the siege again. It will start at any moment."

"You saw this with your own eyes?"

Lukas nodded. "We have very little time. I came to help you with the children."

Christina's body flooded with relief. Had Lukas really chosen her over the knights? "But what about the knights?"

Lukas shook his head and sighed. "I can do little to help them now. But I can do a great deal to help you." He looked around the room. "Where is Sister Angelica?"

"Praying in the chapel. I convinced her to let me tell the children stories."

Lukas's eyes clouded. "I passed by there before I came through the courtyard. She isn't in the chapel."

"She can't have gone far."

"Then we'll find her. We have to get my grandmother too."

Chapter 7

How much time do we have?" Christina asked.

Baby John had felt the tension in her arms and roused. She handed the squirming infant to Elizabet and scrambled to pull empty grain sacks from a high shelf. "We should pack a few things. Food. . .how will I get milk for the baby?"

"We have very little time," Lukas answered somberly. "We must make every moment of preparation count."

"Where will we go?" Christina asked.

"Some place that doesn't look like a house. Some place where the Turks won't think to look for a brood of helpless children."

"If only Angelica were here. Are you certain she wasn't in the chapel?"

Gregory hopped to his feet. "I'll go look." He was gone before Christina could stop him.

"You should go for Devorah," Christina said to Lukas. "Bring her back here. In the meantime, I'll gather some supplies." She turned to one of the older boys. "Charles, go check for eggs."

"We already ate today's eggs," the boy reminded her.

"Right. Of course we did. Lukas, be sure to see what food Devorah has."

Gregory reappeared. "She's not there."

Christina's eyes widened. "Sister Angelica is not in the chapel?"

The little boy shook his head.

Christina spun to look at Lukas. "Do you think something happened to her?"

"Let's not jump to conclusions. I'll look for her on my way to my grandmother's house."

Christina reached up to touch Lukas's cheek. "Be careful. Thank you for coming to help us."

Lukas closed his fingers around Christina's against his face. "You be careful. Wait for me." With one last look full of meaning, he left them.

Christina turned to mobilize the older children. "Marie, we need a lamp and some oil. Judith, we will take some flour, though it will be heavy to carry. Daniel, gather blankets. The nights may be cold."

Lukas clambered across the courtyard and out the back gate, then pushed through the streets toward his grandmother's house. He arrived breathless and did not take time for a proper greeting. "Grandmother, we must go. Now."

"Lukas! I've hardly finished my breakfast."

"Saladin is in the Vale of Jehosaphat. I've seen his troops with my own eyes. They are getting ready to fire rocks, huge rocks, and they have a fresh supply of arrows. I want you to be with me so I can protect you."

"Then stay here."

"I have to help Christina with the children. If the Turks break into the house and find a nun and a young woman with helpless children, they'll have no mercy."

"But my home," Devorah lamented.

Lukas looked around. Childhood memories flooded his mind. He had grown up in this small house. In this house he had said good-bye to his parents for the last time the day of the accident. In this house, he had played childhood games with Christina. Would he ever see it again? He understood his grandmother's reluctance to leave.

"We must go," he said softly. "I don't know if we'll be able to come back. What would you like to take with you?"

"Where is Christina?" Devorah asked.

"She's waiting for us," Lukas explained, his impatience growing. "We will go with the children and Sister Angelica."

"Go where?"

"We will find a place. Please, Grandmother, get your things together. What would you like to take?"

"I have a basket of fruit. Christina will want that for the children."

"Yes, she will appreciate that."

"I must take my cup."

"Your cup?"

"My family—your family—has had that silver chalice for hundreds of years. I will not leave it behind."

"Yes, of course." Lukas stepped toward the mantel and picked up the chalice. He traced the inscription lightly with his fingers, remembering that only a few weeks before he had tried to comfort Christina with its message.

"I will get a shawl to wrap it in," Devorah announced and moved toward the room where she slept.

Lukas could not bear her slow pace. "Just tell me what you want, Grandmother, and I'll get it." He plunged ahead of her into the small chamber.

"I want the warm shawl that I wear every day, and I want the white one that your grandfather gave me for our wedding."

Lukas nodded. He knew where she kept both and emerged with them in his hands within a few seconds.

"Do you have bread?" Lukas asked, scanning the shelves above the fireplace where his grandmother cooked.

"I baked three loaves yesterday."

Lukas found the bread and set the loaves on top of the fruit. He looked at his grandmother and was stabbed by how frail she looked. How would she bear up under the strain ahead of them? His mind raced back to Christina and the children. He had surely underestimated the time it would take to return to the house with his grandmother. And he had not seen Sister Angelica.

In the distance, he heard the din of a Turkish rock engine as it blasted a boulder at the tower of the Jehosaphat Gate.

Christina gathered as many supplies as she thought they could carry. Some of the smaller children would have to be carried as well. She pictured young Marie carrying a bag of flour or cradling baby John and opted to lighten the flour load yet again.

She heard the blast that rattled the Jehosaphat Gate and knew time was short. Where was Lukas? And where was Sister Angelica? She hated to think she might be pressed to leave without her.

"Judith, Daniel, come here, please," Christina said, keeping her voice as even as possible. They came and stood in front of her, eyes expectant. "Sister Angelica has been gone a long time. You are the oldest girl and boy. I am going to put you in charge while I go look for Sister Angelica."

"But what if—"

Christina cut off Judith's protests. "This is a time to be brave and to pray the way Sister Angelica taught you to pray. You stay here in the center of the house. Keep all the children away from the doors and windows. No one is to go outside. Lukas should be back soon. If he gets here before I return, you do exactly as he says. Do you understand?"

Four fearful dark eyes pierced her fortitude, but she held firm. "Remember, stay in the house, then do exactly as Lukas tells you."

She left them there, not daring to look back at the children's frightened faces lest her resolve dissipate. Outside the back gate, she paused to think as Angelica would think. Angelica prayed in the chapel at the house most days because she wanted the children to pray with her. But if she were alone, as she had been that morning, Christina knew the sister would prefer to go to the Church of the Holy Sepulchre. A morning without whizzing arrows might have proven irresistible.

Christina moaned. If only she had not talked Angelica into letting the children hear stories; Angelica would not have left if the children were with her in the chapel. Sighing with regret, Christina set her path north, in the direction of the basilica. With every step farther away from the house, she prayed that Lukas would return to look after the children.

Coming around a corner, Christina gasped. There in the street lay Sister Angelica, a pool of blood spreading beneath her. Christina crouched to cradle Angelica's head in her lap.

"What happened?" Christina asked.

"I wanted to pray. . .one more time. . .in the church," Angelica said with difficulty.

Tears rolled down Christina's face. "Tell me what to do, and I will do it. How can I help you?"

Angelica moved her head from side to side slowly. "Too late. An arrow. . ."

"But Lukas said Saladin has moved."

Angelica breathed rapidly and shallowly. "Then the infidel forgot someone. Turkish arrow. . .in my side."

Christina saw the arrow lying beneath Angelica. "You've pulled it out!" she exclaimed.

"Too much blood," Angelica gasped hoarsely. Her chest rose and fell heavily with each breath. "It does not matter. I am ready."

"But Sister Angelica—"

Angelica opened her blue eyes and looked clearly into Christina's. "I am ready. As the deer pants for water, so my soul longs for God."

"I can carry you back to the house," Christina urged. "Lukas will be there soon. He will know what to do. He's seen many injuries."

But Angelica's eyes were closed again, her breathing stopped completely. Her still, white face lay in Christina's lap. A cry welled up from deep within Christina, and she screamed.

Wiping tears from her face with the back of her hand, she eased Angelica's head from her lap and stood up, blood caking on her skirt. She hated to leave Angelica in the street, but images of the children filled her mind, propelling her back to them.

Chapter 8

Christina hurtled west and south, back to the house. To the east, the rock fire of Saladin's troops rumbled persistently against the tower gate. Tears filled her eyes and spilled down her cheeks. What would she tell the children about Sister Angelica? How could she be responsible for eleven children on her own?

As she came within sight of the house, Christina fought to control her sobbing and wiped her face dry. Quickly she went through the gate and crossed the courtyard. Releasing a final sigh, she pulled the door open and entered the house.

Lukas, standing at the hearth, spun around to face her. "Christina! What happened?" He searched her face, and she knew he saw her grief and terror.

Christina glanced around for the children. "Where. . . ?"

"I told them they could each take one important thing. They went upstairs to choose. Christina, tell me what happened. You're white!"

Impulsively, Christina threw herself against his chest. "I found Sister Angelica," she murmured. "She had gone to pray at the basilica, just as I thought. She died in my arms."

"A stray arrow?"

Christina nodded. "I hated to leave her there, Lukas. But what could I do?"

Lukas nodded. "Right now we must focus on the children."

"And your grandmother?"

"She's here, in the next room."

Christina looked at the baskets and bundles on the rough hewn table. The last of the garden vegetables, yesterday's bread, a little dried meat, one jug of goat milk, Devorah's fruit. It seemed so little for so many people. She forced herself to step back from the comfort of Lukas's arms. "Lukas, where will we go?

"Out the David Gate, to begin with."

"But people have been pouring in from the countryside for weeks, coming to Jerusalem for refuge."

Lukas nodded. "It's clear that Saladin is going to come through the wall on the east side of the city. So maybe it's better to leave from the west side."

"Are you sure it's safer outside the city walls?"

"I'm not sure of anything right now, Christina, except that we are in God's care. But if Saladin is attacking the east side of the city, this seems to be our chance to leave."

"Will we ever come back?"

"I hope so. I pray Saladin will be merciful once he has taken the city."

Christina swallowed the lump in her throat and said hoarsely, "Then let's go."

Together Christina and Lukas gently but efficiently organized the small band of refugees. The older children were given bundles to carry or smaller children to watch. Christina carried baby John in one arm and held Stephen's hand with the other. Lukas strapped more to his back than Christina imagined one person could carry. They began their trek toward the David Gate.

"Grandmother, where are you going?" Christina heard Lukas say, and she turned to see that Devorah had started to wander down one of the market streets.

"I want to see if Hadassah is all right."

"Hadassah?" Lukas asked, puzzled.

"My friend's granddaughter. You've met her. I have been sharing vegetables with her."

"Yes, I remember now," Lukas said. "But Grandmother, we have no extra time."

"Then leave me behind. I will not go unless I see her first."

"Grandmother—"

Christina put her hand on Lukas's arm. "I know who she's talking about, Lukas. Hadassah's Christian husband was killed at Tiberias, and she has a two year old and a new baby."

"Surely there must be someone looking after her," Lukas said.

Devorah shook her head. "She is alone. She left her Jewish family to come here and marry a Christian, just as I did so long ago. You go on if you like. I will not go until I see Hadassah."

Christina and Lukas looked at each other anxiously, their gazes locked.

"We cannot leave her," Christina said quietly.

"No, of course not. I would never think of it."

"Then we must take her to see Hadassah. It is only a few streets from here."

Lukas glanced over the brood of squirming children. "If we try to take everyone, it will take far too long."

"I'll go with her," Christina offered.

"No, it's not safe," Lukas protested.

Christina raised an eyebrow. "And standing here on the street with all the children is safe?"

"No, of course, I can't leave you standing here with all the children."

Christina sighed. "Lukas, you must choose. We cannot send your grandmother alone. Either we all go, or we separate. It will only be a few minutes."

"You've suddenly become very levelheaded."

Christina shook her head. "No. Every part of me wants to scream and run away. But I have to think clearly for the children."

Lukas held out his arms. "Leave the children with me. You have a way with my grandmother sometimes. You will be able to help her see what she must do."

Christina laid John in Lukas's arms and transferred Stephen's grip to the hem of his long shirt. "We will be back as soon as we can."

"We will be waiting under the arch in the market," Lukas said, pointing with his head to a modest shelter behind him.

Christina turned to Devorah. "Okay, Devorah, let's go find Hadassah."

The two women turned down the street toward Hadassah's home. Christina took Devorah's elbow, hoping to quicken the old woman's pace. Devorah surprised her by complying. The slow shuffle that Christina had become accustomed to around Devorah's house, though not eliminated, was masked by Devorah's determination to find her friend's granddaughter. Mentally Christina counted off the minutes. The rock fire continued to rumble on the far side of the city. She knew it was only a matter of time before Saladin penetrated the gate, but how much time?

At last they came to Hadassah's street. Devorah pointed determinedly to the house, and Christina focused on it. She saw no motion on the outside. Was Hadassah huddled inside with her little ones? Or had she already found help? And once they found her, what did Devorah hope to do?

"Christina, is that you?"

Christina turned to see Claude, the market vendor. Claude looked from Christina to Devorah.

"This is Devorah, a friend," Christina explained quickly. "And we are looking for another friend."

Claude nodded. "It is the same everywhere. I have been all over the city today. On the east side you can hear every blast of the rock engines."

"And your family?" Christina asked.

"I am looking for my brother now. We have promised that our families would be together when the time came."

Christina hardly knew how to respond.

Claude continued. "You should find your young man and stay with him," he cautioned. "I have heard the tales of what the Turks will do to young women such as you."

"Claude!"

"I'm sorry if I frighten you. But it is true. You should not be in the streets without an escort much longer. There are so few men, so very few men."

Christina hastened her step. "God be with you, Claude."

"Don't let him frighten you," Devorah told Christina.

Christina glanced over her shoulder at Claude disappearing in the other direction before once again looking toward Hadassah's house. As they drew closer, she heard a crying baby. Baby John had been left at the house when he was four months old. Christina had sat up with him on many nights; she knew the sound of a child who wanted to be fed or held. What she heard now was no ordinary cry of basic need. Something about the cry made her quicken her step and move ahead of Devorah. She knocked lightly on the door when she reached it.

"Hadassah?" she called. No answer came. Christina knocked harder. "Hadassah?" When she still heard no sound from within the house except for the cries of a hysterical baby, Christina pushed the door open. On the floor inside the door was Hadassah with the baby in her arms. Christina rushed in, with Devorah right behind her.

As soon as Christina reached Hadassah and bent over her, she knew that the young mother had been dead for several hours. Her body looked white and thin, one arm stiff around the infant. Images of finding Angelica only a few short hours ago flooded Christina's mind as tears once again filled her eyes as she gently picked up the baby. She stood and turned to Devorah.

"She's gone, Devorah," Christina said hoarsely.

Grief washed across Devorah's face. "She was ill after the baby. After her husband died and the baby came, she did not work hard to get well."

"Isn't there another child?" Christina asked.

"A two year old."

Christina anxiously scanned the room but saw no sign of the toddler. The baby was still screaming and kicking from hunger, Christina presumed, as well as primal terror of having his demands unmet. She thought of the closely guarded jar of goat milk in Lukas's pack. Perhaps there was something in Hadassah's house she could give the baby.

"Devorah," Christina said, her voice trembling as she realized the task ahead of her—caring for yet two more very small children. "Can you sit in this chair and hold the baby? I will look for some milk as well as for the other child. Do you know his name?"

"He is called Levi, and the small one is Reuven."

Hadassah's house was small. If Levi was there, Christina reasoned that she would find him soon enough. She settled Reuven in Devorah's arms, and the old woman began to rock slowly. Still the baby shrieked, his little chest heaving in gulping sobs. Surely he was hungry and probably very wet. As Christina moved to the cooking area looking for milk, she also surveyed the room. She found some milk and a spoon. But would the baby take it? He was no doubt used to his mother feeding him. They would have to try. Christina poured a little milk into a cup and took it to Devorah before continuing her search for the baby's brother.

She found him huddled in a bedroll in the next room, so small that she almost missed him amid the tumble of blankets and shawls. His frightened dark eyes peered out at her. Gently she reached for him. In the background the baby's sobs seemed to diminish.

Chapter 9

Devorah managed to spoon enough milk into Reuven to quell his hysterical cries, at least for the time being. Levi was not so easily coaxed out of hiding, but Christina persisted until she had the two year old in her arms. While she cooed to soothe him, she trembled inwardly. Two more children. A baby who needed his mother's milk. What could she do for these two little boys? Christina quickly rummaged through Hadassah's food shelves, finding some cakes and dried fruit to add to the half-full jar of milk.

"We must go, Devorah," Christina said with more certainty than she felt. "Lukas will wonder where we are. He can't leave the children to find us."

Devorah stood up, holding the baby carefully. "I will go as fast as these old bones will allow."

"Can you carry the baby?"

"Yes, if I make a sling from my shawl."

They left then. Levi buried his face against Christina's chest, but he did not protest being taken from his home. Christina wondered what a two year old understood about death. This boy had lost both his parents in less than four months. Somehow she thought he understood that his mother was not going to wake up.

It was late afternoon. Weighted with the exhaustion of the day, Christina struggled to put one foot in front of the other. Angelica. Then Hadassah. How many more friends and acquaintances would she see for the last time before the siege was over?

Lukas saw them coming and dashed out to meet them.

"Hadassah is dead," Christina explained quickly and quietly. "We had to bring her children. There is no one else to care for them."

Lukas took Levi from her arms. "God sent you to these children, Christina. Many Christians would have left two little Jewish boys to die. But not you."

"They're children, Lukas," she responded wearily. "There was no choice. Her voice began to break. "But I'm not sure what I can do to help them. Will we be able to get through the gate?"

"I'm not sure. We'll have to see if there is anyone to help. We just need a crack to squeeze through."

Christina turned to the rest of the children and consciously unfurrowed her face. "We have two more little ones to take with us. Charles and Judith, please help me with Reuven and Levi. Elizabet, it will be your special job to look after baby John."

The children nodded glumly, and Judith reached for Reuven. Christina added the cakes and fruit to a small food bag and looked over the band of children lined up against the side of a stone building. Involuntarily she looked to the east as another boulder thundered against the tower.

"Lukas, how—"

He shook his head to cut her off. "I don't know how long we have, and I don't know how. . ."

Christina sighed. "What shall we do now?"

Lukas pulled her aside, out of hearing range from his

grandmother and the children. He looked into her green eyes and stroked the dark curls around her face. His eyes did not miss her struggle to keep her tears back. He kissed her forehead. Christina choked on a sob.

"You have seen death twice in one day," he said softly. "I will do my best to make sure you see no more."

Another boulder rumbled through the air and crashed against the tower's stone, startling them both. Lukas clutched Christina against him and spoke into her ear. "I love you, Christina," he said. "Always remember that. I hate to leave you, but I think I should go alone to see if we can get out the gate. Can you manage with the children and Grandmother?"

Christina nodded. Words were beyond her.

"The Turks are not through the wall yet," Lukas said. "Keep everyone close to the building, out of the path of any arrows that might fly over the wall. I will be back as quickly as I can." He took her face in his two hands. "I do not believe it is an accident that God has left these children in your care. He will not abandon us now."

Christina swallowed the lump in her throat and nodded. "Go," she said hoarsely, "and come back."

He turned and left. Christina sighed and turned back to the children.

"Where is Lukas going?" Marie asked.

"He won't be gone long," Christina answered, "and when he returns, he will take us to a safe place."

Lukas knew every inch of the Holy City. He had grown up hearing his half-Jewish mother, Devorah's daughter, claim to trace their lineage in Jerusalem back to the time of King David.

Somehow they had survived the scourge when the Christians took the city in 1099, killing Jews along with Turks. His father's family had come from early Christian Greeks. Generations had come and gone through Jerusalem until his great-great-grandparents had settled in the city. As a boy, Lukas had explored every nook and cranny of Jerusalem. Now his investment in boyhood play would pay off. He surveyed the wall before him, looking for footholds that would take him straight up its side. With a grunt, he hoisted himself up and began the climb. Before long, he had his answer and began the descent.

Christina saw him coming and ached to run to him. But she held herself back, instead choosing to look calm and expectant while she waited for him to reach her. He reached for her hand and pulled her aside, turning his back on the children and speaking softly.

"The gates are bolted shut, and there is no way to open them," he reported. "No amount of money would bribe those guards. I scaled the wall. There is a handful of Turkish troops on the other side. So even if we could get through the gate, we wouldn't get far. It's difficult to be stealthy with thirteen children in tow."

Christina nodded. "I know. The babies could cry at any moment."

Lukas continued. "I want to find a place where you and the children can stay while I cross the city and see what's happening."

Christina gestured down the street. "People from the countryside are already living in the streets. They're beginning to run around half crazy. There will not be enough safe places for everyone."

"There are so few fighting men left in the city," Lukas said. "The women and children are hiding in fear."

"There is plenty to be feared."

"We will not give in to fear," Lukas said firmly.

"Perhaps we should just go back to the house. It's stone, so the Turks can't burn it, and. . ."

But Lukas shook his head. "You are a group of women and children. The Turks will go from house to house looking for defenseless people. Even if I am with you, one man cannot protect you against a band of Turks. No, we must find a hiding place, a cave, or some place underground."

"I know of a place."

Christina and Lukas were startled to see that Devorah had approached them.

"I know a cave," she said.

"A cave?" Christina asked, incredulous.

Lukas nodded. "Yes, Grandmother. I remember. I've been there with you. Grandfather always said he believed there were passageways through that wall."

"Is it far?" Christina asked.

Lukas shook his head. "Very close. I should have thought of it myself sooner. It's almost part of the city wall itself. We will have the strength of the wall to protect us, without the exposure of being in a house."

"Then let's go." In Christina's mind, anything was better than standing in an open street waiting for Saladin to break through on the other side of the city. The need was for immediate safety. She refused to speculate what might happen once Saladin came through the wall, and she was hidden away with the children, running out of food.

Efficiently, Christina herded the children to follow Lukas.

He hoisted the pack on his back once again, and they set off. Daniel, the tallest of the boys, offered an arm to Devorah. Christina carried Levi, who seemed relieved to be back in her arms. He sucked with a rapid rhythm on his thumb as he stared up at her.

When they reached the entrance to the cave, Christina wondered how she could have lived so close to it all her life and never known it was there. The opening was barely wide enough for Lukas to squeeze through, hardly more than a crack. A passerby looking at the wall would likely think it simply a larger-than-usual opening between stones in the wall, never guessing that it led to a secret hideaway.

One by one, they squeezed through the opening and crawled down the steplike stones to a lower level with an open space. Lukas lit a lamp, with the caution that they must conserve fuel. Drawn to the light, the children huddled in a tight circle.

"Miss Christina, can we have a story?" little Stephen asked.

"A story? Right now?"

He nodded. "Are there any stories in the Bible about caves?"

Christina quickly inventoried the stories she had learned at her father's knees. "Yes, Stephen, the Bible has stories about caves."

"Tell us one." Stephen crawled into her lap next to Levi.

Christina glanced at Lukas, who smiled over the oil lamp at her.

"Well, let's see," she said. "When I was little, my father used to tell me the one about Elijah. He was a great prophet who helped all the people worship the one true God. That was a really hard job. Not everyone wanted to listen to Elijah, especially not King Ahab and Queen Jezebel. So Elijah got discouraged, and he crawled into a cave to hide. He even felt like hiding from God.

"But God didn't hide from Elijah. God found Elijah in that cave and told him to stand in the doorway and wait for God to pass by. First there was a great and powerful wind. The wind shook the mountain and tore apart the rocks. But God was not in the wind. Then there was an earthquake, but God was not in the earthquake. Then came the fire. But God wasn't in the fire, either.

"At last Elijah heard a voice, quiet and gentle as a whisper. That was God. And He told Elijah that He still had work for him to do. And Elijah went right out of that cave to do the work God gave him to do."

Christina stopped talking and met Lukas's gaze.

"That was the perfect story," Lukas said quietly.

Christina looked down in her arms at Levi. He had at last released his thumb and fallen asleep.

Chapter 10

Christina hardly knew when evening fell. The dimness of the cave descended to a more subtle shade of blackness. The children, having had no food since breakfast, grew squirrelly, and in the relative safety of the cave displayed the anxiety they must have been suffering all day.

Christina calculated how large a dent an evening meal would make in their food supplies and rationed bread and dried fruit accordingly. She knew some of the older children were not satisfied, but they understood the severity of the situation and kept their complaints to themselves.

Then it was time to arrange bedrolls and settle the children for the rest they needed. Lukas insisted that Christina's spot be deep in the cave, next to Devorah and the smallest children. He would bed down close to the opening, where he could keep vigil. Devorah took Reuven under her blanket, and Christina soothed Levi until he allowed her to lay him down on a blanket next to her. When she was sure he was sleeping soundly, she crept back to the small lamp and Lukas.

He reached out and touched her hair. "Will you be able to sleep?"

She shrugged. "John still wakes up in the night sometimes.

And Reuven. . .I don't know what to expect, but I think he will want at least one feeding in the night."

"And if the babies do sleep, will you sleep?"

Again she shrugged. "Lukas, this was a horrible day. But the most horrible thing is that tomorrow may be worse!"

"We are safe in here."

"For now. But we can't stay in here forever. We'll run out of food before long, and the children need fresh air."

Lukas nodded. "I know. We don't dare burn a fire any more than we have to."

"What will we do next?"

"I don't know. But I think we must have more information about what's happening. If I go out alone, I can try to find out how close Saladin is to coming through the wall."

"Go out! Lukas, it's dangerous. I don't want you to go."

He lifted her hand to his lips and kissed it. "Christina, right now there is no choice that is not dangerous. Please believe that I have in mind the welfare of you and all the children."

Reluctantly she nodded. She did not want him to go. But she knew he must.

Just then John began to whimper. Christina turned to see what he needed as Lukas made his way out of their shelter.

Throughout the night, Reuven, John, Levi, and Stephen seemed to take turns waking up at thirty minute intervals. Devorah tended to Reuven, but Christina could not shut out her movements and soothing coos. She was certain that she wasn't truly asleep for a moment all night, until she heard Lukas's voice and realized she had not heard him come in. She turned toward the sound. He had lit the lamp again, and several of the older children were awake and talking with him in low voices. Having no idea what time it was, Christina roused herself to join them.

Lukas smiled when he saw her crawling toward him. "You were sleeping so soundly I didn't want to disturb you when I came back."

"What time is it?"

"Nearly dawn." He raised a basket. "Look, eggs. I stopped by the house and fed the chickens and collected these."

"The chickens have been so neglected I would have thought they would have stopped laying."

"Well, there are only seven eggs. That's not even enough for the children to each have one, but it's something."

"I'll scramble them. It will seem like more." She took the basket from his hand and turned to find the one pot she had brought. Lukas produced some wood and started a fire against the back wall of their makeshift home.

Gradually the other children awoke. While Christina prepared a simple meal, Lukas stretched out on his bedroll for some overdue sleep. Christina glanced at him frequently in the dim light with its unfamiliar shadows. In only a few minutes his chest rose and fell evenly. Yearning stabbed Christina's heart—yearning to spend a lifetime watching Lukas sleep, taking care of their own children together, once again walking freely through the streets of the city they loved. At the moment she couldn't be sure what the next three hours would bring. Still, she yearned for a future with Lukas.

They fell into a pattern over the next few days. During the day they huddled together in the cave, each bearing a part of the load of caring for the young children, entertaining the older ones, rationing food. When Lukas determined that darkness had fallen outdoors, he helped to settle the children for the night and then crept out.

Every night ripped through Christina's heart. Each time

Lukas crawled through the small opening, she knew that perhaps he would not be back. But each time he returned and not empty-handed. He brought fresh water or food. On the third morning, he brought two chickens plucked and ready to cook. "They have stopped laying eggs," he explained. "We may as well eat them." The meal, two skinny chickens divided among sixteen people, seemed like a feast.

Christina and Lukas continued their hushed conversations. One night Lukas returned with the news that the city leaders had offered fifty thousand bezants to each of fifty men who would be willing to take up arms against the Turks.

Christina gasped, her eyes wide. "That's a huge amount of money!"

Lukas nodded. "I volunteered."

"What! Oh, Lukas, no amount of money is worth your life."

"It's not just the money," Lukas explained. "The knights are doing nothing. Perhaps if men had banded together before this we could have done something."

"But you've said all along that since the fall of Tiberias, there have not been enough men left in Jerusalem to defend the city."

Lukas nodded. "And now there is no doubt. Only a handful of men volunteered, even for that amount of money. They are also offering one hundred bezants for any man willing to keep watch for a night."

"And did you volunteer for that as well?"

He shook his head. "I would be willing to take up arms if I thought there were a chance to save Jerusalem, but just to watch what is happening on the other side of the wall. . .I would rather spend my nights looking for things that will help you, Christina, and the children."

Christina snuggled up against Lukas. "I am unsure of many things, Lukas, but I am sure that you love me. Thank you."

He kissed the top of her head. "We are in God's care," he said, "even when it doesn't feel like we are. Be sure of that as well."

On the seventh morning, Christina woke even before Lukas returned from his nighttime prowlings. Judith and Daniel and Charles were pressed against the opening to the outside.

"Children!" she reprimanded them. "Get back!"

"But Miss Christina, the rock fire has stopped."

Christina hurried to the front of the cave. Careful to keep herself out of sight, she looked out onto the street. The rock fire had indeed stopped, and the streets were swarming with Jerusalem's inhabitants. What did it mean?

"Woe to us miserable people. We have no gold! What are we to do?" came the moaning from the street.

"What do they mean, Miss Christina?" Judith asked.

"I don't know," Christina murmured, scanning the crowd for Lukas. Finally he appeared and pressed himself through the opening.

Lukas scanned the faces of the older children around Christina.

"Listen carefully," he said in a hushed voice. "I don't want to frighten the younger children."

"What's happening, Lukas? Is it over? Is Saladin through the wall?" Christina's mind swirled with questions.

Lukas was nodding. "The tower has crumbled, and the Turks have taken the city."

"Why are those people out there talking about gold?" Charles asked.

"It seems the city leaders have been trying to strike a deal with Saladin. They wanted him to accept them as allies."

"Allies!" Christina called. "How could Jerusalem be an ally to the Turks?"

Lukas shrugged. "Perhaps they thought it was better than being slaughtered."

"Are we going to be slaughtered?" Judith asked, her voice thin with fear.

Lukas shook his head. "Let's pray not."

"Sister Angelica always prayed in Latin. I don't know enough Latin to pray."

"Then you shall pray in French," Lukas assured her. "And God will hear you just the same."

"Lukas, please, more details," Christina implored.

"Saladin refused the offer of an alliance. I don't blame him. We really have nothing to offer him. Then Balian, Ranier of Naples, and Thomas Patrick offered him one hundred thousand bezants if he would receive them. Still Saladin refused. Finally they asked what terms he would agree to."

"And?"

"He wants tribute. And they agreed. The gates are closed; Turkish guards are posted. No one can leave the city until the tribute has been settled."

"I don't understand, Lukas," Christina said. "Are Balian and the others going to pay tribute to Saladin?"

Lukas shook his head solemnly. "Each person must pay individual tribute. I'm sure they agreed to the terms because they have plenty of gold and can pay tribute for their entire households, even servants. But for many people, it will be more difficult."

Christina's voice was barely audible. "How much is the tribute, Lukas?"

"The price is ten bezants for older boys and men, five for women, and one for the children."

Christina could scarcely take it in. "That is a great deal of money."

Lukas nodded. "We have forty days. Anyone who can pay is free to go. We can even leave the city and go out into the countryside. Anyone who cannot pay becomes booty at the mercy of the army's sword. The Orthodox Christians can stay. But Saladin wants no more European Christians in Jerusalem."

"So we will be slaughtered!" Judith exclaimed.

"No," Lukas insisted. "We will find a way. We have forty days."

Chapter 11

The days crept by, first one, then two, finally enough to begin counting weeks. One week, then two.

Christina and the children moved back into the house the day the terms were announced. She made beds for Levi and Reuven. Devorah wanted to take Hadassah's children home with her, but Lukas persuaded her that they would wear her out if she were caring for them on her own. He suggested that she come to the house during the days to help with the children, as he planned to do. But at night she could return to her own home to get the rest she needed.

Levi still seemed calmest in Christina's arms. Too many changes in too few days had produced an almost constant state of anxiety in the little boy. Stephen spent a lot of his time hiding under furniture.

Christina determined to establish a routine for the children. They sat down together for meals at regular times. The older children were given responsibilities for chores or caring for the smaller ones.

Jerusalem slowly came to life. After breaking through the tower at the Jehosaphat Gate, Saladin had done relatively little damage to the rest of the city. He wasted no time removing

Christian symbols and reestablishing Muslim mosques. The headquarters of the Hospitaler Knights, for whom Lukas worked, became a Muslim college.

Rather than facing physical destruction of their homes, Jerusalem's families faced the oppression of the tribute. The markets were busy again, but rather than the usual wares, vendors hawked valuables. Few people had any real gold. They might sell most of their worldly goods but never gain enough to pay tribute for their households.

Christina anguished over Lukas and Devorah as much as for the children and herself. Lukas had no money, not even enough to ransom himself. And if he had ten bezants, the price of an adult male, he would give it to buy other lives rather than his own. Over and over Christina remembered the conversation when Lukas had had the opportunity to stand watch for one night and receive one hundred bezants. He could be free right now if he had chosen that path. But he had chosen to spend his nights taking care of Christina and the children, and that choice might now cost him his life.

When the tribute was announced, Christina immediately calculated what she owed. Daniel, Charles, and Gregory were old enough to demand a grown man's ransom of ten bezants. Stephen, Reuven, John, Levi, Louisa, and Leah would each owe one. Judith, Elizabet, Rebekah, and Marie were close enough to womanhood to warrant the women's tribute of five bezants, along with her own price. Altogether, Christina needed sixty-one bezants for herself and the children. Devorah and Lukas would owe another fifteen, and Christina resolved to do whatever she could to raise their tribute as well.

But how could she possibly raise seventy-six bezants in the remaining twenty-six days? The vegetable garden was ransacked, the hens unproductive. Besides, no one wanted to spend money on food if they could find it any other way. Christina herself counted carefully the few coins she found in Angelica's kitchen jar and used them wisely to buy staples.

On the fifteenth day, Christina heard Marie calling wildly down the upstairs hall and ran to see what was the matter.

"Miss Christina! Look!" the girl cried. "I was sweeping just as you asked me to, and look! I found two coins. Is it enough? Is it enough?" She pressed the small coins into Christina's hands.

"Marie, thank you!" Christina said enthusiastically. They would need much, much more than what these two long lost coins represented. But Marie was doing her best to help, and Christina wanted to acknowledge that.

The days ticked by: fifteen, sixteen, seventeen, eighteen.

Christina systematically went through every room of the house, looking for anything of value, anything that the Turks might take in exchange for money. The large floor vase in the common room gave her hope. It was only a beginning, but she was sure the artistry of it would be recognized even by the Turks. Christina remembered Angelica remarking once that it was quite old, though she was unsure of its origin. In the kitchen Christina found a plate with a gold rim that had arrived with a crate of odds and ends of donations. Christina had little experience with gold, but even she doubted that the thin line around the plate was very good gold, and in any event it was a very small quantity. But it was gold, and perhaps the plate itself would have some interest for a Turkish guard.

The day came when Christina forced herself to enter Angelica's room. She had never been in the large room at the end of the upstairs hall before. Angelica always kept the door closed, and it had remained closed since her death. Christina paused with her hand on the door handle. It seemed somehow disrespectful to enter, but she knew she must. Christina knew almost nothing about Angelica's personal life, her family, where she had come from before opening the Children's House single-handedly. What should she expect to find in her room? She turned the handle and pushed open the door.

Christina stood in the doorframe and surveyed the room. The room was large, and the sparsity of its furnishings only accentuated its size. She saw a simple pallet on the floor, not even a proper bed, though Angelica had always insisted that the children have beds. Above the pallet on a bare wall Christina saw a crucifix and a painting of Pope Urban II, who had been head of the church during the time of the successful crusade that had brought her own great-grandparents from France to Jerusalem. Across the room was a small round table and a plain wooden chair.

Christina crossed the creaky planks of the floor to examine the contents of the table: prayer beads, a half-burned candle, and a milk jar. She picked up the jar and was surprised by its weight. Christina had supposed it to be empty, but clearly it was full. Seeing the coins in the bottom she suddenly realized that she had stumbled upon the cache of coins that Angelica had used to try to pay Jacob for the goat milk he brought so faithfully—until a few weeks ago.

So often Jacob had left without glancing at the coins that Angelica set out for him, much less picking them up. After Jacob was gone, Christina would see Angelica pick up the coins and drop them in a pocket. She had always supposed that Angelica used the money Jacob refused on other household expenses. Now she understood that Angelica had methodically dropped the coins into this jar.

It looked like quite a bit of money. It was not likely to add up to the ten bezants Jacob would need in order to have the privilege of ever entering the city again, but Christina determined to find a way to give it to Jacob. He had not come to them since before Saladin began his siege on the eastern side of the city. Christina prayed he was safe. He would need the money now, and she was determined that he would have it. She refused even to count the coins, lest she be tempted to calculate how many children's lives they would redeem. That money belonged to Jacob.

Christina looked up at the crucifix on the wall and held Angelica's prayer beads in her hands. She had run into Claude in the market again, and he had been quick to tell her that he had found Angelica's body and overseen the proper handling of it. He promised to show her the burial spot when it was safe. Angelica had learned Latin from a priest at the Church of the Holy Sepulchre and had prayed fluently in the language of the church. Christina herself knew only enough Latin to mumble the appropriate responses during mass. But she was sure God understood French, and in her heart she prayed in French, giving thanks for Angelica's life and seeking courage for the days ahead.

Day nineteen, twenty, twenty-one, twenty-two, twenty-three, twenty-four, twenty-five.

The children seemed happier now. The younger ones, of course, did not truly understand what was happening. They were simply grateful that predictable routine had returned. Christina provided as much security and routine as she could muster for them. The older children she kept occupied. They understood, and she wanted them to be so busy that they didn't have time to ponder their troubles and so weary that they fell promptly asleep at night. Daniel and Charles, the oldest boys, had tried to find odd jobs to earn money, but no one was paying for jobs that were not urgent.

In her own room, Christina tugged on a trunk that she had not opened in nearly five years, long before her parents and brothers died. She knew that her dowry was in that chest. Her family was not wealthy. They had always had enough food to eat and clothes to wear, but there was no extra money. Her father had given her the trunk when she was eleven years old and told her to start storing things in it for her wedding. Along with her dowry, the trunk held a quilt her mother had made and a dress she had always hoped to marry in.

At nineteen, she was nearly an old maid. She and Lukas had hoped to marry when she was seventeen and he twenty. But his parents had died, leaving him to look after his grandmother and try to earn an income on the fringes of the army at the same time. Then Christina's family had fallen ill and died, and she had come to work at the house. Her hope to marry Lukas had never dimmed, but somehow the time had not seemed right.

Christina wore the key to the trunk around her neck, and now she used it to unlock the latch. She had never asked the amount of her dowry; she was simply satisfied to know it was there, and when the day came that she and Lukas could wed, the money would give them a good start. Without the dowry, it might be years more before they could marry. Lukas knew about the money. Perhaps he had even discussed the amount with her father. He knew the money would become his property when he married Christina. Would it make a difference?

And then of course there were the thirteen children. She could not abandon them, yet she couldn't ask Lukas to take on responsibility for them. If she didn't have the money but she did have thirteen children, would Lukas take her as his wife?

Desperately she wanted to believe he would.

With trembling hands, she opened the trunk and pushed aside the dress to find a pouch of coins. Her stomach rose to her throat as she lifted it and opened it. Would it be enough? Could she ransom everyone? Save sixteen lives, including her own? She let the coins spill into her hands. It was not so much as she might have imagined.

Perhaps half. It was enough to save perhaps half the lives. Even combined with the plate and the vase, it was not enough.

Chapter 12

Day thirty-six, thirty-seven, thirty-eight, thirty-nine. Day forty.

Christina waited until the last day to stand in the tribute line. Many of the wealthier citizens of Jerusalem had paid their tributes immediately and used the remainder of their wealth to finance a journey to a new home. Christina thought only one day at a time. If she could not afford to pay tribute on herself and thirteen children, how could she possibly pack their belongings and lead them into an unknown future?

Lukas had not come by the house for three days. Until then she had seen him every morning and evening as he escorted his grandmother back and forth. Devorah was determined to be of help to Hadassah's children, and along the way she had become markedly attached to most of the younger children. Though she still moved at snail speed, she had a spark in her eye that Christina hadn't seen in years. Being with the children was clearly good for Devorah, and Christina was convinced being with Devorah was good for the small children.

Lukas looked for work. He had earned a good amount of money helping a wealthy family pack their belongings before their departure. But when he appeared one morning with sacks of food, she suspected that he had spent most of his earnings on their supplies. She avoided asking him directly if he had fifteen bezants to ransom himself and his grandmother.

In the early weeks, they held hushed conversations in the courtyard each evening, speaking with optimism. So much could change in forty days, they told each other, or thirty-five days, or thirty days. Lukas, a displaced soldier, might find work. Saladin might change his mind and be even more merciful when he realized that many of Jerusalem's inhabitants could ill afford the tribute he demanded.

But as the weeks ticked by, Christina's hope faded. There was no reason to hold Lukas responsible for thirteen children. It was up to her to find the tribute for them. After day thirty, she wouldn't speak to Lukas of tributes, except to urge him to do what he could for his grandmother. After day thirty-five, she found it difficult to speak to him at all. Just seeing his face reminded her of their lost future.

So now Christina supposed that he stayed away because she had treated him so distantly. She didn't blame him.

The line was long. Christina was at once encouraged and frightened that so many people had scrounged up tribute money. She strained to hear stories of mercy from people leaving the tribute office but heard none. Clearly those who did not have the required tribute had not come to stand in line. They would face the consequence of their poverty from their homes.

Christina looked down at the bundle in her arms. A large vase, which was beginning to feel heavy, the plate, and the dowry pouch. The dowry would pay half of the tribute she owed. It seemed unlikely that the vase and the plate would cover the rest, but she prayed—in French—for a miracle. And she prayed that God would not ask her to make a choice. If she did not have enough money for all thirteen lives, how could she possibly choose which names to list? She would sacrifice her own life for any one of the children; but how could she choose among them?

She felt a nudge at her elbow and turned to see Lukas standing beside her. Relief flooded through her at the sight of him, followed closely by guilt and anxiety for her recent rejection of him.

"That vase looks heavy," he said. "May I hold it for you?"

She released her load into his willing arms, seeing that he had a bundle of his own. Perhaps he had come up with the tribute. Perhaps he would be all right after all! She held onto the plate and the pouch.

"Thank you," she said awkwardly.

"Christina, what's come over you?" he asked softly. "I thought maybe you didn't want to see me anymore. You seemed relieved to see me leave each night. But I can't stay away from you. Please tell me what's wrong."

"I'm sorry, Lukas. Sorry I've treated you badly. Sorry I've not appreciated everything you've done for the children. I hate to think what all that food you brought us cost you. . . ." She left the thought unfinished and glanced toward the front of the line. "I'm afraid, Lukas," she finally admitted. "Afraid for us, for the children, for all of Jerusalem."

"Have I not told you often enough that we are in God's care?"

"Yes, Lukas, but I am here standing in line, and I know I do not have enough money to pay tribute for everyone. It will soon be my turn to go to the table."

"Even there you are in God's care, Christina."

"Lukas, I've been praying for hours, even days." She laughed nervously. "When you assured Judith that God hears prayers in French, I decided to believe you."

Lukas smiled broadly, and Christina looked at him, puzzled.

"I have something to show you," he said. "Here, take my bundle and open it."

She took the small bundle from under his arm and slowly folded back the cloth. Within the soft cloth lay a gleaming silver chalice.

"Your grandmother's chalice!"

Lukas nodded. "She always said that she was going to give it to me on my wedding day. And I would have liked that. But what is the point of a family heirloom if you are not there to share it with me? That's what Grandmother said when I refused to accept her chalice."

"I know how much this means to her."

"You mean more to her, Christina. And the children have come to mean more to her."

"But this has been in your family for hundreds of years."

He nodded. "And perhaps this was God's purpose for it all along. Do you remember what the inscription says?"

Christina turned the chalice in her hands, careful not to leave fingerprints or smudges. "You said it was a Christian inscription. 'I will pour out my blood for you.' "

"That's right. You have poured out your life for those children. It seems only right that this cup should pay your ransom and theirs."

"Oh no! I couldn't let you do that!" Christina protested.

Lukas raised an eyebrow. "I know your parents raised you to be proud, Christina, but do not reject a gift of grace when it stands before you in the street."

Christina couldn't help but smile. She held up her own little pouch. "My wedding dowry."

"Ah," Lukas said. "Have you pulled back from me because

you thought I would not marry you without your dowry?"

She looked away from him, not wanting to admit the doubts of his love that had overwhelmed her. "It turns out it's not much after all."

"I told your father years ago that it did not matter how much money he put into that pouch. I wouldn't let him tell me how much it was. I didn't care if he didn't have anything for your dowry. I've wanted to marry you since we were children, Christina. That hasn't changed."

"But I suddenly have thirteen children, Lukas. They're depending on me. If you marry me. . ."

"Then they'll be my children too."

They had come to the front of the line. Tears streamed down Christina's face as Lukas placed the chalice on the table and listed the names of the ransomed, beginning with her own.

Christina tucked her arm through Lukas's for the walk back to the house, pausing to look at the Church of the Holy Sepulchre. While Saladin had begun tearing apart Christian churches on the east side of the city, he had promised not to destroy this church.

"Angelica loved to pray in that church," Christina said softly.

"Because it gave her hope to do so," Lukas responded. "Before we leave Jerusalem, we will marry in that church and remember her hope, our hope."

Christina looked up at him. He still carried the awkward vase and looked a little silly. Warm love flowed through her. She knew it always would, no matter how silly Lukas might look. She held up her pouch.

"Let's not wait any longer, Lukas."

He nodded. "We'll tell the children—our children—and I'll make the arrangements with the priest."

SUSANNAH HAYDEN

Writing under a pen name, Susan Martins Miller is a wife, mother, and editor for Cook Communications who lives in Colorado Springs, Colorado. She has partnered with Barbour Books on many successful writing projects

Cup of Honor

by Marilou H. Flinkman

To Barry Fell,
my friend and advisor on Jewish religion

All scripture in *Cup of Honor* is taken from the Hebrew Bible according to the Masoretic Text.

"And I will bring you in unto the land,
concerning which I lifted up My hand to
give it to Abraham, to Isaac, and to Jacob;
and I will give it to you for a heritage."
EXODUS 6:8

Chapter 1

Early 1948

Leah stood on the crowded deck of the rusted tramp freighter. Sixteen hundred Jews overloaded the old ship renamed the *Star of David.* She kept a protective arm around her younger brother. "We're going to make it, Reuven. We're going to find a new home in Palestine."

Reuven pushed away from Leah. At seventeen he stood nearly a half-foot taller than his sister. He didn't need protecting. "Look," he pointed to the British cruiser approaching them. "Looks like we have an escort."

Leah brushed back the tendrils of black curly hair that had escaped her braids as she looked to the American captain of the *Star of David.* He picked up the loud speaker and announced, "Keep calm, everyone. There's no danger."

"They can't touch us until we are within three miles of land," Reuven told his sister.

Leah tried to act calm, but she felt sure everyone could hear her heart pounding. *We have survived the Nazis to get this far. Dear God, don't fail us now,* she prayed silently, still clutching the rail. "I better get back to the children," she told her brother. "They'll be frightened."

Before she got to the ladder leading below deck, the captain stopped her. "There's enough fog for me to make a run for the beach. Bring the children up on deck. We'll get them to shore first."

Leah started to protest but thought better of it. She nodded to the captain. "I'll get them ready."

Working with the other nurse and doctor on board, Leah tried to explain to the children that they would be dropped over the side of the ship and must swim for shore. There the Palmach, the Jewish secret army, would gather them up and get them safely into Palestine.

Excitement filled the air as the first glimpses of Eretz Israel, the Land of Israel, could be seen in the wind-driven swirls of fog. The old boat churned at her greatest speed toward the secluded beach. Leah saw the white water around the jagged rocks near the shore and tried to find Reuven to warn him to be careful. She couldn't spot his flaming red hair in the crush of people. The old freighter creaked and shuddered as her timbers smashed into the rocks. Confusion reigned.

"Quick, quick, get to the people waiting on shore." One by one the children were handed over the side to waiting arms below. In all the disorder Leah lost sight of her brother.

"Leah, go. Go, now," the captain shouted.

Looking around, she realized she was one of the few left on board. She went over the side. The cold water swept over her, taking her breath away. She struggled to the surface and swam for the shore. She could see flashes of light and people rushing up the beach to safety. In the shrouds of fog, she searched for Reuven. She hit the rocks along the shore, and when she tried to stand, she fell back on the jagged edges.

Finally gaining her footing, she looked up to see four uniformed British soldiers. "No, no!" she screamed as they reached for her. "I must find Reuven. I must take care of my little brother." She kicked and hit at the men trying to subdue her. When one man put a hand over her mouth to quiet her screams, she bit him. A truncheon came down against her head, and she fell into blackness.

Leah came to with a splitting headache. Trying to raise her head sent waves of nausea over her. She could feel the gentle sway of the cot she lay on. "Where am I? Where is my brother?"

She got no answer. Again she tried to sit up, swallowing back the bile in her throat and thinking only of finding Reuven.

"You starting to wake up are you?" a kindly voice asked. "You've been out so long I worried how much damage those soldiers had done to you."

Leah looked up to see the nurse she had worked with on the *Star of David*. "Where are we?" she whispered.

"On our way to Cyprus."

"Cyprus!" Dizziness sent Leah back on her cot.

The cool hand of the nurse felt the knot at the side of Leah's head. "Better lie still. You have a concussion."

"My brother. Where is Reuven?" she asked in deep concern.

"I haven't seen him on this boat. Wasn't he one of the first off the *Star of David*?

"I don't know. The captain sent me below to help get the children ready to run for shore, and I never saw him."

Again the cool hand rested on her forehead. "He must be one of the lucky ones who made it to the waiting Palmach."

"What will happen to him? I need to take care of him," Leah protested.

"He looked like he could take care of himself," the nurse said kindly. "Reuven is big and strong enough to face whatever comes."

"I've failed," Leah moaned.

For the rest of the trip, she refused to speak at all unless it was to ask about her brother. She followed the refugees as they were led into the camp at Caraolos on Cyprus. Barbed wire and tents didn't faze her. She could only worry about Reuven. Was he safe?

The horrid conditions of the camp didn't lend to her getting any special attention. No one seemed to care about her or her brother. She went to the tent assigned to her, sank down on the cot, and turned her face to the canvas wall.

She didn't know or care how long she stayed there. "I've failed," she would moan over and over. "I promised Oma I would take care of little Reuven, and I have failed."

The light in the tent went dim. Leah turned toward the door to see what blocked the sun. Holding back the flap of the tent stood a giant of a man. *He must be well over six feet tall,* Leah thought. His wild black hair framed a weather-beaten face that held ice blue eyes.

"Are you Leah Shapira?" he demanded in a deep voice.

Pulled by his strength, Leah sat up and nodded her head.

"Are you a nurse?"

"Yes," she whispered.

"We need you," he stated.

Chapter 2

"Who are you?" Leah swung her legs over the side of her cot and pulled on her shoes.

"Joshua Ben Ami. I'm a Palestinian, and we need your help."

"All I want to do is find my brother," Leah said weakly.

"Who's your brother? Is he in this camp?"

Leah shook her head from side to side. "I don't know. No one will help me," she moaned.

"We don't have time to help weeping women. Get up," he ordered. "Let me show you what it's like here. If you decide to help us, I'll try to find your brother."

Sighing in resignation, Leah got off the bed and walked toward the giant in her doorway. He looked like a wild man with his bushy black hair and mustache. In spite of her lethargy, she felt a tingle of interest in this man giving her orders.

"Where are we going?" she asked.

Joshua took hold of Leah's arm in a viselike grip and led her into the sunshine. He held on to her while she became accustomed to the bright light. "Walk with me."

Leah barely came to his shoulder and had to look up to see his face. The sun had baked lines into his young face that aged him beyond his years. "Why are you doing this to me?" She hurried to keep up with his pace.

"See that tent?" He pointed to one standing a bit apart. "That's the synagogue. Not much more than a mezuzah at the door, but we do have ritual candelabra. Do you keep the Shabbat?"

"Oma taught us to keep the commandments," she whispered. "I don't know what day it is. Is this Saturday?"

"No, you are not breaking the Sabbath. I must admit, we aren't as good as we should be in keeping the rituals in this place."

"Why are you here?" she asked in curiosity. "You said you were a Palestinian. Did the British capture you?"

His booming laugh made Leah smile. "No. I break into their camp to bring what aid I can."

"You break in?" she asked in wonder.

"They don't keep a very close guard on the garbage dump. If they see me out there, they think I am picking through their waste rather than coming in the back door."

He stopped in front of another tent. "This is where you are needed. Just walk through with me and look. Then decide if you can turn your back on your duty." Joshua pulled her into the shade of the canvas structure.

Leah didn't feel him release her arm. She walked slowly between the cots. Her mind and soul filled with horror at the conditions. "Why are they so dirty?" she asked Joshua.

"We have a choice. We have enough water to drink, or we can keep the patients washed."

"No water?" She looked at him in disbelief. "You have a hospital with no water?"

"The British didn't think water was a priority." His voice dripped with bitterness.

Leah continued to walk past the patients. When one or two reached out to her, she took their outstretched hands and murmured words of comfort. She saw faces yellow with jaundice, festering sores, and what looked like tuberculosis.

"What's being done?" she demanded.

"We get no help from the British," Joshua growled. "What money we get is from Jews around the world. We buy medicine and smuggle it in."

"What do you think I can do? I have no money. I lost my only family when Reuven disappeared. I don't belong here," Leah protested.

"None of these people do. Like you, they dreamed of a new start in Palestine. This is what they got." He looked down at her. "Can you deny them what little comfort you can offer?"

Leah did not answer. She continued to walk to where she heard children. "Their heads are shaved," she exclaimed.

"Some of them needed to be deloused. That's the only method we have to get rid of the lice."

Looking into eyes blank of emotion, Leah felt torn. Is Reuven in a place like this? Who is helping him?

"What is it you want of me?" she asked Joshua.

"We have so little we can do for these people. You could offer comfort," he suggested softly.

And who will comfort me, she cried silently, wondering if she would ever see her brother again. She followed Joshua out of the tent into the heat of the sun.

Joshua put his arm around her, pulling her shoulder into his chest. "I know you can bring hope."

"Hope? What hope do we have here?" she asked in disgust.

He smiled. "I manage to smuggle a few out of here into Palestine."

She pulled away, putting her hands on his chest. "I want to go," she demanded. "I need to find Reuven."

"If you'll spend a little time here, helping nurse the sick, I promise I'll look for your brother."

"I need to find him now," she cried desperately.

"You don't know the land. You have no idea where to start." He grabbed her fluttering hands in one of his.

Feeling the calluses on his hand holding hers, Leah sensed the strength of this man. She looked into his eyes that before had seemed the color of ice. Now they looked like the blue flowers that grew in Oma's garden. "How long must I stay here?"

"Now you want to bargain with me." His deep chuckle warmed a part of her that had been cold for a very long time.

Leah did not pull her hands away. She liked the feel of this man. *He will help Reuven and me,* she reasoned, then said, "I will serve my time. After all, I am in prison, aren't I?"

He smiled. "Not my prison. Even the British call it a camp. Were you in the camps in Germany?"

She shook her head. "Our parents got Reuven and me to our grandmother in Switzerland. We didn't suffer as these people did." She motioned toward the feeble bodies sitting in the shade of the tent. "Will they see Eretz Israel?"

"That's the dream that keeps them alive. That's the promise that God made to our people. A land of our own." Joshua's words held passion.

Leah looked up at this man and listened as his booming voice quoted the prophet Ezekiel: " 'Thus saith the Lord God: I will even gather you from the peoples, and assemble you out of the countries where ye have been scattered and I will give you the land of Israel. . . . And I will give them one heart, and I will put a new spirit within you; and I will remove the stony heart out of their flesh, and will give them a heart of flesh; that they may walk in my statues, and keep mine ordinances, and do them; and they will be my people, and I will be their God.' "

The listless people, who moments before had sat with drooping heads, stood trying to hold their backs straight and cheered the Word of God.

This man is a leader, and I will follow him, Leah declared to herself as she joined in the cheering.

Chapter 3

Leah rose early. Using the water sparingly, she prepared for the day. Breakfast consisted of weak tea and stale bread. "British don't offer much in the way of food," a woman sitting across from Leah in the mess tent commented. "Haven't seen you before. You new here?"

"Yes." Leah did not feel comfortable admitting she had stayed in bed for days. The nurse from the boat had brought her food and insisted she eat even the foul soups. "Now I need to go to work."

"What do you do?"

"I'm a nurse." She smiled wanly. "A nurse with no medicine and not even water to bathe the patients. Maybe I can hold their hands." She took her cup back to the kitchen and walked slowly to the hospital, hoping to see Joshua.

At the hospital she found her friend from the *Star of David.* "Thank you for taking care of me," she told the woman.

"You find your brother?"

Leah shook her head. "Not yet. A Palmach who broke into camp dragged me here." She motioned to the patients in the tent around her. "He said if I would help here, he would look for Reuven."

Her friend laughed. "You must have met Joshua. He has a way of getting things done." She put her hand out. "If we are to work together, we should be friends. I'm Sarah."

Leah took the offered handshake. "I'm Leah. Thanks for being so good to me." Curious, she asked, "How do you know Joshua? Did he drag you in here too?"

Sarah laughed. "No, he caught me taking food."

"Really?" Leah couldn't believe what Sarah had confessed.

"I guess I'm to blame for you being here. I had to tell him I wasn't stealing food for myself but for you. That's how he found out where you were."

"You stole for me?" Leah felt a wave of guilt. "I've been very selfish."

Sarah patted Leah's arm. "You've been worried about your brother. Now let me show you what little we can do around here."

Sarah knew the patients by name and stopped to introduce Leah to some of them. "We have some medicine that Joshua smuggled in. We dole it out to those who need it most." She looked at Leah with tears in her eyes. "Sometimes only to the ones we know we can help."

"Is there nothing we can do? Can't we protest to the British government?"

"It's been tried. Takes long months to even get an answer. In the meantime, good Jews in America send money to help us. That's the reason we have a school and a synagogue. We set them up ourselves."

"Does Joshua come often?" Leah tried not to show her personal interest in the man.

"He is just one of the Palmach who sneak in with supplies. He is one of the more important leaders, and I've been told he travels all over Palestine, helping settle refugees."

"Maybe in his travels he'll find Reuven." Leah felt new hope for her brother.

At the back corner of the tent, Leah looked at the children and saw dull eyes that showed no life. She turned to Sarah. "What's happened to them?"

"Trauma from the war." Sarah sighed. "Some of them have been hidden in attics in Germany and never played in the sun. Most have lost their parents. They have nothing to live for."

"The Aliyah Bet helped Reuven and me. Did they bring these children here?" Sadness filled Leah as she looked at the listless children.

Sarah nodded. "They want youth to grow and make our new homeland strong."

Leah shrugged. "And they wound up in another camp." Sighing deeply she reached to brush the face of a child. "What can we do for them?"

"You can teach them to play and to sing," came the deep voice of the man who had dragged her from her cot just a day before.

"I don't know how to sing." Leah turned to face her tormentor. His deeply tanned face and wild black hair did not go with the gentle look in his blue eyes.

"You and the children can learn together," he said, putting a hand on her shoulder. "We have only our faith to share with them in this place."

Faith? I am not sure I have faith anymore, Leah thought. "Maybe I can remember the songs our mother sang to us as children."

He squeezed her shoulder. "Do what you can to bring back their spirit. They are the hope of tomorrow."

Leah looked at the listless, pinched faces and wondered

what kind of a tomorrow any of them would have.

"I am on my way to the garbage pit," Joshua told the women.

"When will you be back?" Leah asked with more than casual interest.

"Depends on what I find in the kibbutz we are building in Galilee. Others will be coming in with supplies as they are available."

"Thank you for the drugs," Sarah said quietly. "We appreciate all the help the Palmach gives us."

"Thank the good people who support us." Joshua turned to leave. Looking back, his glance held Leah's. "I will ask for a Reuven Shapira. You said he had bright red hair?"

"Yes. He looks like our father."

"And he is seventeen?"

"Yes," Leah answered.

"If I find him, I will send word," he promised.

Something deep inside of Leah wished Joshua would come back to see her. "I would appreciate knowing of your progress."

Joshua waved. "Until we meet again."

May that be soon, Leah's heart prayed.

Sarah looked after Joshua as she whispered to Leah, "Don't give your heart to that one. He's married to Palestine."

"I heard him quote the words given to Moses, promising that we will have a homeland. He's a strong leader," Leah said wistfully, watching Joshua disappear out the back of the tent.

"And what do we have here?"

The women turned to see a British officer walking toward them. "You can't be sick," he said leering at Leah. "You are much too pretty to be in here."

"I am a nurse," Leah stated firmly.

"Oh, a pretty little Jewish nurse. Welcome, my dear, to the

British camp for refugees." His tone dripped with sarcasm.

Leah gritted her teeth, sensing it would be best to say nothing to this arrogant fool. When he reached out to touch her, Leah stepped back, wondering if she would have to tolerate his unwelcome attentions.

"Oh, you visiting us again?" Sarah asked, stepping between Leah and the offensive officer. "What can I do for you today?"

"Nurse Sarah to the rescue?" he asked.

Leah stepped forward, letting anger take over her reason. "I don't need protection from someone who would abuse sick old people and children." She motioned around the tent. "Is this your idea of a jolly good time?" Her voice held the fury she felt.

The man backed up, showing surprise at her outburst.

Leah stepped closer, hands on hips. "You won't even give them water to drink. Would it take away from your afternoon tea to share with us?"

"Where did you come from?" he asked in wonder.

"It took four of your mighty British warriors to capture me. Will they get a medal for that?" she asked with no less sarcasm than he had shown.

The officer stood straight and smoothed his spotless uniform. "You say you need water?" he asked in a soft voice.

"Yes, so even though we have no medicine we can at least put a cool cloth on the head of the suffering."

He backed up, trying to show dignity. "I'll see what I can do."

"You do that," Leah growled at him.

Chapter 4

"Is it safe to breathe now?" Sarah stood with her hand over her heart.

Leah looked at her pale friend. "Are you all right?"

"You about gave me a heart attack talking to a British officer like that," Sarah scolded.

"That pompous windbag? What could he do? Throw me in a dungeon?" She wiped the perspiration from her forehead. "It might be cooler than here."

Sarah took a deep breath, then started to chuckle. "I don't think anyone has ever stood up to that one. Do you think we might get more water?"

"If we don't, I will go to his commander and complain about his harassing me as a woman."

"You are a feisty one. Two days ago, I didn't think you would ever get off that cot, and now you are standing up to the British Army."

"We'll have to if we are to force them to recognize the Balfour Treaty."

"We have to get to Palestine first."

"And we have to keep these people well so they can go too." Leah started to walk back through the patients, taking time to speak to each one.

"You did a good job," one withered old man told her. "It was the ones with spunk like yours that survived the Nazi camps."

"That must mean you," she told him, patting his hand. "Let me go find some water and a cup and bring it around."

By late afternoon, the temperature in the tent was approaching one hundred degrees. "Let's get the ones who can walk, outside," Leah suggested to Sarah. "In the shade of the tent, they may find the air less stifling." Leah gripped the arm of a woman sitting on the edge of her cot and helped her stand.

Sarah and Leah moved several of the patients into the fresh air.

"It may be hot, but at least they can see something besides canvas," Sarah noted.

"Barbed wire," Leah said, looking at the fence around the camp.

"We've seen lots of that, Miss," murmured one old man. "At least here we are closer to Palestine."

Hearing a clear voice singing, Leah looked around to find its source. She spotted a young woman not much older than herself. "Join me," the woman urged, walking closer to where the people sat in the shade of the tent.

Leah listened to the words and then joined in:

Onward! Onward to Palestine
In happiness we throng,
Onward! Onward to Palestine
Come join our happy song!

"We learned that on the boat. We'll make it to our homeland even if it is by way of Cyprus," the young woman shouted to

Leah and the others gathered in the shade.

"Do you know other songs? Could you teach the children?" Leah asked, remembering what Joshua had instructed her.

"I help in the school. Do you mean those children?"

"I was thinking of the ones in the hospital. Maybe we could teach the ones in school first, and they could get the ones in the hospital interested in learning."

"Worth a try," her new friend said.

Joshua will be pleased when he comes back, Leah told herself.

A few days later as Leah administered what few medicines they had, she looked up from a sick bed and saw a British officer. Standing up to get a better look, she recognized her antagonist. "So, you came back," she said, wiping her face with the back of her hand.

"Will this be a help?" He put down a five-gallon container.

"This is water?" Leah asked.

He nodded. "I'll try to bring more."

Leah looked at his face. He seemed to be sincere. "Thank you. I can bathe at least their hands and face. Feeling clean can be healing." She looked pointedly at his crisp uniform and clean-shaven face. Leah was rewarded with a blush on the officer's cheeks.

"I apologize for my behavior," he stammered. "You're a very attractive woman, and I'm sorry I offended you."

"It's all right to offend the unattractive?" She couldn't keep the sarcasm out of her voice.

"I didn't mean it that way. I only meant to say you are a beautiful woman."

"Thank you. I would look a lot better if I could take a bath and wear clean clothes, but that seems to be limited to the British. Jews are riffraff to be locked up."

"I don't always agree with what my countrymen do."

"But it didn't bother you to try a little Jew-baiting yourself." She looked at the water and back to the officer. "I appreciate what you have done. Anything that alleviates the suffering of my people is appreciated."

"I'll try to talk to my commander and get more help for you. I know I'll be able to bring water from time to time."

"Thank you. I'm sorry if I didn't treat you with respect when you were here last. I lost my temper."

He smiled. "You do have quite a temper, and I'll try not to be the brunt of it again." He stood with his hat in his hand. "I'll leave so you can get back to work. May I know your name?"

"I'm Leah. Thank you again for the water. It will bring comfort." She lifted the heavy container and started for the back of the tent.

The young woman from the school brought a dozen children to the hospital to sing. The elderly smiled. Some sat up to listen. Leah heard a noise from the children's area and saw several of the young ones had come to listen. She went to them and urged them forward. "Come on. We'll learn the songs too."

The sound of music brought a feeling of hope. The older people talked about when they used to return to the synagogue after Yom Kipper to sing and dance all night.

"And we will sing and dance in our own land," Leah told them. In her mind she dreamed of dancing with Joshua. *Do you think you will ever see him again? Did he just coax you into the hospital with the promise of finding Reuven?* Shaking such gloomy thoughts away, Leah went back to the children who sat with blank faces and did not appear to hear the songs.

As she used some of the precious water to bathe their hands and faces, she sang to them. *Someday those eyes will sparkle again,* she told herself. *We must keep our faith.*

That night Leah tried to sleep, but thoughts of Joshua crowded her mind. Again and again she heard his voice as he spoke to the people. " 'And I will give you the land of Israel.' "

Turning over, Leah promised herself, *I will follow this man as my ancestors followed Moses.*

Chapter 5

Leah worked day after day. More supplies were smuggled in, but Joshua did not appear.

"Do you know the Palmach Joshua Ben Ami?" she asked one of the men who had brought medicine.

"Everyone's heard of Joshua. Last I knew he was in the North. There's been trouble draining a swamp to set up another kibbutz near the border."

Leah thanked the man but dared not ask more. "Why did I think he would come back? All I hear is how important he is. Why would he remember me?" she muttered to herself.

Just then the young woman Deborah who taught the children songs arrived with a group of children. "Are you busy? Should we come back?" she asked Leah.

"No, please lead the children inside. They bring hope to faces where I never thought to see a smile again." She put down the basin she carried. "How are the children from here doing in school?" Leah asked with concern.

"Good, considering some of them didn't speak a word for months. They at least listen with interest, and someday they'll be able to join in," Deborah encouraged.

Leah shuddered. "I don't want to know what horrors sent them into such deep trauma."

Deborah agreed, then led her group of singers into the tent. Leah took the basin out to empty. When she came back, she saw a familiar giant of a man standing in the doorway, watching.

"You came back." She walked up behind Joshua, repressing the urge to throw her arms around him.

"Did you doubt me?" he asked, turning to face Leah.

She felt her face grow hot from the guilty thoughts she had harbored. "It's been a long time," she mumbled weakly.

"I brought you good news."

"Reuven. You found my brother." Excitement filled her mind, blotting out her memories of doubting Joshua.

He led her outside the hospital tent. "He's in a youth camp in northern Galilee."

"Is he well? Tell me about him," she urged.

"He's fine. Seems to fit right into the kibbutz lifestyle. Works with the others to grow crops and take care of the younger children," he told her.

"How soon can I leave? How long will it take me to get to this camp?" Passion rose in Leah's breast. "I can't wait to see him."

"Slow down." Joshua took her fluttering hands. "Your brother is fine. You know where he is and that he's well cared for."

"But he needs me. I must get to him at once." She struggled to free her hands.

"Reuven is a fine young man. He doesn't need a keeper."

Leah pulled her hands free and rested them on her hips. She felt the heat of anger rage through her being. "What do you know of my little brother? I promised Oma I would take care of him, and I will do it," she shouted.

"Leah, your little brother is nearly six feet tall. He likes the life he has in the kibbutz. He doesn't need a big sister."

"I don't believe you. I want to go to him now," she demanded.

"Reuven is doing fine. You should be proud of him. He can

take apart a rifle and put it back together faster than anyone in his group."

"Guns. You gave my brother guns?"

"Leah, that is enough. Quiet down and listen to me." He put his hands on her shoulders. "There will be war. Do you want your brother to be able to protect himself or not?"

"War? We just fought a war," she cried in frustration.

"Look around you, Girl. You live in a prison camp. Do you expect the British to say, 'Sorry, just a mistake, let us hold the gate for you?' "

"What about the Balfour Treaty? They have to give us a Jewish homeland," Leah insisted.

"Leah, that treaty was signed in 1917. What makes you think they're going to honor it now?" Joshua asked in exasperation.

"But war? You're going to send my brother into war?" Standing with her hands on her hips, she fought back tears of desperation.

"We don't want to fight. We're trying to work with the government. It's more than the British. The Arab chiefs who fear us set their people against us. We have come in and made the desert bloom. They have left their people to scrape in the dust for centuries. They don't want them to learn our ways and become independent. The chiefs would lose their power," Joshua explained.

Tears escaped her eyes. "What are you going to do?"

"I'm going to keep helping refugees find a place to live. I am going to smuggle supplies into this camp. I am going to encourage young men like Reuven to live in peace but to be ready in case of war."

"I still want out of here," she insisted quietly.

"So does everyone in this camp. We're trying to get word into the international press. If we can put enough pressure on the British, they may ease up on the quotas of people they allow to migrate to Palestine. In the meantime, we need you here."

"Why?" Tears of frustration poured down her cheeks.

"I've talked to the people here." He pointed to the tent where the sounds of singing and laughter filled the air. "I'm seeing people who a month ago wouldn't sit up. Now they are standing and clapping their hands. Some are even singing." Joy sounded in his voice.

"Deborah taught them," Leah muttered.

"She helped, but I hear the stories of your compassion and love. These people need and deserve you. Will you deny them?" he asked sternly.

"I don't know."

"Leah, living by faith means believing that God is generous and that we ought to be generous as well. Would your grandmother want you to go to Reuven, who doesn't need you, or would she encourage you to help your people?"

Leah sighed deeply. His question stirred up memories of Oma.

Joshua let go of her and looked to the heavens. " 'I command thee this day to love the Lord thy God, to walk in His ways, and to keep His commandments and His statutes and His ordinances; then thou shalt live and multiply, and the Lord thy God shall bless thee in the land whither thou goest in to possess it,' " he quoted from Deuteronomy.

Leah looked into his face which glowed with faith. *How can I refuse? I have vowed to follow the commandments given to Moses.* She shook her head, trying to clear her thoughts. *But what of Reuven? Shouldn't my family be my first concern?*

Joshua's hands dropped to her shoulders again. "You know what you have to do."

Chapter 6

Do you have the letter for Reuven ready?" Joshua asked later that day.

"Yes." Leah pulled the document out of her pocket. "When will you see him?"

"I probably won't see him, but I'll send this with someone going that way." He looked into her face, his expression so gentle it twisted her heart. "You're doing what's right, Leah. A little while longer and you will be joining him," Joshua told her gently.

She swallowed hard, not wanting him to see how much she hurt. Looking into his weather-beaten face and shining blue eyes, she knew she was as sorry to see him go as she was not to see Reuven. "When will you be back?" she asked quietly.

He shrugged. "Never know. Palestine is in such turmoil, I'm running from one place to another trying to keep things together."

"I'll miss you," she admitted out loud.

His hands still rested on her shoulders. "And I'll look forward to seeing you again." His usually rough voice held tenderness.

Could he care for me? she wondered.

Squeezing her shoulders gently before he released her, he smiled and turned to go.

"Where would you like the water, Leah?" The British officer's question startled both of them.

Joshua looked back. Leah stood between the two men.

"Could you carry this for the lady?" the officer asked Joshua.

Looking from Joshua's scowl to the officer's smile, Leah intervened. "I can carry it." She reached to take the container.

Joshua grabbed it first. "What is this?" he growled.

Leah looked at her feet. "I demanded water, and this man has been bringing us an extra five gallons each week." She looked up to the officer and tried to smile as she murmured, "Thank you."

Joshua looked at the uniform. Fury filled his face. "And how does he manage that?" he demanded.

The officer seemed stunned at Joshua's reaction. "I save the water given me to wash. Leah said she needed it to bathe some of the patients."

"Humph." Joshua turned to Leah. "Where do you want this?"

"Where we keep the medicines in the hospital tent," she told him.

The officer looked after Joshua. "I'm sorry if I made him angry. Why would he object to your having more water?" His face showed open curiosity.

"I don't think it is the water that made him angry," Leah explained softly.

Seeing Joshua returning, the officer tipped his hat to Leah. "I'd better be going. I'll bring more water when I can." He left hurriedly.

"How did you meet that dandy?" Joshua demanded.

"He came into the hospital. I found him rude and lost my

temper." With her eyes, she pleaded for his understanding.

"It doesn't seem to have scared him off. How long has this been going on?" Joshua's face was black with rage.

Leah cowered in front of him. "Nothing is going on. I demanded more water, and he has been bringing it. That is all. What did you think, I would get down and beg for supplies?"

"I don't like you being friendly with the British."

"I am no friend to my jailers. I found a way to get more water, and I took it. Do you want me to deny a sponge bath to the dying?" Anger rose in her at his suggestion that she would do anything improper.

"I guess five gallons of water is a help," he admitted reluctantly. "What will you ask for next?"

"Nothing," she stated firmly, "and I will give nothing either."

Joshua appeared to relax. "I have seen your temper," he smiled. "I am only surprised your officer didn't bring a tanker truck of water."

"It happened when I first got here. I may not have worked up enough rage yet." She let her stiff spine relax.

"I must be on my way. I just hope that officer doesn't come looking for me in the next few days."

"Maybe you should stay," she suggested hopefully.

"I'm needed elsewhere. He'll just have to look and wonder."

"Do they look for people you smuggle out?" Concern filled her voice.

"He probably will when we take you out. We'll have to think up an excuse for his little spitfire having deserted him." Joshua smiled.

Leah felt the blush. "I hope you have a safe trip."

He waved as he walked toward the garbage area and the way out.

During a quiet moment that evening, Leah told Sarah her brother had been found. "He's in a youth camp in Galilee."

"That must be a great relief to you. Is he your only family?" Sarah asked.

"Yes." Leah paused. "I wonder if he kept the knapsack he carried." Looking at Sarah, she explained to her friend how she and Reuven had been able to save the chalice that had belonged to their oma. "She said it had been in her family forever." Leah smiled. "We loved to hear her tell about smuggling the cup out of Russia when she escaped the pogroms there. When we left to look for our parents, we took it with us."

"Is your oma alive?"

Leah shook her head. "No. She died just before the war ended." Sadness filled her when she thought of her grandmother.

"And you never found your parents?"

"No. We ended up in a refugee camp in France. The Aliyah Bet helped us get to the *Star of David*. And now I'm here." Leah shrugged her shoulders.

"I'm glad you stayed. I know you wanted to go to your brother, but we need you here," Sarah told her.

Leah smiled at her friend and turned back to sorting medicine that Joshua had brought them.

Thoughts of the gentle giant tugged at her mind. *He's married to Palestine. He will never have time for you.* She sighed. *His faith is so strong. He must know the Torah by memory. And I don't even have the holy books to read. I'll talk to the rabbi and see if I can borrow something to study.*

Putting the bottles in order, she remembered how she had hated having to go to Hebrew school. *Oma dreamed Reuven and I would make it to Jerusalem. She instilled us with the faith of our fathers. I wonder who taught Joshua?*

"Get him out of your mind and go to work," Leah ordered herself softly as she went to check on a child she heard crying. Seeing the flushed face and feeling the fever burning in the small girl's body, Leah went to get a basin of water and a cloth.

"Joshua may not like him, but the officer's gift of water makes life a little better for a few," she murmured as she bathed the child's face with a cool cloth. "I must be thankful for even the small blessings," she murmured, then began to croon a lullaby to the sick child.

Chapter 7

Sarah and Leah spent long hours with their patients, trying to bring comfort to their bodies and healing to their wounded souls. The heat remained unrelenting. One day melted into the next as they struggled on.

When Leah walked through the hospital tent, checking on her people, she spoke to them in Yiddish, a dialect of the German she had learned as a child. Most of the Jews in the camp used Yiddish as a universal language.

One old gentleman called out to her. "Could I ask you a question?"

Leah bent over his cot and responded in the same language. "What can I do to help you?"

"You speak Hebrew?"

"Yes," she nodded, taking the hand he held out to her.

His eyes lit up. "Do you by any chance read it too?" he asked with hope in his voice.

Leah smiled and nodded yes. "My oma insisted my brother and I learn Hebrew. She dreamed that we would someday live in Eretz Israel, and Hebrew would be the official language."

"Your grandmother is a wise woman. Is she here?" he asked.

"No. Oma died before the war ended, but my brother and

I hope to make her dream come true."

He pulled back the hand she held and reached for a book under his pillow. "My eyes fail me now, but I have kept my Torah. Could you sometimes read to me?"

Leah touched the holy book with awe. "I haven't seen the laws given to Moses in a long time." She looked through mist-filled eyes at the man holding the book. "I would be honored to read to you. Perhaps you can help me understand the words."

He chuckled. "I am no rabbi, but I will share my ideas with you."

The friendship was sealed. Leah spent every spare moment reading to those who wanted to hear the words God gave to Moses. Some listened who didn't understand the Hebrew but knew the words were the laws they lived by. Her old friend would talk to the people about what had been read when Leah had to return to her duties as a nurse.

"You have a separate synagogue started here?" Sarah asked.

Leah smiled. "Not me. Our friend with the Torah has brought new hope to the people. Joshua can quote the words given to Moses, but most of us can't. With the Torah we can read them."

"You mean you can read them, and the others can listen." Sarah patted Leah on the arm. "You give them something to think about besides the heat and how much longer we will be kept here."

When more supplies were smuggled into the camp, one of the Palmach members sought out Leah. "I have a letter for you," he told her, handing her a parcel.

Leah felt like hugging the man when she saw the familiar

scrawl. "Oh, thank you, thank you. I feared he was dead."

The man shrugged. "I just brought the package. Is this your lover?"

Leah felt the blush stain her cheeks. "No, this is my brother. We got separated when the boat we came on crashed on the beach."

"Glad I could bring you good news." The man wandered off to talk to others.

Leah hugged the letter to her chest and ran to her tent to read in quiet.

Dear Leah,

Your friend Joshua brought news that you are alive. I hope you will soon be out of Cyprus and here in Palestine with me. I love living here.

Eagerly Leah read Reuven's descriptions of his work and friends in the kibbutz.

Joshua took some of us with him to help dig ditches to drain swamps in the camp they are building north of here. We dig channels for the water to drain into a basin. Then it can be routed to irrigation ditches. It was very hot, and I got sunburned. Anya brought ointment and healed me.

Jealousy filled Leah. "Anya! I should be the one there to take care of him. Who is this Anya?" she sputtered in anger.

Reading the letter again and again, Leah felt close to her sibling. *He calls Joshua my friend. What would give him that idea? Unless Joshua told him we are friends.* But then her conscience warned her, *Only friends, Leah, no more.*

Days filled up weeks, and still Joshua did not come back. Her British officer did, however. He appeared each week with five gallons of water.

"We have come to depend on the extra water you bring us," Leah told him, trading an empty container for the full one he held out to her.

He looked down, hat in hand. "I have been given orders. I'll be going back to England." Then he looked up as if seeking her approval. "I've talked to some of my friends in the barracks, and they have agreed to give up part of their rations and bring them to the hospital. You'll still get extra water when I'm gone."

"That's very kind of you. Thank you for finding help for us." Leah sincerely appreciated his goodness. "May God bless you and give you a safe trip home."

The officer blushed. "I'll miss seeing you," he told her shyly.

"You won't miss my temper tantrums," she retorted with a chuckle.

He smiled in return. "No, I won't, but neither will I forget the lesson you taught me."

As Leah watched him leave, she determined to make herself scarce when others brought the water so they wouldn't start looking for her when she left the camp.

Days later, when Joshua finally returned, he grabbed Leah in a bear hug and swung her around. "I missed you. No one scolds me like you do."

Smiling at the sight and touch of him, Leah could only laugh at his charges. "I only scold when you need it."

"Like when you don't get your own way?" He grinned.

"Ouch! You know me too well." She threw her hands up.

"Not nearly well enough." The softness of his tone sent a shiver down her spine in spite of the heat. "Could we spend some time together after the evening meal?" he asked.

Leah couldn't speak. With dismay she realized she had no clean clothes. With the heat and lack of water, she struggled to keep her body clean. She shrugged. Joshua was no better off than she. "I would like to spend time with you," she whispered at last.

"No other boyfriend going to interfere this time?" he teased.

Leah put her hand to her face. "Yes, there is, but I'll put him off till tomorrow."

"More British solders?" he asked in a growl.

"No. I have been reading the Torah to some of the patients in the evening," she explained.

Joshua's look of pleasure sent a new thrill through her.

"One of the patients has a Hebrew Torah, but his eyes are too bad for him to see." She looked down at her clasped hands. "I have been reading to any who want to listen." She looked up at him. "You have the words memorized, but most of us do not."

"I know some of the words, but not all. What you're doing is wonderful. How is it you read Hebrew?"

"Oma insisted Reuven and I attend the Hebrew school, and Hebrew is all she would speak at home." Leah smiled. "She wanted us to be ready to live in the Jewish homeland."

Joshua took her hand. "Let's find a place in the shade. We'll have our chat now so you'll be able to read to your admirers this evening."

"They are my patients, not admirers," she protested.

"I won't argue with you. I do want to know more about you. How is it you and your brother escaped the camps? I know you said you stayed with your grandmother." They sat in the shade of the hospital tent.

Leah sighed. "Oma lived in Switzerland for her health. My

father owned a factory in Germany, so summers Mother would take Reuven and me to visit her mother. Father made uniforms for the German army, and he didn't think the Nazis would bother him. Mother didn't trust them. When Reuven was eight and I was eleven, she took us to visit Oma for the summer and left us there."

Leah looked into the distance without seeing. "For a long time we got letters from our parents. Father sent money to Oma to take care of us. Then the letters stopped." She looked up at Joshua, who sat beside her. "Oma died, the war ended, and Reuven and I went to search for our parents." She tried to smile. "We never found them. The records showed them going into Auschwitz but never coming out."

Joshua squeezed her hand but did not speak.

"Now it's your turn to tell me about you," Leah urged.

Chapter 8

Joshua pulled Leah to her feet. "No time now. The evening meal is being served. Do you have to feed your patients?"

"No. There are others who bring them meals and, if necessary, feed them."

"Then will you dine with me?" He bowed before her.

Standing in the dust, looking at the barbed wire, Leah could only laugh at his dramatic flair. "I know the perfect spot. They serve the worst soup you have ever tasted."

Joshua sat next to her in the mess tent. "I think they mixed up the dishwater and the soup pots," he said, putting his spoon down. "You'll have to come visit my parents. My mother will serve the best lamb roast you have ever tasted."

"It would be no matter. I have forgotten what lamb tastes like. Reuven and I haven't been able to have a real Seder dinner in many years." Leah looked unseeingly out the door of the tent. Coming back to the present she smiled. "But thanks to you, I know where Reuven is. He'll be able to celebrate the Seder next spring."

"Did you hear from him?"

"Yes. His letter is full of how much he likes the kibbutz—though I do want to know more about Anya. He sounds much too interested in a girl for his age."

Joshua threw back his head and roared with laughter. "Most Jewish mothers would say the same thing. No woman is good enough for their sons." He took her hand. "Reuven is almost eighteen. He's had a lot in his life to make him grow up fast. Don't hold him back." He squeezed her hand reassuringly. "If you do, you will lose him."

Joshua stood up to greet some of the people in the mess tent.

"Will you read to us?" one withered old woman asked Leah.

Leah looked up at Joshua. He made an impressive figure. His gentle manner with the people around them belied the strength that showed in his massive body. His forearms rippled with muscle. She stood beside him and put her hand on his deeply tanned arm. "Would you read to the people?"

Word traveled fast, and a crowd gathered outside the hospital tent. Joshua stood before them, his arms raised to God, and read from Genesis: " 'In that day the Lord made a covenant with Abram, saying: Unto thy seed have I given this land, from the river of Egypt unto the great river, the river Euphrates.' "

Joshua's voice boomed over the listening crowd. From Exodus he read to them the story of God delivering His people from Egypt. "We read this story every year at Passover as a reminder of all our God has done for us." He held the worn leather book up so they could all see it. "The Torah shows God's handiwork in too many crises of the past to doubt His help now."

Tears streamed from many eyes. All voices were raised in praise to God.

Leah's eyes were filled with tears as she stood proudly beside this powerful man. *I will stand by his side as long as he will let me,* she promised herself, but then wondered if she would only be in the way of a man who was so obviously being used by God to do great things.

"How soon do you have to leave?" Leah asked as Joshua walked her back to her tent.

He faced her and took her hands at the doorway. "Would you like to go with me?"

Leah's heart leaped in her chest, but she was too excited about the proposed journey to say anything.

"We'll go out at dusk. That's when the British are having their evening meal and are less likely to be watching the garbage dump. You won't be able to bring much," he apologized.

Leah smiled. "I have nothing to bring."

He bent down to brush a kiss across her cheek. His mustache tickled. The thrill of his kiss wiped out any urge to giggle.

The next day, news of Leah's imminent departure traveled through the camp. Making her rounds in the morning, she received the blessings of all her patients. Even one of the mute children reached out to be hugged. "It's hard to leave," Leah told Sarah.

"Go. The word is that the British are getting so much pressure from the free countries in the world that they will soon let us into Palestine. We will meet in Eretz Israel." Sarah wrapped her arms around Leah.

"Who will read to us now?" her old friend with the Torah asked.

"I will," came a soft voice from the darkest corner of the tent.

Leah went to the side of the man lying there. He had rarely spoken before. "You'll read the Torah to the people?" she asked eagerly.

He wore his humility like a cloak. "I have turned away from God too long. You and your young man have shown me the way back."

The man who owned the book of the Torah reached out to shake the hand of his new friend. "Welcome back to God's world. You read Hebrew?"

"I used to be a rabbi," he admitted in a soft voice. "The camps stole my faith."

Leah knelt beside his cot and put her arm around his thin shoulders. "God sent you here. We need you."

He reached up to pat her hand on his shoulder. "You woke me from a long, dark sleep." He looked up, smiling through his tears. "I will do what I can."

"Come," the other man urged. "Let's sit outside and visit. I'll bring my book, and we may even read a little together." The two old men made their way slowly to the door of the tent.

Leah stood with tears running down her face.

"Will you be too sad to leave?" Joshua asked when he saw her tears.

She smiled and told him what had happened. "It's wonderful what the Word of the Lord can do." She turned to him. "You're like Moses," she said, patting his cheek. "These people would follow you anywhere."

He grinned. "Will you follow me to the garbage dump tonight?"

"I will be there." She didn't add what her heart was shouting. She would follow Joshua Ben Ami to the ends of the earth.

As quietly as she could, Leah took leave of the place that had been home for several months. She walked slowly to the edge of the camp, not daring to look around to see if she had been followed. Her heart pounded so hard she felt sure the British guards would hear it.

"Over here."

Startled, she obeyed the voice she knew so well.

"Just stay behind me. Look down as though you are trying to find something good in the garbage," he instructed her.

Leah noticed the pack on his back. He carried medicines in it when he came to the camp. Now he acted as though he scavenged for things to put in it.

It seemed to take hours to make their way out of sight of the refugee camp. Joshua turned and took her hand. "How does it feel to be free?"

Leah took a deep breath. "It will feel better when I know I am in Palestine."

"It will be a few days before you touch Eretz Israel. Then I plan to take you to my parents' home in thc Jezred Valley." He put a hand up to quiet the protest she started to voice. "It is on the way to Reuven's kibbutz. You will be with your brother soon."

Chapter 9

"We're here." Joshua's soft voice woke Leah from her slumber.

Sitting up from her corner in the back of the jeep, she looked around. Shaking the dust off her blouse and brushing back her uncombed hair, Leah tried to blink the sleep out of her eyes. "Where are we?" she asked.

Joshua laughed. "You're in Palestine." He pointed toward the house they were parked in front of. "My friend Rachel lives here. You can stay with her for today. I'll be back for you at dusk."

"Do you only travel at night?" Leah asked, still groggy from her nap. They had boarded a fishing boat in the dark of the night on Cyprus. When they'd landed, she had kissed the ground of Eretz Israel. Following Joshua to the jeep, she had fallen asleep in the backseat while he drove.

"I have people to see today, but we can continue on our way tonight."

"How can you go without sleep?" she asked in wonder.

"Shimon will be our driver tonight. I may try to catch a nap before we get to the Jezred Valley."

A young woman came to the door. "Welcome, Joshua. Who have you brought to me this time?"

Leah looked at the woman greeting Joshua. Inwardly Leah groaned. *She's pretty, and she's clean. Could this woman be Joshua's girlfriend?* Suddenly Leah's mind became alert.

"Rachel, this is Leah, the nurse I told you about."

"Welcome, Leah. Come in, and I'll make tea."

Leah took the hand offered her. It felt soft against her callused and dirty fingers. "I'm glad to meet you," she whispered. Leah followed Rachel into the cool interior of her home.

"I'll be back this evening," Joshua called, pulling away from the curb.

Rachel laughed. "He's always so busy. The country needs a dozen more like him." She guided Leah to a chair in the kitchen. She looked her guest up and down. "What am I thinking? I offered you tea when what you would really like is a bath and clean clothes."

Leah looked down at the clothes she had worn for days. "A bath would feel wonderful, but I have no other clothes."

"Not to worry. Come, let me show you where you can find towels and soap."

An hour later Leah sat in the kitchen with the promised cup of tea. "I feel like a new person," she sighed in pleasure. She shook her long hair back over her shoulders. "I'll braid it again when it's dry."

"Your hair is too pretty to hide in a braid. I'll find a bit of ribbon you can tie it with."

Leah looked at her crisp white blouse and blue shorts. "You have done too much already."

Rachel laughed. "Not me. It's the donations we receive from America that make it possible for us to take care of refugees." She nodded toward the clothes. "You are wearing the uniform of the kibbutz."

"Really?"

"Makes you look like you belong. The patrols won't take notice of you, unless it is to admire your beauty."

Leah sputtered and felt the heat rise to her face. She wanted to like this friendly woman, but thoughts of Joshua intruded. *He never said you were the only woman in his life,* her mind nagged.

"The men will be here soon. I'll fix a meal." Rachel chuckled as she took dishes from the shelf. "They may not take time to eat, but at least I can offer."

"Fresh vegetables," Leah exclaimed.

"Want a raw carrot?" Rachel offered, holding out one she had just peeled.

"Yes, please. I haven't tasted anything fresh in months. First a bath, then clean clothes, and now fresh vegetables. If this is a dream, I don't want to wake up."

"You'll get lots of vegetables and fruit in the kibbutz. They raise almost all their own food."

"No wonder my brother loves it there." Leah crunched the last of the carrot.

"We're here," a voice shouted from the front door.

"Shimon!"

Leah watched Rachel run into the arms of a man dressed in the same tan pants and shirt that Joshua always wore. Shimon didn't stand as tall as Joshua, but his skin gave evidence that he spent long hours in the sun.

"Leah, this is my husband," Rachel said, introducing the man who still held her in his arms.

"And our driver," Joshua added as Leah reached to shake the hand Shimon offered.

"I have food cooked," Rachel offered.

"A quick meal and we'll be off," Joshua said, taking Leah's hand in his. "You look like a true sabra."

"I'm clean for the first time since the British pulled me out of the water." She chuckled.

"Let's celebrate your freedom with one of Rachel's good meals." He led her to the kitchen.

"I'll be back in a few days," Shimon told his wife a short while later as they prepared to leave.

"Thank you for everything," Leah said, hugging her new-found friend. "I don't know how I can repay you."

"By helping someone else. That's the way of the people here."

"Even the sky welcomes me." Leah pointed to the colors of the sunset. She sat in front with Shimon while Joshua tried to take a nap in the back of the jeep.

It seemed like they traveled over bone-jarring roads for hours. Leah lost track of time. Instead she tried to concentrate on the country they drove through. When it became too dark to see, she watched the road.

"We'll be there soon," Shimon told her. "Levi and Ruth have a nice place in the Jezred Valley. Fertile land there."

"Do they live in a kibbutz?" Silently Leah wondered what she was getting into.

"No, they live in a moshav. It is like a kibbutz in that the land is farmed as a commune, but they have their own cottage. They do have a small private vegetable garden. Ruth always sends vegetables to Rachel."

"I hadn't tasted any fresh food in months. The vegetables were the best I have ever eaten."

Shimon laughed. "That's what all the refugees say who come

to stay with us. Makes Rachel feel good to share with them."

Joshua stirred in the backseat. "Almost there?"

"Couple more miles," Shimon answered.

When they pulled into the settlement, Leah tried to see in the dark. Shimon parked in front of a small cottage, and two elderly people rushed out to greet them.

A man with flowing white hair pulled Joshua into a hug. He stood nearly as tall as Joshua, and the light from the doorway showed his face had been creased by years in the sun. The rotund woman at his side had her head wrapped in a scarf. She looked lovingly at Joshua when he bent to kiss her withered cheek. "Mama, I have brought Leah to meet you."

"Come into the house, Child." Ruth reached out to touch Leah's arm and guide her into the lighted room. "You must be tired from the long drive."

Leah could feel the love that filled the house. Tears built behind her eyes as she looked at Ruth and saw her oma. *I have come home*, she thought, looking into the soft blue eyes of Joshua's mother.

"The men will want to talk politics. Let me pour them tea, and then we can get acquainted," Ruth told Leah, patting her arm.

"Joshua told us you are a nurse," Ruth said a few minutes later, putting a cup in front of Leah and sitting down with one of her own.

"Yes. Oma thought I would always be able to find work if I could take care of the sick."

"A wise woman. Are you going to the youth camp?"

"My brother's there. We were separated when the ship we came in crashed on the beach. Reuven escaped, and Joshua found him here."

"He told us how worried you were." Ruth sipped her tea and shook her head sadly. "So many people looking for loved ones. I'm glad you have found your brother."

"I understand what you are saying. In the camp on Cyprus I heard many stories that made me thank God Reuven had survived. I can't wait to see him." Leah put her cup down.

"You rest here tonight. Joshua will take you to join your brother tomorrow." Ruth put her hand over Leah's, filling her with a warmth she hadn't known since Oma died.

Chapter 10

Joshua and Shimon returned from the dormitory where they had spent the remainder of the night. Leah had been up since early light. She helped Ruth serve fresh bread and coffee to the men.

"He's a good boy, my Joshua," Ruth said, pouring out mugs of coffee for Leah to carry to the men.

Leah smiled at this mother's pride. "Yes, he is a fine man," she agreed. "He has a wonderful knowledge of the Torah. He would quote passages to the people held in the refugee camp."

Ruth looked out the window and sighed deeply. "It is every mother's dream that her son will become a rabbi. He studied as a boy, but then came the war." She shook her head sadly. "That changed many things."

"He's like a modern Moses. People want to follow him." Leah shared her feelings freely with this kind and loving woman.

Ruth looked at Leah. "Yes, and like Moses he faces frustration, disillusionment, and even failure." Her parchmentlike face shown with pride. "But Joshua has one goal in life. He will pour out his blood if necessary to secure the land God has promised to His people."

Leah stopped with a cup partway to her mouth. "Oma's

cup. It has those words inscribed on it."

Ruth looked puzzled.

"My grandmother had a silver chalice we used at Seder. Reuven and I took it with us when we went to look for our parents."

"Do you have it now?"

"I don't know. Reuven had it in his knapsack when our boat crashed on the beach. I haven't seen either one since then." She looked at Ruth and smiled apologetically. "Your words made me remember the chalice."

"Those words have been true for many, and I fear many more will give their blood before God fulfills His promise of a Jewish homeland.

Joshua stood in the doorway of the small kitchen. Leah looked at him and sighed. *I pray to God that Ruth's words don't come true. I don't want his blood spilled for any reason.*

"Time to move on." He reached down to hug his mother. "I'll stop by on my way back through."

"And Leah?" Ruth asked.

"She is to be nurse at the children's camp above Galilee," he explained, letting go of his mother.

"You will come and see us," Ruth ordered Leah. "The camp is in the hills near here."

"I would like that," Leah responded with honesty. "To come here would be like coming home." When she thought of the words she had spoken, Leah put her hands over her cheeks. "Oh, I didn't mean to be rude."

Ruth took Leah's hands away from her face. "You are not rude. This will be your home whenever you want to come here. You are welcome as the daughter we never had."

Leah felt the tears press her eyelids. She put her arms

around Ruth and hugged her as she would have hugged Oma. "I will come back."

"Let's go," Shimon called. "I want to get back to my pretty wife."

Joshua laughed. "Our driver has spoken. We'd better be on our way, or we'll be walking."

The road to the children's camp climbed into the hills. The view back over the valley took Leah's breath away. "It's beautiful," she said with awe in her voice.

"This from a girl who lived in the Alps?" Joshua teased.

"This is different. This is the land God gave His people."

"Convince the British of that," Shimon said with sarcasm.

"Even the British will bow to the Lord God," Leah stated with conviction.

The closer they got to the camp, the more excited she became. *Will Reuven have changed? He sounded happy. Maybe he won't want me to live in the kibbutz with him.* Worries skittered through her mind. When the jeep came to a stop in front of what appeared to be the dining hall, Leah jumped out without waiting for Joshua to help her. "Where is he?"

Joshua laughed. "Probably working in the fields. He didn't know you were coming."

"Didn't know? Why not?" she demanded.

"Leah, if something had happened, if I hadn't been able to get you off Cyprus, he would have lost you again. Now you can reward him with a pleasant surprise."

What Joshua said made sense, but still Leah looked over the area, searching for the bright red hair she knew so well.

"Joshua and Shimon, welcome. And who is this lovely creature?" A short man of middle age, topped with a head of unruly gray curls, offered Leah his hand.

"The nurse I promised you," Joshua said. "This is Leah Shapira, Reuven's sister." Turning to Leah, he introduced the man who held her hand. "This is Dr. Weismann."

Leah looked straight into his soft brown eyes. "How do you do, Doctor."

"Kathy is going to be very pleased to have you here."

Leah must have looked puzzled.

"Kathy is my wife and also a nurse. She's missed having another woman to be friends with here." He turned, pointing to another building. "She's giving shots to children who have just arrived."

"More children?" Joshua asked.

The doctor nodded. "The children are the leaders of tomorrow. It's up to us to keep them healthy."

Leah looked up as an attractive blond in the same uniform she wore walked across from the building the doctor had pointed to.

"Here comes the love of my life now," Doctor Weismann said.

Leah looked from the middle-aged little man to the willowy woman who looked to be in her thirties. Before she could draw any conclusions, the blond lady offered her hand. "Welcome. I'm Kathy, and I'm sure you are the new nurse."

"I'm Leah." She shook the hand Kathy held out to her.

"You men go talk war or business or whatever it is you spend so much time discussing. We women have things to do."

Leah gave Joshua a look of appeal.

"I'll find Reuven and bring him to you. Where are you planning to hide Leah?" he asked Kathy.

"I'll show her to her quarters," Kathy said with lifted eyebrows. She looked at Leah and grinned. "Men never think about the little things like where a girl is to live."

Bewildered, Leah followed where Kathy led. "Won't I live in the dorm like the others?"

"No. As a nurse you get a private cottage." Her laugh rippled over the air. "Not fancy, but you do get a room of your own and a shared bath. We take our meals with the others, so you don't need to cook."

Kathy opened one of the many doors scattered across the front of a large building. "Welcome home," she said, standing back so Leah could enter.

"Oh," Leah exclaimed, looking around the simple room. "It's bigger than any room I've had since I was a child in Germany." She turned to Kathy, who still stood in the door. "For months I've lived in a tent."

"Life can be hard here, but for most it is far better than where our people came from. Some of our children will never recover from the horrors they have been through."

"I saw them in the refugee camp." Leah shook her head with the sad memories. "I don't want to know what grief left such deep scars."

"Where are you, Leah?" The shout startled both women.

"Reuven, is that you?" Leah ran out the door, past Kathy, into the arms of her brother. "Oh, you've grown taller." She pushed him back to get a better look. "And fatter," she teased.

"These are muscles," Reuven protested. "I've worked hard to earn them." He hugged her so tight she cried out in pain.

"All right, I believe you."

"You two have a lot of catching up to do. I'll see you at supper," Kathy said, leaving the happy pair.

Chapter 11

Leah listened with rapt attention while Reuven chattered about all he had done. "When I got off the ship, the Palmach took care of me. They brought those of us under eighteen to this place."

Seeing the glow of happiness on her brother's face brought joy to Leah. "Will you be able to stay here now that you are eighteen?"

"We help with the younger children and work in the fields." He grinned. "Takes a lot of vegetables to feed all these people." He gripped his sister's shoulders. "Someday I will fight for the Palmach."

"Fight? There's no war," Leah protested.

"There will be before we gain our rights as a nation."

Leah didn't want to hear about war. She wanted to protect her little brother. "I pray you are wrong," she murmured. A bell broke into her uncomfortable thoughts.

"Dinner time. Come on, I want you to meet Anya." Reuven grabbed her hand and pulled her toward the dining hall.

Leah looked around. The room seemed so orderly for the numbers of energetic children it served. She followed Reuven toward a young woman in charge of a group of what looked like three- to four-year-old girls. Her heart contracted when she saw the look of love that crossed the stranger's face as she spotted Reuven.

"Anya, this is my sister, Leah."

Leah shook the hand of the slender young woman with hair as black as a raven's wing. Her nearly black eyes sparkled. She looked so young. "I am pleased to meet you," Leah said, automatically falling into the polite habits her mother and grandmother had drilled into her.

"Reuven has talked about you so much. I'm glad you're here," Anya said sweetly. Her voice reminded Leah of music.

Looking at Reuven, Anya pointed to the little ones standing in a line. "I must get back to my children. I'll see you later," she called over her shoulder.

"She teaches the smallest children," Reuven explained.

"She's a teacher? She doesn't look old enough to be out of school herself."

Reuven grinned. "She is my age and has been to school just as we have. She spent the war years with a family in Belgium. They passed her off as their daughter so she was not locked up as a Jew."

"How did she wind up here?" Leah asked.

"Same as you and me. Looking for her parents and her heritage." Reuven took his sister's arm. "Let's sit over here."

Leah enjoyed the fresh vegetables. "The food is good, and it's healthy. No wonder you are getting fat," she teased her brother.

"I'll get you into the fields and see if you still think this muscle is fat."

It felt so good to be back bantering with her brother. But much as it felt like old times, Leah realized both she and her brother had faced too many hardships for life to ever be like it was in their childhood.

After the meal, Reuven took his sister around the kibbutz.

Impressed with how orderly and clean everything looked, she asked, "How long has this camp been here?"

"Less than two years. People like your friend Joshua have worked hard to set up places for refugees. Thousands pour into Palestine with nothing but the clothes on their backs. Many die getting here and leave children without family."

"It seems overwhelming to me."

"With God all things are possible," Reuven told her softly. "Moses led our people out of Egypt into the desert. Two thousand years later we are making a homeland out of that desert."

"There you are."

Leah's heart skipped at the sound of Joshua's voice. "Thank you for bringing my brother and me together."

"It's not often we can put families back together." He motioned to the kibbutz. "The best we can do most of the time is bring people to a community where they feel they belong."

"Reuven has shown me around. I'm awed that you have made a garden in the desert."

Joshua laughed. "You make it sound poetic." He clapped Reuven on the back. "Your brother and I know the hard work it takes to set up irrigation canals." Then he looked down at Leah, sending ripples of joy through her being. "I came to say good-bye."

"Oh." Her disappointment echoed in the sound. "How soon do you leave?"

"At daybreak. Shimon and I have to check the progress of the kibbutz being built farther north."

Swallowing her feelings, Leah asked, "When will you be back?"

"Never know. I live from day to day and place to place doing whatever I can to help." He put his hand on her cheek. "I'll be in contact. There may be times when you can come to visit me."

"I would like that." Leah felt a little better about his leaving if he would invite her to join him.

"Can I go north with you?" Reuven asked eagerly. "I can work hard."

"I know you can. You've proven yourself, but your sister would never forgive me if I took you away so soon after your reunion." Joshua took his hand from Leah's face to shake Reuven's hand. "Your job now is to take care of Leah."

As the days progressed, Leah found Reuven did not need her. He had his own life, and it didn't include her. The hurt went deep.

"Let the boy grow up," Kathy advised. "He's found himself and a life here."

"Did that growing up have to include Anya?" Leah asked bitterly.

Kathy's laugh rippled through the room. "You're jealous." Turning serious she asked, "What does Reuven think of you and Joshua?"

Leah felt her face flush. "I don't know that there is any Joshua and me. He's married to Palestine and the dream of a Jewish homeland." She looked sadly at her friend. "I'm not sure there is any room for romance in his life."

"If that were the case, the Jewish people would not have survived all these years without a homeland. I stand in awe of your people."

Leah looked at Kathy in wonder. "What do you mean, my people?"

Kathy raised her eyebrows. "I'm a Christian. I thought you knew that."

Leah shook her head. "Why are you here with a bunch of Jews?"

"Jesus was a Jew. How can I be a good Christian without being a Jew in spirit? I must respect the heritage of my Lord." Kathy spoke with conviction.

"Your husband?"

"Is a Jew." Kathy smiled. "Growing up my mother always told me not to fall in love with a Jewish boy because he wouldn't marry me. I found the one exception."

"May I ask how you wound up here?"

"We're Americans. Ben and I worked in a hospital in New York City. We saw some of the refugees coming through and wanted to help." She stared down at her hands. "I can't have children." She looked up with a sad smile. "We came here to take care of orphan children. My secret dream was to adopt one or two to take home."

"Do you still want to do that?" Leah felt drawn to this woman.

"How could I choose? If I stay here I can love them all," Kathy said, waving her arm to take in the whole kibbutz.

"And it doesn't bother you to be among Jews?" Leah asked, trying to understand how Kathy felt.

"I grew up in New York. I have been around Jews all my life. I admire your people." She smiled and took Leah's hand. "Here I am in the land where my Lord taught. I can walk the same sand Jesus did when He preached. The Sea of Galilee is my God's own sea. Here the Bible comes to life. I can see places where the things written about two thousand years ago really happened." She squeezed Leah's hand. "And your Jewish heritage goes back even farther. I want to learn more about your Scripture too. It's what we call our Old Testament."

Leah reached out to hug Kathy. "We can explore this country together."

Chapter 12

Leah tried to be friendly with Anya but was honest enough with herself to realize she had decidedly mixed motives. Much as she disliked the idea of her brother being interested in any girl, she hoped that, if Reuven cared for Anya, he wouldn't join the Palmach. He'd stay on the kibbutz where Leah could keep an eye on him.

Sighing, Leah approached the building where Anya and Esther looked after many of the young children. A little girl had been brought in the day before, and Leah wanted to check the status of the new child's health.

"Her mother died on the boat bringing them to Palestine," Anya explained sadly before she called the girl to see Leah. "We'll give her lots of attention until she feels secure."

Leah looked out the window where the children played in the yard. "Which one is she?"

Anya pointed out a pale little girl standing in the corner. "I don't know if it's just all the strangers or not, but she doesn't seem to feel well. She doesn't complain, but Esther thought Becky felt hot when she checked on her in the night."

"I'll look her over. Maybe I should take her temperature to be sure she doesn't have some infection. The conditions on those refugee boats are appalling."

Anya went to the door and called to Becky. She and Leah watched the child walk slowly to the door.

"She looks so forlorn," Anya said, kneeling down to hug the little girl.

Leah felt the compassion of the young woman as she comforted Becky and realized once again how unfair she was being about Anya.

"This is the nurse who wants to meet you," Anya said, carrying the little girl to Leah.

"What's your name, Sweetheart?" Leah asked gently.

"Rebecca," came the soft answer. "Mommy called me Becky."

"May I call you Becky?" Leah smoothed the dark brown hair back from the girl's forehead. She looked over Becky's head to Anya and frowned. "She feels hot."

Anya set the child on the edge of a table while Leah picked up her bag. "Can you slip her T-shirt up so I can listen to her heart?"

"Hmmm, look at this," Leah said as she put the stethoscope on the little chest.

Anya looked where she was told. "What are those spots?"

"It looks like measles to me. We'd better take Becky to visit Dr. Weismann."

Dr. Weismann played with Becky and even got her to smile. Looking at Anya he asked, "How long has she been in camp? Who has she been in contact with?"

"She came here yesterday and has not been out of the dormitory. We brought supper to her." She gently rubbed the child's back. "I thought she would do better not to be part of the noisy dinner hall the first night."

"Good, good. Now you must get the girls in her room back into the dormitory and keep them under quarantine." He smiled at Anya's look of shock. "We have measles here, and we don't need it spreading throughout the compound."

Leah carried Becky back to Anya's building. She watched the young woman gathering up the other little girls. Ten three-year-old children to entertain for how long? The experience would show what Anya was made of. Leah pushed back her unkind thoughts. Instead she asked Anya, "How may I help you?"

"I need to let Esther know what's happened. She'll have to keep the four-year-old girls to themselves." Anya seemed to be thinking out loud. "Would you stay here while I find her?"

"Of course." Leah sat down so she would be on the same level as the circle of children around her. "Do you like to sing songs?" she asked.

A few heads nodded. Most stared at this stranger in front of them.

Leah took a deep breath and tried to sing one of the songs she had learned on Cyprus.

"Anya sings better," one child told her matter-of-factly.

Leah had to smile. "Will you help me so it sounds better?" She kept the children happy until Anya returned.

"Esther will take over the other room and keep them out of here. We don't think they were around Becky yesterday. Now I need to put something over the windows. Dr. Weismann said to protect their eyes."

"I don't think you need to do that until they come down with the measles."

"Becky already has," Anya reminded Leah quietly as she pulled the muslin curtains over the windows.

Within ten days, other girls were showing signs of the disease. Leah went by each day to check on the children. She always found Anya cheerful and trying to keep her charges entertained.

She does sing better than I do, Leah admitted to herself one morning. She has the voice of a sweet bird. Pulling Anya aside, she again asked if there was anything she could do to help.

"No, thank you. It's nice of you to check my girls every day."

"Do they eat their meals here, as well?" Leah asked.

"Yes, Reuven brings the trays of food for me to feed them." Anya cuddled one of her charges in her lap.

Leah chafed at the sound of her brother's name.

Later at lunch, Kathy asked about the measles.

"The one who started with them is well," Leah explained. "Now the others are breaking out."

"Any with serious problems?"

"No." Leah smiled. "Some with more spots than others."

"Then why are you so glum?" Kathy looked puzzled.

"Anya is just too sweet. She stays unruffled with ten sick children. Each time I go in, she is singing to them or telling them stories."

"Leah, you are wicked. You can't admit this girl is right for your brother. Be thankful she is sweet and good. Reuven could have fallen in love with a Gentile," she teased.

Smiling, Leah asked, "Am I that transparent?"

Kathy nodded. "Have you heard from Joshua?"

"You trying to distract me?" Leah asked with a grin.

"Maybe. So have you heard anything?" Kathy persisted.

"No. Only more and more rumors of skirmishes." Leah turned to Kathy. "I'm sure he's in the fighting."

"I'm glad I married a doctor. He doesn't fight, just patches up the wounded." Kathy reached out to put her hand on Leah's arm. "Why don't we go visit Joshua's parents? They must be worried too."

"And maybe they have heard from him," Leah added with a

trace of hope in her voice. "But I can't leave with the measles still running rampant."

"We'll be through the worst of it in another week. Let's start to plan our trip to see this country. We can start with the Ben Ami home and move on from there. Maybe Levi will help us decide where to go."

"I don't think Joshua's father is going to send us to Christian shrines," Leah objected.

Kathy laughed. "I wasn't thinking of that. We'll go to some of those when we go to Jerusalem. Palestine is a small land, but every inch holds ghosts of blood and glory. We need to seek them out."

"Every inch?" Leah exclaimed.

"I dream big." Kathy laughed. "We'll get out the maps and our Bibles tonight and decide on the important inches."

Reuven slid into the seat next to his sister. "I picked up the mail and brought you this."

"Thanks." Leah felt a glow of pleasure at the sight of Joshua's handwriting. She looked at Kathy and Reuven. "Do you mind?"

"Would it matter if we did?" Kathy teased. "Go ahead and read it."

Leah read through the text about where Joshua had been, noting that he didn't admit he had been in the fighting. "Oh, listen to this," she said suddenly to the other two at the table. "He says he'll be in Jerusalem in ten days and wants me to join him." She looked over the letter toward Kathy. "Looks like we'll see the sites of Jerusalem first."

Chapter 13

"The doctor has declared the children no longer contagious." Anya's excitement matched that of the children playing around her. She walked to where Leah stood watching.

"I think it has been good for Becky to be shut in with the others. She seems to have adjusted well." Leah watched the once sickly, pale child playing tag with her new friends.

"Reuven tells me you and Kathy are off to Jerusalem."

"Yes. We leave day after tomorrow." Leah no longer cringed when Anya spoke of Reuven. She wasn't sure if it was because she was growing to truly like the girl or if it was simply the prospect of visiting Joshua that was making her more tolerant.

"I hope you have a safe trip."

Leah sighed. Stories of fighting came more often and were more violent all the time. Dr. Weismann had already warned Kathy and her of which routes to avoid. "We'll be careful."

A couple days later, Kathy drove the jeep down the winding road out of the hills. She and her husband had visited Joshua's parents, so the way was quite familiar to her. Leah had been surprised to learn that Ruth would have no advance notice of their visit.

"That's the way it is here," Kathy had explained. "No one can predict their schedule with any degree of accuracy, so we welcome visitors whenever they may show up."

When they arrived, Ruth Ben Ami rushed out the front door to greet them. "Welcome, girls. Come in, and we'll have tea and cakes."

"Ruth, how do you know when we are coming and always have fresh cake?" Kathy hugged the cheerful woman.

Over cups of tea, Kathy explained the trip she and Leah had planned. "This land makes me feel the Bible is a living, breathing thing undiminished by time. We want to stop at several places, so we have left extra early to meet Joshua in Jerusalem."

"You should go to the church at Kafr Kanna. That is where your Jesus performed His first miracle," Levi told them as he joined the women for tea and cakes. Reading Leah's expression he smiled, "This small piece of land is holy to many. We must learn to tolerate each other and our beliefs before there will be peace."

"Will there be peace?" Leah asked thoughtfully.

"The Lord God has promised it. Remember His Words in Jeremiah? 'I will remember you, and perform My good word toward you, in causing you to return to this place. For I know the thoughts that I think toward you, saith the Lord, thoughts of peace, and not of evil, to give you a future and a hope.' " Levi's voice resounded off the walls of the cottage.

"Joshua must have learned from you," Leah said in awe of the man's knowledge. "He could quote the Word of the Lord and encourage the people too."

"We all pray for peace," Ruth stated, "but we must be prepared to fight for our Promised Land."

Leah could not speak. Her heart hurt with the thought of

Joshua in danger. Yet she realized she must be brave and prepared to fight beside him.

Kathy put down her cup. "We should get back on the road. We have much to see."

"You will come for the Passover Seder next month?" Ruth invited.

Leah nodded and looked at Kathy, who stood with a look of consternation.

"My husband would welcome a real Seder."

"You must come too," Ruth insisted.

Kathy's face glowed with a smile. "You would welcome me? I'm a Gentile."

"Didn't your Jesus celebrate the Passover?" Levi asked.

"Oh, yes. I know it is my heritage, but Ben's family never accepted me." She looked down. "He wouldn't go without me."

"Then it is settled. You will come and bring Leah. We will pray Joshua can be home too." Ruth held her hands out to the girls. "Please come as often as you can."

"They are so warm and welcoming," Kathy said with a sigh as they started back on the road. "It has been hard for Ben to be shut off from his family."

Turning to look at her, Leah could see tears in her friend's eyes.

Kathy gave a shaky smile. "It shows me how much he loves me."

A while later they stopped to see the small church at Kafr Kanna. "To touch the places where the stories I grew up with took place two thousand years ago makes me realize what the term 'holy land' really means," Kathy said.

They drove on toward Nazareth and into the past. "This is all dried out and barren," Leah remarked. When they went to look at the places that were supposed to have been Mary's kitchen and Joseph's carpenter shop, they shuddered at the dirty conditions of the town. "It hasn't changed since Jesus lived here," Leah commented.

"And most of them haven't had a bath since then." Kathy held a handkerchief over her nose. "Let's get out of here."

The road took them through Samaria into the hills of Judea. "We must be getting close to Jerusalem. I can feel the pull of the Holy City," Leah said with wonder.

"I feel I only have to scratch the sand and history will flow out. The stories of my youth seem to whirl in my head as I see where they took place. This land is incredible."

It was late afternoon when they made their way into the city. "You'd better get the map out," Kathy told Leah. "We need to find King David Avenue."

A short while later, settled in their room at the King David Hotel, they plotted their route for the next day. "Let's have a meal and get some sleep. We need to start out early." Leah suggested.

Kathy laughed. "Are you afraid we won't be here when Joshua comes?"

Leah smiled. "I don't think he will be here until day after tomorrow. We'll be able to sightsee for a couple days."

"I agree." Kathy patted Leah's arm. "I like to tease you. I never had a younger sister to pick on, so I take it out on you."

In the morning, the women walked through the narrow streets of the city. "So many religions started here," Leah said, pointing to the hundreds of shoes on the steps of the Mosque of Omar, the Dome of the Rock. Close by they saw bearded Jews weeping and praying at the Wailing Wall of the Great Temple.

Kathy pointed to the barren hills around the city. "Those hills have seen Romans and Crusaders and Greeks and Turks and Arabs and Assyrians and Babylonians and British. All this in a city of Jewish kings. Is it holy or is it cursed?" she asked Leah.

Leah looked to the hills. "It is the center of civilization and contains both good and evil. Only the Lord God can know where it started and where it will end."

Kathy sighed. "You're right. We have to trust Him to lead us." She picked up their map. "Now I want to go to Calvary and Gethsemane."

"It sounds gruesome, but I will go with you." Leah looked over Kathy's shoulder at the map. "Isn't the room of the Passover Seder near there too?"

"Yes. I am so excited to be going to a Seder next month. Will you stay close to me and explain what is going on? My Hebrew isn't very good. I don't always follow what's being said."

When they came to the Holy Sepulcher, Kathy followed the footsteps of millions of Christians before her. Leah waited while her friend knelt and kissed the marble tomb, traditionally believed to be that of Jesus Christ.

Wiping away her tears, Kathy rejoined Leah. "I appreciate your going with me to the places of my faith. I never felt right asking Ben to go, and I didn't want to go alone."

"But now I have a better understanding of Jerusalem. It is the center of not just Jews, but of Muslims and Christians. How will we ever learn to live together?"

"Only God knows the answer to that question," Kathy said. "But now we'd better get you back to the hotel in case Joshua got in early." Kathy took Leah's arm, and they started back to the King David Hotel.

The lobby of the hotel was supposed to look like King David's court. Leah felt a rush of joy when she saw a giant of a man with wild black hair and mustache waiting for her. She longed to run into his arms but walked sedately to him instead. "Have you been here long?" she asked Joshua.

"Long enough to get settled in my room. Have you two been out shopping?" he asked as Kathy joined them.

"We've been sightseeing," Kathy told him.

"I'd like to hear about it. Why don't you join me for dinner in an hour?" Joshua invited.

Over dinner the women told Joshua all the places they had seen. Leah wondered at his silence but attributed it to fatigue.

Kathy placed her napkin on her plate. "I have things to do. I'll leave you two to visit awhile longer." She looked at Leah. "I'll see you in our room."

Joshua watched Kathy leave. Shocked, Leah saw his face turn black with rage. "I don't want you with that woman. She is trying to make a Christian of you," he thundered.

"No. You're wrong. She's my friend, and she wants to know more about Jewish beliefs. We don't talk about her religion."

"I don't believe you. You've spent the day at her shrines. How can you say she isn't trying to convert you?"

Tears filled Leah's eyes. "I don't want to talk about it now." She rose and stumbled to her room.

Chapter 14

Leah sobbed on Kathy's shoulder. "How could I have been so wrong?"

Kathy patted Leah much as she would a child in the kibbutz. "Why do you think it's you who is wrong? Are you sure you understood Joshua?"

"Yes." Leah sat back and wiped her face with a tissue. "He's intolerant. I thought he was a man of God, but I was wrong," she sniffed.

"Have you seen him angry before?" Kathy asked gently.

Leah thought for a moment. "Yes. On Cyprus he got very mad at me for talking to a British officer." She took a fresh tissue from the box and wiped her eyes again. "The man brought us extra water." She tossed the balled-up tissue into the wastebasket and looked at Kathy thoughtfully. "After I explained, Joshua understood what I had done."

"And you don't think it's the same now?"

"No, I don't. He knows you and your husband. He knows you're not here to convert Jews. You're here to help heal the sick. For him to say such things is unforgivable." She stiffened her spine. "I could not love a man who is that intolerant."

Kathy sighed. "I think you should take a shower and try to

relax. We aren't going to solve anything tonight. Get some sleep, and we'll both talk to Joshua in the morning."

"Aren't you angry with him?"

Kathy smiled. "I'm a Gentile in a Jewish land. He's not the first one to be suspicious of me." She reached to push Leah's hair back from her face. "Just as you have had to learn to live with intolerance in Europe, I have felt it here. It makes it easier for me to understand the Jews' longing for a land of their own."

Leah lay in the dark, thinking of Joshua. Could he be jealous of anyone she paid attention to? Not a woman, her mind argued. But why was he so angry with her for sightseeing with Kathy? It was all so harmless to share a friend's pleasure. Unable to solve the riddle, eventually she drifted off to sleep.

Getting dressed the next morning, Leah watched Kathy comb out her blond hair and put on makeup. Kathy looked at her in the mirror. "I am going shopping this morning. I'll stop for coffee in one of the little cafés. You go meet Joshua and see if things don't look brighter in the light of morning."

"I'm not sure that's a good idea."

"Try it and find out. I'll come back here at lunchtime, and if he's still angry, we'll go out together."

A short while later, Leah had run out of excuses to delay going down for breakfast. Her mouth felt dry as she walked into the lobby of the hotel.

Joshua came up to her at once. "I feared you wouldn't come down." He took her arm. "Will you have breakfast with me?"

Leah looked into his vivid blue eyes, and her resentment melted. "I would like that," she said quietly.

"Is Kathy coming?" he looked behind her.

"No. She's gone shopping. I'll meet her later."

"Did she ask you to go?"

Leah felt the heat start to rise. "You mean did she want to coax me to more Christian shrines. No, she sent me to talk to you to see if you are as intolerant as I said you were last night." Leah put her hands on her hips and stared at him.

"I'm wrong. Kathy is a sweet woman who is giving her time and talent to help our children. You told her what I said?" He looked ashamed.

"Yes. Did you think I would lie to my friend about you?" She stood stiff and angry.

"Please, Leah, let me explain." He took her arm and coaxed her into the coffee shop.

As soon as they were seated, Leah continued to press her point. "I can't stand intolerance. I've seen what it has done to my people in Europe. I didn't come to Palestine to see it go on against Jews or anyone else."

"Leah, please let me speak. I don't know why I lashed out at you. I guess I resented Kathy showing you Jerusalem when I wanted to be the one to take you around the city."

"Joshua, I will live my own life. You can't keep me in a box and only take me out when you have time."

"Leah, you must understand. I haven't had time for women in my life. All this is new to me, and I don't know how we'll fit together. Will you be patient with me while I learn?" he begged.

She reached out to take his hands on the table. "We'll learn together."

When Kathy came back at noon, Joshua had gone to a meeting and Leah sat on the terrace. "Did you find lots of bargains?"

"Funny how quickly the vendors learn to speak English when they see American dollars," Kathy said, chuckling. "Here, I brought you a present."

Leah opened the bag to pull out a beautiful blue patterned scarf. "It's lovely."

"You need something to hold your hair back so you don't have to braid it."

When Joshua returned, he joined them for tea and cake. "Do you have your map, Kathy?"

"Yes." She pulled it out of her pocketbook. "Ben warned me which areas to avoid because of fighting."

Joshua laid the map out between them. "If you take this way back, you could go through Bethlehem."

Kathy looked at him with a smile. "Thank you, Joshua. I would like that."

A few weeks later, Reuven crowded between Leah and Anya in the back of the jeep. Dr. Weismann drove with his wife beside him. "Which of you children is the youngest?" the doctor asked Anya and Reuven.

"I am a week older," Anya said with pride.

"As the youngest you get to ask the questions at Seder, Reuven."

"I've done it before. Guess I can remember my part."

"I'm the one with the questions," Kathy said.

"We'll sit together, and I can explain what is going on," Leah offered, trying to stay involved in the conversation even though her mind was filled with thoughts of Joshua. She still didn't know if he would make it to the Seder.

Ruth and Levi had the door wide open to welcome friends and strangers on this special occasion. The house smelled of roasting lamb as the group entered.

"The table is beautiful," Kathy said, crossing to the long table set with white linen and silver.

"Reuven, you saved it," Leah cried, falling on her knees in front of the table. "Oma's cup, you saved it." Tears coursed down her cheeks.

"It has a small dent where I hit the rocks when I escaped the *Star of David*." He put an arm around Anya. "But Anya polished the cup so well it hardly shows."

"What does it say?" Kathy asked, looking at the silver chalice.

"I will pour out my blood for you," Leah translated.

Kathy knelt beside Leah. "This could be the cup Jesus blessed at the Last Supper. He poured out His blood for me." Her voice held awe.

"This is the Elijah cup," Levi explained as the girls stood and wiped the tears from their faces. "We fill it with wine, believing that Elijah will join us before our Messiah comes."

"As children we would watch to see if the wine disappeared," Reuven said with a smile. "We always thought the level went down in the cup."

"Gather around the table, and we'll start the prayers," Levi instructed them.

Ruth looked at the door, and her face shown as though a candle had been lit behind her eyes. "Joshua." She breathed his name like a prayer.

Leah turned to meet his gaze.

"I couldn't miss Seder with my loved ones," he said, looking into her eyes.

"Welcome, my son. We are about to start the prayers so we can get to your mother's good meal."

"This is the Seder plate," Leah explained to Kathy when they sat down. "Reuven will ask the questions about why the different things are on it, but let me tell you in English."

"Thank you," Kathy whispered.

"The shank bone symbolizes the Passover lamb. We also think of it as the arm of God. The boiled egg is the symbol of new life. The bitter herbs or *maror* remind us of the bitterness in life. We eat them once to remember the suffering of the slaves in Egypt and again we dip them in horseradish and eat them between the *matzo* or unleavened bread. That was the practice when the temple was still in existence.

"Now this is the good stuff." Leah pointed to a sticky brown square. "I haven't had this in many years. It's dates, almonds, and honey ground together. As children, Reuven and I would wait for this part. It's to remind us of the blessings of this life. To us it meant sweets and the promise that the long prayer service would end soon." Leah laughed. "The service moves slowly, and you will hear the story from Exodus. We go slowly to remind us of how as slaves in Egypt, the Hebrews were always pushed to hurry." She hugged Kathy. "Now that is more than you ever needed to know about Jewish Seder."

"The Last Supper," Kathy said softly. "It's my heritage too."

After the final benediction had been said, Ruth served a sumptuous meal of lamb, rice, and vegetables.

The men turned to talk of politics. "How bad is the fighting?" Levi asked Joshua.

Shaking his head, Joshua told them, "As soon as they heard the United Nations passed the resolution giving us the right to a land of our own, the Arabs entrenched to fight." He shook his head sadly. "I had hoped we could live together in peace."

"The resolution was passed last winter. Why don't the leaders declare a Jewish State in Palestine?" Reuven asked.

"I believe it will come soon," Joshua told them. He reached

out to take Leah's hand as she removed plates from the table. "Will you walk with me?"

She felt the heat of a blush rise to her face and looked down to hide it from the others. "I'm helping your mother," she murmured.

Anya leaned over the table and whispered, "Go. Kathy and I will help Ruth."

Walking hand in hand with Joshua in the spring moonlight, Leah pushed back all fears of the fighting and the dangers Joshua faced.

"Will you come to Jerusalem again?"

"Yes." She looked up at his weather-beaten face.

"I'll be there in three weeks. Please don't tell the others, but I have reason to believe the Jewish State will be declared then." He turned to pull her into his arms. "I want you with me when we have a homeland."

Chapter 15

Three weeks later, as promised, Leah stood in the lobby of the King David Hotel. Joshua rushed up to greet her. "You came alone?" he asked, looking around for other familiar faces.

"Reuven taught me to drive." She longed to touch Joshua, but in the crowded hotel lobby she maintained a respectful distance.

"Let's get you checked into your room. Do you need help to carry your things up?"

"No." She held up her small backpack. "This is all I have." She grinned. "My wardrobe is not very large."

"As soon as you are settled, I'll meet you on the terrace."

Leah slipped on the dress she had borrowed from Kathy. *I hope the wrinkles fall out*, she fussed as she brushed out her hair and wound the blue scarf into a band to hold the riot of black curls off her face.

She stood at the edge of the terrace, looking for Joshua. As she noted all the European women dressed in lovely dresses and slack suits, she felt glad that she had let Kathy talk her into borrowing a dress.

Joshua came up behind her. She jumped in fright when he

took her arm. "Didn't mean to startle you," he apologized. "I just wanted to claim the prettiest girl on the terrace. Come sit down where we can talk."

After finding seats and ordering tea, he asked, "How bad was the attack? Were many hurt?"

Leah sighed and looked into her cup, remembering the attack on the kibbutz a week earlier. "The men." She smiled and looked at him. "Boys like Reuven had dug trenches around the kibbutz. We put the children in the center building." She looked at his concerned face. "You planned for something like this didn't you?"

"What do you mean?"

"You put the dining hall in the center of the compound. You knew it would be the safest place for the children."

"We hoped it would never come to that. Now tell me what happened."

"With all the fighting, we've been keeping lookouts. They alerted us that the Arabs were massed on the hill below us." Leah felt the tears behind her eyes. "When they got close enough to fire on us, I could see them. I knew those men," she said with anguish in her voice. "They were the fathers, uncles, and even brothers of the children Kathy and I gave immunization shots to in the Arab village. We spent hours with the women, teaching them basic hygiene." She reached out to take Joshua's hand. "Why, why do they want to kill us?"

He held her hand in both of his. "The people don't want to hurt us. They welcome what we bring them. It's their leaders who fear they will lose their power. They want to keep their subjects dependent on them."

"Will it ever change?" Leah asked.

Joshua shook his head. "I don't know. We can only pray that

peace will come. We don't want to take away their land or their homes. We only want to make this a better place for all of us."

"But we will fight," she stated sadly.

"The United Nations resolution gives us undeniable legal possession of this land. We have waited two thousand years to return to the land God promised us. Yes, we will seek peace, but we are prepared to defend what is ours."

They turned at the commotion in the hotel lobby. "Come, everyone. Come hear this," someone shouted.

Leah and Joshua crowded into the hotel, where a radio was turned to full volume. A voice broadcast over the radio announced, "We hereby proclaim the establishment of the Jewish State in Palestine, to be called the State of Israel." Shouts filled the air, drowning out the radio.

Joshua took Leah in his arms. "The Lord God's Word has been fulfilled." He threw back his head and shouted the words of Jeremiah: " 'Therefore, behold, the days come, saith the Lord, that they shall no more say: As the Lord liveth, that brought up the children of Israel out of the land of Egypt; but as the Lord liveth, that brought up and that led the seed of the house of Israel out of the north country, and, from all the countries whither I have driven them; and they shall dwell in their own land.' "

A resounding "amen" filled the air.

Joshua and Leah escaped the crush of people to return to the terrace. He kept hold of her hand as they stood looking out over the valley to the Old City.

"In the silence of dawn you can hear the muezzin call his people to prayer from a minaret down there," Joshua observed. "On the Christian Sabbath you can hear the bells of the churches. Our combined heritage goes back centuries."

"What will happen now?" Leah looked over the quiet

beauty of the ancient city.

He put his arm around her. "Only God can show us the way to live together in peace." He hugged her close. "We have to pray there are enough people listening to make it work." He tipped her chin up and kissed her. "I don't know what the future holds, Leah, but I know I want you in it as my wife."

"I will be at your side. We will raise our children in the State of Israel." She melted into his arms and lifted her lips for the kiss she longed for.

Epilogue

Joshua put aside his Biblical studies to help found an independent country of Israel. Leah continued to be close friends with Kathy after her marriage, and the women encouraged Joshua to again study scripture. He kept remembering Kathy's words when she first saw the silver chalice they used for seder and started researching the meaning of its inscription, "I will pour out my blood for you." Kathy still felt it could be the cup—or a superior replica of the one—used by Jesus at the Last Supper and encouraged Joshua in his study. The more he studied the more he came to believe the Messiah had come. Jesus had poured out His blood for them as the cup's inscription said.

Joshua gave his heart to Christ, and Leah soon followed him. They believed the Son of God would come again and bring peace to the land of Israel.

Having the chalice as a focal point in their home had blessed them with a new focus of faith. And that faith did not deteriorate even when the cup was lost.

MARILOU H. FLINKMAN

Marilou lives in Washington State with her best friend who happens to be her husband. Now that her husband is retired, they spend winters in Arizona where Marilou is able to write full time. The Flinkmans continue to tavel. Many of those trips are to visit their six children who are scattered throughout the northwestern states, including Alaska and Canada.

Marilou remains active in the Kairos Prison Ministry. This ecumenical program reaches out to those behind bars to bring them to Christ.

When her husband retired, Marilou gave up teaching creative writing at two local colleges. When she is not traveling, Marilou writes full time.

Cup of Praise

by Jane LaMunyon

Chapter 1

Jerusalem, October 2000

Late again. Sarah Reuben closed the massive oak synagogue door and hurried to the seat beside her family. This was the last day of Sukkoth, the feast of booths commemorating forty years of her people wandering in the wilderness after deliverance from Egyptian slavery.

Sarah always felt the sadness of the Israelites as they watched Moses ascend the mountain, this time never to return. How alone they must have felt and how frightened, losing the only leader they'd ever had. She looked up at the light above the Ark, glowing in its censer, a reminder of God's presence.

The scroll was closed, another Torah opened, and its first lines read. "In the beginning God created the heaven and the earth. . . ." There seemed to be a sigh of relief from the congregation. The creation story started the cycle all over again.

Afterward, on their family's terrace beneath a canopy of cut branches and palm fronds put up for this one special week, they gathered for coffee and dessert. Sarah sat at one of the tables beside her aunt Florrie, facing her sister Rachel and her friend Nina.

"I heard that Michael Van Gelder is back," said Nina, leaning forward as though she had told a great secret. Her big brown eyes glowed as she glanced at each of them.

Sarah's heart leaped. She nervously pushed a strand of auburn hair behind one ear. Ten years ago he'd gone to school in America.

"Someone should have kept him from his terrible fate."

Sarah grabbed a glass of water to steady her hand. She lowered her lashes to conceal her eagerness to hear what Nina couldn't wait to say.

"What fate?" asked Rachel, her lovely face pinched with concern.

Nina looked around, making sure she wasn't heard by anyone outside their circle. Sarah leaned forward, wanting to hear but hoping the news wasn't as dreadful as Nina hinted. Tension surrounded their table while the rest of the family walked around them, visiting and talking.

In a voice so low they all had to gather close, she said, "He's betrayed his family. Broken his mother's heart! He. . ." She glanced to either side, as if the rest of what she was going to say would get her in trouble.

So intent were they on hearing Nina, they missed Aunt Paula's approach.

"Acch! Such serious looks you girls have on your faces. We're not talking about troubles, are we?" Her loud voice broke their concentration, and Nina settled back in her chair, her cheeks blushing guiltily. Her troubled brown eyes pleaded for the others to remain silent.

"No, Aunt Paula," replied Rachel, smiling up at the older woman. The brown curls surrounding her face gave it an elfin appearance. "Just girl talk."

Aunt Paula waved her hand at them and said, "So, don't be so serious! There's lots more to eat; you girls go get something." She pulled down on her snug-fitting red suit jacket. "Forget your silly diets."

Sarah followed Nina closely to the long table and picked up a plate. As they pondered platters full of delicious calories, she leaned toward Nina. "What, exactly, did Michael do?"

Nina glanced back, but Aunt Paula had circled the room and was staring at them from the other side of the table. With a wide knife, she offered them cheesecake. "Here. Eat. Eat. Both of you." She pointed to the raspberry blintzes. "Go on."

Sarah picked out carrot and celery sticks and reluctantly took one of the blintzes. She and Nina hurried away from the table, stepping around curly-headed children who watched a bright blue- and red-striped top spinning on the tiles at their feet. They found seats near the trellis. Before Sarah could hear the news, Nina's parents came for her, and Sarah had to say good-bye.

Plate in hand, she circled the room, making small talk with her relatives. Her father said Mother was having a wonderful time with Aunt Betty in London.

She returned to the balcony, watching the afternoon sun reflect off the walls and spires of her beloved city. What could Michael have done that was so bad Nina was afraid to mention it? Michael, his gray eyes like a Mediterranean storm, once picked her up from school, taking her downtown for a fudge sundae. For once, she had had him all to herself.

Her grandfather interrupted her reverie, telling her it was time to go home. After saying their good-byes, they started the long walk home, a pleasant Sabbath sacrifice. The streets were quiet, with very few cars around and most stores closed because it was Sabbath. They acknowledged other people with the traditional greeting, "Shabbat Shalom."

Walking beside her grandfather in pensive silence, Sarah rebelliously entertained thoughts of Michael. His ready smile, his eyes twinkling at her as he called her Gnat because he said she was always hovering in the one place where she wasn't needed or wanted. She tried to be as grown up as her sister, but it was Rachel he'd always come to see. Rachel had been eighteen when he left, and Sarah only fourteen. She'd often wished she were the oldest sister, the one he came to see.

She and grandfather stood at the street that separated the new Jerusalem from the old. She looked up at the ancient walls while waiting for the light to change so they could cross. Grandfather took her hand, and she knew they both shared the awesome delight and humility of living behind those walls. It was a privilege to live and work in Old Jerusalem, where space was at a minimum and special permits were granted to only a few residents.

Grandfather owned and operated a rare bookstore. In the mornings they shared a small breakfast of sweet rolls and coffee. Then they'd go to work, he to his bookstore, she to the Heritage Museum.

She sighed. She should be happy. She'd just celebrated her twenty-fourth birthday, and everything was going well. But a cloud was approaching to hang over her head. Her mother and aunt Paula were conspiring to enlist a shadchen, or matchmaker, to find her a husband. All her protests of being too busy, not interested, needed by grandfather only fueled their determination to find her a good man.

Nina had laughed, saying they didn't have shadchens anymore, but Sarah knew that if there was a shadchen anywhere in Jerusalem, her mother and aunt Paula would find her.

As they wound their way through the narrow streets, brick

walls rising on either side, past the gates of their neighbors' homes, Sarah asked, "Zayde, did you know that Michael Van Gelder is back?"

Her grandfather's face tightened, and he looked away. His gray eyebrows met together over suddenly fierce looking eyes. "I know."

"Why wasn't he at synagogue today?"

Grandfather opened their gate. "Enough of him! Talk about something else."

The way he almost spat the name made Sarah shudder as she stepped back to allow him room to reach the door on their small enclosed porch. "But—"

"Did you eat one of Aunt Paula's blintzes? They were terrific."

She followed him inside, touching the mezuzah on the doorpost. His change of subject squelched any further discussion of Michael.

While Sarah hung up her sweater and picked up her book, her grandfather turned on his stereo. Music from Verdi's *La Boheme* flowed through the rooms. Although Sarah enjoyed this opera, worry over Michael kept her from concentrating on her book. Closing her eyes, she lifted her heavy hair over the cushion behind her and leaned back. The minutes ticked by with ever increasing monotony.

When the sun finally set, bringing an end to Shabbat, she put her book down. "Zayde, I'm going to the museum for a little while."

Nodding his gray head, her grandfather smiled. "Remember, little one, with God and the Torah we are never alone. We cannot hide from ourselves or from God." He touched her shoulder, his brown eyes filled with a melancholy she couldn't understand.

She put on her sweater and went out the door, thinking about what he'd just said. Grandfather's cultural proverbs always made her stop and ponder their meaning. This one must apply to Michael. Or was it for her? What exactly was he trying to say?

She continued walking through the Jewish Quarter near the steps leading down to the Western Wall of the old temple. She was seized by a desire to descend the stairs and join the women in their prayers. Instead, she turned toward the museum, breathing her own silent prayer. *God, I ask that whatever trouble Michael is in, he'll be able to overcome it. And help me find him.*

Why hadn't he come to see her? What was the mystery surrounding him? She let herself in with the key, straightened the desk in the anteroom, and lined up pamphlets on the table near the door.

She went through the showroom past displays of Moses' tabernacle, the temples of Solomon and Herod, charts and diagrams, dioramas and copies of temple artifacts. Opening the door to the room being remodeled, the smell of sawdust and new wood swirled around her. An empty carpenters' table stood near the back wall, and boards were stacked in the corner.

She carefully picked up a goblet that had been donated by a young couple who discovered it in their basement when they rented their apartment. They said it looked old and had brought it to the museum. They were promised that as soon as its age and origin had been determined, they'd be compensated.

She gazed at it, lovingly tracing the Hebrew letters etched on it. *I will pour out my blood for you.* What did it mean? Its design and other symbols made it decidedly a Jewish memorial cup, but it certainly never had held blood—that was forbidden by Jewish law. Why had this phrase been engraved on the cup?

She placed it gently back on the shelf and sighed. So many questions. So few answers.

A half hour later, satisfied that the place was presentable, she went to the entry area and picked up the phone to call Nina. She heard a soft clinking sound. Her fingers froze over the phone. No one should be in the building but her. She listened for a few seconds and heard nothing but sensed tension in the silence. With slow, quiet steps, she approached the showroom, glanced inside, then stepped through the doorway. A hand closed over her mouth. Her heart hammered as she struggled against the intruder.

"Be quiet," he whispered, his breath feeling warm on her ear.

The clinking noise sounded again, this time from the storeroom. Panic began to create an icy knot in her stomach. She struggled, but the strong arms tightened.

"I'm a friend," he whispered. "Not with them. Be still, and I'll explain."

Sarah ground her heel on his toe. His grip didn't loosen as she'd hoped. Footsteps shuffling in the back room stilled her. *Oh, God, protect me!* Her captor pulled her into the entry room and backed up against the wall. She felt a hard, flat chest heaving with the exertion of holding her still.

They heard the click of the back door. Still holding his hand over her mouth, the man managed to turn her so she could see his face. Shock ran through her. She was looking into the smoky gray eyes of Michael Van Gelder.

Chapter 2

Don't scream." Michael loosened his hold and glanced back toward the storeroom. Sarah gaped at him, her tense nerves quivering.

"Stay here, and don't call the police. Yet." He stepped away from her. "I'm going after them."

She watched his broad back walk away. His dark blue jacket stretched across massive shoulders, fitting snugly over a trim waist. She followed him into the storeroom. He was quietly closing the outer door when she glanced around.

"It's gone!" she cried. The cup was missing. There were other empty spaces on the shelves as well.

She clenched her fists. "They can't have it!" she muttered. She touched her cell phone, but Michael had said not to call the police. If anyone else had told her not to call, she'd have ignored them. Instead she ran out after Michael. Her trembling fingers fumbled, but she managed to lock the back door. Michael had just turned the corner.

He headed straight into the Jewish Quarter instead of turning right and going down the stairs to the Western Wall. Midway down the long flight of steps to the ancient site, soldiers checked backpacks and tote bags. The thieves wouldn't want that. Families strolled past her, black-robed fathers with long forelocks, their sons beside them, dressed the same except wearing yarmulkes instead of the tall, black hats. One of the wives pushing a baby stroller raised her eyebrows as Sarah hurried by.

She'd taken her gaze off Michael for a moment, then panicked because she didn't see him among the people ahead. She ran over the brick walkways, through the square, and there—she saw him. She picked up her pace.

Michael turned right, toward the Muslim Quarter and the bazaar. Now she had to catch him or lose him in the crowd.

He slowed, staying behind two young men who casually strolled through the streets.

When she caught up with Michael, he glanced quickly at her, reluctant to take his eyes off the two he was following. "I told you to stay put."

"I couldn't." Sarah shook her head. "They took the cup. I must get it back."

The two thieves turned onto Tanur Street.

"Why don't you stop them?" asked Sarah.

"I'll tell you later." He moved quickly until he and Sarah were only five feet behind them.

She shuddered. The thieves had probably been in the museum when she came to straighten it up. They could have been hiding in the restroom or the supply closet.

Strolling behind them, she wondered which one had the cup in his backpack. She itched to tackle one of them, hope he was the right one, and take her cup back. She'd begun to think of it as "her" cup, because it was special to her. If it turned out to be valuable, she'd learn its history and proudly tell visitors.

Barely wide enough for three or four people to walk abreast, the narrow, worn-brick lane between the bazaar shops was well lit, inviting tourists to stop and look at T-shirts, beads, fans, clocks, carved items, key chains, and other souvenirs. Every few feet the lane had a step downward into the heart of the Old City. Sarah and Rachel used to walk down this long street, ogling the mix of cheap and expensive jewelry, trinkets, statues, clothes, exotic foods, and fabrics crammed into shops no larger than eight feet wide. The two men turned off onto one of the lanes branching off the main bazaar.

Continuing toward the Via Dolorosa, Sarah felt secure walking beside Michael. To look at him, he seemed the same. But what horrible thing had he done to make himself outcast among his family and friends?

The two men turned again, but when Sarah and Michael turned the corner the men were gone. Disappeared, as if into thin air.

This street was a little wider than the main bazaar street. Michael's eyes narrowed at the three shops nearest the corner. "They must have gone into one of them."

Sarah grimaced. One of the shops was a market, displaying a goat's head, skinned, looking like a rubber replica. In the shop next to it racks of Levi's hung from a pole to catch the buyer's eye. Beneath were boxes of brand-name athletic shoes.

Inside the market an old woman stood at the counter, talking to the clerk.

Inside the jeans and tennis shoe shop the proprietor, a dark-haired man with a large mustache, came toward them, smiling. Behind him were more American items, including purses, backpacks, and watches.

"You like the Levi's?" he asked hopefully. "I have prices you like."

Michael shook his head. "No, we just got separated from the two guys we were with and thought they might have come in here."

Michael's voice had deepened since she'd last seen him. It

flowed through her, soothing her, even almost assuring her she'd have her cup back soon.

The man gestured behind him. "No one here but me." He picked up a colorful purse which looked like a huge plastic crayon box. "Just the thing for a girl like you."

Sarah shook her head. "I don't think so." They moved on. The next shop displayed pottery, dishes, and colored egg-shaped rocks on its shelves. A few people were in there, picking up and examining small carved camels and stones in the bins while the owner rang up a sale.

Back in the street, Sarah and Michael scanned the three stores. Their quarry had to have gone into one of them.

"Did you get a glimpse of either of their faces?" asked Sarah.

"Yes. I saw one of them while he was prowling around the work room." Michael's gaze was fixed on the doorways.

The man in the Levi's shop straightened a stack of T-shirts, glanced at them, then held up a shirt for two teenage girls passing by.

"That's very suspicious."

"What?" asked Michael, gazing oddly at her.

"I'll bet he's in cahoots with the two robbers. He's a lookout. We'll have to stay here watching everyone going in, and if someone comes out who didn't go in, we'll know it's them."

Michael's mouth curled in a smile. "If that man is a lookout, he'll tip them off, and they won't come out while we're here."

"Oh, I guess that's right." Sarah turned to face Michael, her back to the shops. "I'll just pretend I'm not interested."

Michael smiled but didn't answer.

"Don't look at me! Watch the people coming out of that shop."

He glanced up, scanning the three entrances. His gaze settled back on her face. "Yes, Ma'am."

Sarah couldn't stop looking at him. His dark hair contrasted with his sparkling silvery eyes. "You don't remember me!" She tugged at the ribbon holding her hair at the nape of her neck. Then bending forward, she ran her fingers through it and stood straight, throwing her head back. She'd seen it before in the mirror. Her curly auburn hair would be fanning out wildly in all directions. She put her fist on her hips. "Michael Van Gelder, you said you'd never forget me!"

His eyes twinkled with amusement. Peering closer, he exclaimed, "Gnat! It's you!"

"Humph. No one but you called me Gnat."

"No one but you could be all over the place at once and always in the way." Laughter came up through his throat. "It was an affectionate nickname, and you always laughed."

Being with him gave her joy, and her heart felt lighter. "I did laugh. Sarah. That's my name. Really."

He tightened his lips and forced a serious expression on his handsome face. "I know that, and I knew it was you." Glancing back at the shop entrances, he added, "It's very good to see you, Sarah."

"You too," she said, suddenly feeling shy. A group brushed past them, part of the growing crowds looking for bargains before the shops closed.

"Come on." He cupped her elbow in his hand. "They've probably gone out a back way, and we won't catch them tonight."

Sarah refused to budge. "I'm not leaving!" She looked up, boldly meeting his gaze.

He showed no reaction. "What is this cup you mentioned?"

She pulled her hair to the back of her neck, wrapping the ponytail holder around it. The ribbon went in her pocket. "It's a special cup. Donated to our museum a couple of weeks ago."

She leaned sideways, peering intently at a dark-haired man

coming out of the market. Michael glanced at him and shook his head.

"Anyway, about the cup," Sarah continued. "They thought it looked old and brought it to us to find its age and origin."

"Surely you've had many interesting items. Why was this cup special?"

"I can't explain why it was special only to me. It's as though the minute I saw it I felt—" She glanced up to see if he would scoff, but he had a thoughtful expression on his face. "I felt as though the cup had come home. That, even though it would belong to the museum, it was there for me. Can you understand that?"

Michael took her chin in his thumb and forefinger, lifting her face. She actually leaned into his hand. "Ahh, little Gnat. I mean. . .Sarah. You always were a dreamer."

Heat from his fingers traveled up to her hairline. Backing away from him, she protested. "It's true! The cup is special." *Get hold of your emotions, Sarah-girl. He might be married. Rachel is. Goodness! What if he was about to be a parent too, like Rachel?*

With an air of calm, Michael said, "I'd like to hear more about this cup. Let's talk on the way back to the museum."

"But, those men, the things they stole—"

"Those two are long gone. Let's go see what's missing besides your cup."

Sarah walked beside him, her mind whirling with questions. She grabbed his arm. "What were you doing in the museum? How did you get in?"

Michael looked down at her affectionately. "I was following the thieves and slipped through the back door after they jimmied the lock."

She stopped walking and waited for him to notice. When he looked back, she planted her fists on her hips. "Who do you think you are, Michael Van Gelder? You scared me half to death with your cloak-and-dagger routine in the museum. I'm not moving a step forward until you answer some questions, starting with, what have you done to alienate your family and friends?"

Standing beneath a light over the door of a closed jewelry store near the Jaffa Gate, he calmly regarded her. "Are those your only questions?"

"No. I have dozens more."

Michael took her arm. "Let's keep walking. There are things I can't talk about, but I'll answer as many questions as I can."

They walked through the high arch of the Jaffa Gate and out of the Old City. He turned to look past her at the wall on their right. "I missed this place. There's nowhere on earth like it." When he glanced down at her, the light in his eyes touched her in a way she had only imagined but never experienced.

She gulped. "I know. When I returned from England and my feet touched the ground in Tel Aviv, it was as if I were part of a grand symphony, and by touching the ground a chord resounded that sang all the way to heaven."

He laughed. "Yes! That's exactly what I—and so many others who come here for the first time—felt. No matter where they've been born, a Jew knows this is home."

Crossing the busy street, they continued up Jaffa Road. It felt so right to be with Michael after all the long years.

"What have you been up to since I last saw you?" he asked.

"When I graduated from school, I went to London for a year, living with Aunt Betty and Uncle Jack while I studied and did student research at the British Museum and Victoria and Albert Museum. When I got back home, I served the required time in the military." She glanced at him. "Enough about me. What were you doing in the museum?"

He raised his eyebrows, glancing at her.

"And not just because you were tracking thieves." She

lifted her left hand, palm up. "Why my museum?"

"Sarah, I'm an investigator, and I can't talk about what I'm working on."

"Investigator? Of what? Where have you been the last ten years?"

"America, studying and working."

They passed city hall's large courtyard. Lights gleamed overhead, erasing the darkness and shadows. Sarah frowned. She'd asked him three questions, and he'd avoided them all.

"So, what are you investigating?"

"Oh, whatever looks interesting." He shrugged his shoulders. "I told you I can't talk about it."

"I'm involved! They took my cup." They stopped for a traffic light to let a steady stream of cars exit from a one-lane street into the Jaffa Road thoroughfare.

"It belongs to you?"

"I told you! That cup is somehow involved in my destiny. I can feel it."

They continued down the narrow sidewalk toward Zion Square. "Listen, perhaps we should go down that way." He pointed across the street to a lane between the bank and a block of stores. "Remember the Nargila Café? We can talk there."

They crossed the street, and Sarah greeted two uniformed soldiers strolling the area, their guns at their sides. "Joel! Benjamin! How are you?" The two greeted Sarah and looked warily at Michael. "This is my friend, Michael Van Gelder," she said.

Michael nodded, and the two men glanced at each other, then said, "Duty calls. Take care, Sarah." They walked away.

Sarah looked back after them. "That was odd." She looked into Michael's nonexpressive face. "Do they know you?"

Michael sighed. "Come on. I think it's time I told you a little about where I've been for the last ten years."

Chapter 3

In the dimly lit café, half the tables were filled with young people, most dressed in popular American-style dress. One couple had dyed banana-yellow short tufts of hair and matching earrings. Michael and Sarah found a table near the window.

A thin young man with black hair, dressed entirely in black, brought them a menu. Michael leveled his gaze at Sarah.

She tried to wait for him to speak, but when his eyes filled with sadness, she asked, "All that time you were gone. Did you do something to disgrace your family? Did you commit some crime?"

He sighed. "No. Nothing illegal. But to my family, worse." Their waiter returned, and Michael handed him the menu. "Just coffee. Sarah? Order whatever you want."

The waiter took her menu. "Coffee will be fine for me too." She leaned on her forearms. "You have my undivided attention."

"I'm surprised you haven't heard by now."

"No one will talk about it. Did you commit a crime? Marry a Martian?"

"There's that imagination again. No. None of the above. All right. Here it is. And I'm not sorry for what I did. Only sorry that my family can't understand."

Sarah held her breath.

"When I was in the States, I met some other Jews who believed that Messiah has come. I argued with them; we talked far into the night many times. They met with a rabbi to study the Torah and the Tanakh and invited me to come and simply listen. I knew if I went there I'd find a flaw in their argument."

"You went to a goyim Bible study?" Sarah shuddered. "How awful!"

"They were all Jews, not Gentiles. It was awful at first." Michael stared at a spot on the floor, lost in thought. "I was armed with all my knowledge, and in my smugness, I sat away from the group while they studied and discussed the Scriptures. They don't know what they're talking about, I thought. I'll show them the truth."

He looked back at her with wonder in his face. "They were coming across verses I'd never heard in *yeshiva* or synagogue. Soon I was leaning forward, flipping through the Law and Prophets, finding what they were talking about."

An icy premonition settled over Sarah as she guessed where this story was going.

"Don't look at me like that," he said. "It's all there. And history supports the fact that Yeshua fulfilled all the prophecies. All of them! There's no way to doubt that He was and is God's Son, our Messiah." His voice was low and sincere, with no hint of uncertainty or confusion.

Sarah's chest tightened, and she found it hard to breathe. She searched his calm face for a full minute. The rocking beat of another song punctuated the air, while the storm gathered in her heart. "I don't believe it!" she said, glaring at him. "You know history. You know how through the centuries the rapes, murders, and pogroms all done by. . .Christians." She almost spat the word at him.

He reached for her hand, and she recoiled. "Did you become a Nazi too, while you betrayed your people?"

Michael shook his head slowly. "Sarah, it isn't like that. Men did those things. It wasn't God's will."

"Right. They cheerfully sang to their God while torturing and killing us. Have you lost your mind?" There seemed no other explanation. She frowned at his yarmulke. "You're not a Jew anymore." His betrayal to his family and his people rocked her to the core. "I could never have imagined you'd do such a thing! I could forgive you most anything, but this is far beyond a crime. You've denied everything we are!"

"Please don't think that way. Let me tell you why I am now a completed Jew."

Sarah pushed her coffee away. "I'm not thirsty anymore, and I won't listen to any more heresy." She stood as if jolted upright.

"Are you afraid? What if it's true? Study and find out. If it's not, you haven't lost anything. But if it is true and Yeshua is Messiah and you never find out, you've lost everything."

Trembling with increasing rage and shock, she narrowed her eyes and leaned her hand on the table. With her face level to his, she said, "You don't get it, do you? You're the one who lost everything."

"No." He sadly shook his head. "I've found everything. I wish you could see. . ."

"Good-bye, Michael. I can't even say have a good life because you've already messed that up, and I'm sorry for you." Before he could answer, she stalked out of the restaurant without looking back.

In the cool night air she stopped suddenly. She hadn't found out what he knew about the cup and why he was involved. She wondered if she'd dare approach him on a strictly business way.

No. He was *oysvorf*, unclean. An infidel. A deep wave of sadness rolled through her. All that potential. Wasted. She shook her head and walked on. The presence of soldiers on the street made her feel secure. Finally arriving back home, she opened the door with a heavy hand. The room's thick warmth swept over her.

Her grandfather looked up from his cup of hot chocolate, his eyes dark with anger. "I told you to forget about a certain person whose name I will not say. So you were with him tonight. Why?"

Sarah pulled her sweater off and headed for her room. "I don't want to talk about him, Zayde."

"Oh. So now you won't talk about him. Two hours ago you wanted to hear everything."

She paused with her hand on her bedroom doorknob. "I'm sorry, I—"

"You were seen by good, upright people. Think of what you're risking!"

"I didn't know."

He pounded his fist on the table, making the cup bounce. "If you'd listen to your elders you'd know a lot of things. I haven't lived on this earth for over sixty years without gaining some wisdom. I try to impart some to you. But you're acting like an addlepated little girl!"

Sarah listened, her head downcast. She dared not talk back to him.

"Go to your room."

She entered her room and shut the door, then with leaden feet walked to the upholstered chair beside her dresser and slumped into it. She covered her face with her hands. *Oh, Michael. I've prayed so often for your return. But not like this.* Tears dropped through her fingers.

In the restaurant his sincere, thoughtful eyes had seemed so serene and confident. She leaned forward, knowing she must let him go but unable to. He had rooted himself in her heart when she was a girl, and she was sure they were meant for each other. Maybe it was all childish imagination, but it pained her to think of trying to tear him from her heart.

She awoke and stiffly rose from her chair. The house was very quiet, and her digital clock said one-forty-five. She stepped out of her clothes, leaving them on the floor, and pulled her nightgown over her head, then slipped into bed.

Michael watched Sarah walk out. Shock and grief held him immobile as he watched her rush away from him. He groaned, thinking of her wide-eyed eagerness as he began his story, then seeing her innocent wonder turn to horror.

When he'd heard she worked at the museum, he'd planned to see her and tell her of his newfound faith. She used to hang on his every word as if it were the most important news in the world. He knew she'd had a school-girl crush on him, but he'd never thought the loss of her friendship would hit him so hard. When he was in America, he missed the times with her and Rachel. Later he found that it was Sarah he missed the most. With her sparkling eyes, her keen intellect and quirky imagination, she was a unique mix of whimsy and innocence.

He paid for their coffees and went home. In his studio apartment, he turned on his computer and sent messages to his agency, telling them of the theft of the cup. He requested a meeting the next morning to discuss the thieves and their possible contacts.

After midnight he finally lay back on his pillow and stared up at the ceiling in the quiet stillness surrounding him. *Father, I really botched it. Please soften Sarah's heart and give me another chance to tell her about You. And help me next time to do it right.*

The next morning, Sarah and her grandfather ate breakfast in strained silence. Walking past the bakeries with their sweet-smelling pastries and the small restaurants just opening, she keenly felt his disappointment in her and tried to think of a way to make it up to him. Her footsteps followed those of ancient ancestors who'd walked these very streets, so much a part of her and her heritage. How could Michael turn his back on it?

Mr. Silverman was in the back of the museum's showroom, measuring. He planned to prominently display the model of the new temple which he dreamed would be completed in his lifetime. He looked over his shoulder at her.

"Ah, Sarah!" Sitting back on his heels, he pointed to the temple model on the floor before him. "We'll have a marble slab and upon it a pedestal." His blue eyes danced. "It will be the gem of our collection. We'll set it off with a blue velvet curtain behind. We'll put lights there and there." He pointed at the ceiling.

She nodded, thinking of the cup.

"Why the sad face?" He stood and looked intently at her.

"Mr. Silverman. It's the silver chalice."

He patted her shoulder. "It's missing. I know. But we have very skilled and determined people who will find it."

"You know?"

"Got a call this morning." He rubbed his palms together, dusting off his hands. "How did you know?"

She told him of her adventure last night, omitting Michael's name, and ending at the part where they lost the two thieves.

"Oh, you shouldn't have followed them. You could have been hurt!" He took off his wire-rimmed glasses, held them up to the light, blinking his eyes as he looked for a smudge. Settling them back in place, he regarded her closely. "You're all right now?"

"Of course." Sarah followed him back to the small office they shared. "Are you sure the people looking for it are competent? Don't you think I should have called the police?"

He leaned over his desk, moving papers from one side to the other, looking for something. "Of course, that would be the usual thing to do, but in this case, I think you did the right thing—not by going after them, but by not calling the police." He pulled a paper out from beneath a book. "The agent who called explained it all to me."

If it was Michael, she wanted to hear how he was going to find her cup. "Do you have his phone number?"

He patted his vest pockets, dug into his pants pocket, and ruefully looked at his desk. "I wrote it somewhere, on one of these pieces of paper." He shrugged. "Not to worry. He said he'd be in touch with us before we close tonight. Meanwhile, you can make some of those fund-raising calls you're so good at. I have another list of names." He held out a sheet of paper.

Sarah took it, went to her desk, and turned on her computer. While she waited for it to boot up, the phone rang. She picked up the receiver, and before she said a word, the voice on the other end said, "I'm coming over there, and I want to talk to you."

"Good morning, Aunt Paula." An ear-splitting click was the only response. Sarah held the phone away from her ear and winced. She sighed, then entered her password.

Checking her E-mail, she noted that her friend from the

British Museum had something on the history of the cup. From the photos and description she'd sent, he surmised it was made in the first century by a Roman silversmith named Demas. He said he'd have to see it for confirmation and that his colleague would be in touch with the museum soon.

In spite of her concern for the cup, Michael intruded into her thoughts. He'd been trained from an early age to understand the scorn and contempt for those who abandoned their faith. Though she'd never known one, she joined in mocking those wicked traitors. A deep sorrow welled up again. Her hand began to tremble, so she put the paper down and closed her eyes for a moment to gather her composure. With a deep sigh she reached for the phone to call the first name on the list. In her sorrow she'd placed the paper upside down, and scrawled in pencil on the back was a phone number.

Maybe it's Michael's, she thought, dialing the number.

"Hello?" A woman's voice answered.

"Good morning. I'm calling from the Heritage Museum."

"Yes?"

Sarah paused, thinking quickly. This may just be a friend or relative of Mr. Silverman. "We actively seek and save the precious antiquities of our country." *May as well ask for a donation.*

"Is this about the chalice? Have you found it?"

Speechless for a second, Sarah quickly regained her composure. She couldn't admit the cup was gone. "I'd like to talk with you about it. When would be a good time?"

"I'm volunteering at the retirees home at noon, but I have a few minutes this morning."

"I'm writing this down. I'll need directions to your home. Oh, and how do you spell your last name? I want to get it correctly."

"Ben Ami." The woman gave Sarah an address in Beersheva.

Sarah thanked her, told her she'd be there soon, and hung up. She sat, staring at the phone. The woman had mentioned the cup. Sarah would find out what her connection to it was.

She gathered up her purse and keys, then looked in the exhibition room. No visitors yet, but Mr. Silverman was busy measuring. She was about to tell him that she'd be out for a little while when the outer door opened.

She turned, expecting to see a visitor. Aunt Paula strode in, looking from side to side, probably being sure no one else was there to hear her.

"Hello, Aunt Paula." Sarah clutched her keys. "I'm sorry I can't talk now. I have an appointment."

Aunt Paula crossed her arms over her formidable chest. "It can wait. I have something to say to you, young lady. It's a good thing your mother isn't here." She rolled her eyes. "Do you know how it would have hurt her to know you've been seen with. . .with a certain despised person?"

"But it was—"

Aunt Paula threw her hands up. "What was she thinking?" she asked the ceiling. She leveled her gaze to Sarah and pointed a long finger at her. "Be careful, or you'll be another one. Banned from the family. Your name never mentioned. The grief of your parents." She shook her head and began to enumerate more dire consequences of being seen in Michael's presence.

Just then the subject of her tirade walked in. Aunt Paula stared at him, then backed up as if a horde of tarantulas had crawled in under the door. She was speechless until indignation kicked in.

"You! Snake in the grass! Betrayer of all that is holy! How dare you come around decent people?" She pointed to his head. "Take off the yarmulke! You aren't worthy to wear it."

"Good morning, Mrs. Rosten." The look he gave her was so tender, Sarah looked again to be sure she'd seen it.

"Well!" Aunt Paula sputtered, then glared at Sarah. "This is all your fault! You should have never spoken to him." Refusing to look at Michael, she shook her head and left. Sarah and Michael stood in silence for a few seconds, then Sarah turned back to the exhibit room. "Mr. Silverman. I'll be gone for an hour or so. Museum business."

He waved one arm back at her as he wrote dimensions with the other.

"Sarah, we need to talk."

"No, we don't. Unless you want to tell me who those men were and how you expect to get the cup back."

"I can't tell you anything right now. It's an ongoing case, and I am restricted from talking about it."

"Well, I'm on a case myself and don't have time for chit chat." She stepped around him, but her arm brushed his and a tingle raced up to her shoulder, warming her. Shocked, she looked up to see if he'd felt it too. A mistake, she learned too late. His gray eyes looked deep, seeming to penetrate her heart. She looked away quickly and forced herself to leave.

Chapter 4

Michael watched Sarah leave him again. He knew he'd offended her family by his conversion, but he'd never thought Sarah would shun him. She'd always been inquisitive, never stopping till she found answers. She'd said she was on her own case. Did it involve the cup?

After a hasty hello to Mr. Silverman, he left. He knew where Sarah parked her car, so he hurried down the steps to his, which was parked near the Dung Gate. Sure enough, in a moment Sarah's car emerged from the resident parking area and turned onto Maale Ha-Shalom.

Following her, he prayed, *Lord, please restore our friendship. And if by some miracle I'll have another chance to tell her about You, open the way.* As they drove out of Jerusalem, he had a hunch where she was going. Following her little blue Opel, he thought of all the times they'd laughed and played together as children. She made every game or story more fun with her bubbly personality and active imagination.

Although he and Rachel were closer in age, it was Sarah who'd gotten to his heart. At first when he'd viewed her as a younger sister, his urge to protect her had been born. Now, after seeing her again, that image of younger sister had faded away. She was a lovely young woman.

He didn't need to follow closely behind her now. He knew where she was going. Soon they pulled up in front of the Ben Amis' home. He leaped from his car before she could knock on their door.

"Sarah, wait!" He hurried to her side. "You just can't barge in on them. They're the original owners of the cup. I shouldn't even be telling you that much, but—"

"I know they're the owners." She started for the steps to their door. "Now, if you'll excuse me?"

He reached out and touched her elbow. "They don't know it's been stolen, and they must not know. When I get it back, it won't matter, but now, it would cause them unnecessary worry."

She looked to heaven. "Really, Michael, do you think I'm a total nutcase? Of course I won't tell them. I just want to know more about it, and I think they can tell me."

Michael struggled with himself. He could tell her a lot more than Leah and Joshua, but because of his investigation into its theft and the danger to her of revealing too much, he had to keep silent.

"You go about finding it your way, and I'll work in mine." She stepped onto the first of six steps to the front door.

Her remark shocked him. "You're not going to hunt for the cup. It's a dangerous business. Stay out of it."

"I'm not speaking to you." Sarah turned up her nose and took the next step up.

"You could get hurt. This isn't the hide-and-seek we played as children. Leave it to trained investigators. I'll find the cup soon, maybe even in the next couple days."

She took another step, then turned. Now at eye level with him, she narrowed her eyes. "You know where those two thieves are?"

He shook his head. "I can't tell you that. Just let me handle it."

"I'm not afraid. And I'm not stopping my search." Her blue eyes darkened as their gazes met and held.

The door opened, and a lovely gray-haired woman stood facing them. "Michael! How nice to see you again." She looked at Sarah. "You must be the person who called from the museum." She extended her hand to the interior. "Come in!"

Sarah lifted her head and stared triumphantly at him. He closed the gap in two steps. "Gnat! Always buzzing around where you shouldn't be."

She whispered back, "Michael Motorcycle! Always telling me what to do."

They touched the mezuzah on the doorpost and entered Leah's home as she led the way with sedate dignity.

While Leah went to get coffee for them, Michael relaxed, wondering what Sarah would think of her and wishing she could meet Joshua too. Watching Sarah's baffled expression, he asked, "Are you surprised that I'd receive a warm welcome in a Jewish home?"

"Maybe they're liberal or don't know of your betrayal."

She looked so curious and sparkling with life, he had to smile. "They are very religious. And they know."

Leah returned with a tray and coffee and set the refreshments on the round coffee table before them. Sarah's blue eyes widened when she saw a Christian Bible among the books beneath the glass-topped table. She flicked a glance at him, and he grinned.

Leah sat in the overstuffed chair between them and asked, "You're together, so I assume you found my cup at the museum?"

"No, it's not there." *Now if only Sarah doesn't mention the theft.* She seemed flustered and appeared to be collecting her wits. Did the sight of the Bible upset her that much?

"I have every confidence that you'll find it soon. Now, Miss Reuben, you said you wanted to talk about our cup?"

Sarah sat straighter, a sense of reserve covering her. "Yes. You see, I've developed an interest in it and want to know all I can."

"How did you hear about it, may I ask?"

Michael was about to intervene, when Sarah quickly answered, "I have photos of it in my office. It's very unusual and beautiful." *Good for her.* She'd told the truth without exposing the fact that she'd actually seen and handled the cup.

Leah smiled. "There's a story to the chalice. Would you like to hear it?"

"Oh, yes!" Sarah's eyes danced with anticipation. Michael settled back to hear the story again, content to watch the play of emotions on Sarah's face as Leah told the history of the cup. She leaned forward, eagerly listening, flinching at the mention of Yeshua, how He gave them peace in the midst of chaos. But she leaned forward again, asking a question or two as she was drawn back into the story.

When it was over, the coffee had gone cold, and Leah looked at her watch in surprise. "Oh, my! I have to rush. I'm late."

Michael and Sarah stood. "We won't keep you," he said.

"Yes, and thank you for the story," said Sarah. "It was fascinating."

"Let's have a quick prayer before we part." Leah reached out both hands to them. Sarah glanced at her, then looked to him, and he nodded. They held hands and Leah prayed for their safety and asked the blessings of Yeshua to go with them. Michael saw Sarah's face redden, wondering if it was from shame or surprise. But he echoed the amen. Leah gave them both a hug and told them they were welcome to come visit any time.

Outside on the sidewalk Sarah slowly shook her head. "She seemed like such a nice woman. I wonder how much of her story is true. I mean, that the cup has Christian significance."

"What do you think the inscription 'I will pour out my blood for you' means?"

She reached into her purse for her keys. "I don't know, but I intend to find out."

"So long as you keep that the focus of your inquiries."

She lifted her head and gave him a haughty look. "I'll go wherever my inquiries take me."

"I told you, don't put yourself in danger."

"Why, I didn't know you cared."

He followed her to her car and opened the door for her. Before closing it, he repeated, "I do care, little one. Don't mess with something you don't understand."

"Bye!" She started the engine, and he closed the door.

As he watched her drive away, he smiled, thinking of her expression as she listened to Leah tell her story, including references to Yeshua. *Lord, You've given her a lot to think about. Help me find the cup and keep her from danger.*

He drove away, hurrying to his office to make calls on a secure phone, check with Interpol, and search the network of antiquities for sale. He doubted the cup would be there, but he might find a clue. He figured it was taken for a private buyer and was destined to be smuggled out of the country and lost forever. He had to work fast.

Chapter 5

After lunch with her grandfather, Sarah walked thoughtfully back to the museum. He didn't show anger or try to make her feel guilty. Yet as he patiently explained that although he grieved for anyone who decided not to be a Jew any more, it was a disgrace to be friends with such a person, Sarah felt her guilt increase.

She felt sad for Michael and guilty for wanting to keep him as a friend. He'd done nothing to harm her, and she felt the same as she always had toward him—attracted. It must have been painful to choose to walk away from his heritage. Even though she could never do the same, she owed him an apology for her quick rejection when he tried to explain it. She wanted to understand and to let him know that although they could only relate in a professional way, she would not reject him as a person.

"Phone!" said Ruth.

"Thanks."

"Sarah! I've been trying to get you all morning!" Nina's voice was breathy, as though she'd been running.

"I've been very busy."

"I heard you were with Michael last night. Tell me all about it! How did he look? Did you ask him about changing sides? What did he say?"

Glancing at her computer screen, Sarah saw that she had E-mail.

"Sarah!"

"Oh. Listen, Nina, I am in the middle of something I can't put off. I'll call you back, okay?"

"Bah! All right. But call me as soon as you can."

"I will." Sarah hung up and checked her messages. One was from her mother, telling her to stay away from a certain *meshugganer*.

The other, from her former coworker at the British Museum, told her that her inquiries about the chalice had gotten the attention of antiquities people from several countries and there were numerous requests to find out where it was. It could be a very valuable Israeli artifact. "Put it in a vault for safekeeping until we can tell you more. It must not fall into the hands of a private collector, and it is illegal to be shipped out of the country."

Sarah groaned. If only she'd known that yesterday. She e-mailed back, asking for the names of some of the inquirers. Turning to her assigned duties, she picked up the list of possible donors and began making calls. She dialed the first number and turned the sheet over. Drawing circles around Leah and Joshua's phone number, she thought of the sweet lady with the same look in her eyes as Michael's, almost as if they'd seen heaven itself.

"Hello. I'm calling from the Heritage Museum." Sarah gave herself a mental shake and got down to business. When she'd called everyone on the list, she carefully went over the names of inquirers after the cup. One sounded familiar.

She called a friend with whom she'd served in the military. "Moshe, how are you?"

"Hey, I'm good. Are you going to take my offer and play soccer with us?"

She laughed. "Nice try. Believe me, the team won't miss me."

After small pleasantries, she asked him, "Do you know anything about Amir Endrawos? Does he or his family have a business in jewelry or antiquities?"

"Just a minute." When Moshe came back to the phone, he said, "No. The family owns a meat market in the Old City. Why?"

"Nothing. Just for curiosity sake, is it near El-Wad Road?"

"Yes. Right around the corner from the bazaar."

Sarah took a deep breath. "Nice talking with you, Moshe. Tell Elaine and the kids I said hello." When she hung up, she sat for a moment with her hand on the phone. El-Wad was where she and Michael had lost the thieves. She longed to talk with him, and if she knew his phone number, she'd call him now.

What am I thinking? I can't even be seen with him. Is this what the fascination of the moth for the flame is like? She felt so drawn, she could hardly resist the pull. She recited a childhood prayer. "I am thankful before thee, King, who lives ever lasting. . . ."

Late that night, Sarah lay in bed for a long time, thinking. Michael had said God was very personal to him. How could that be? She believed in God, but not in the way Michael suggested. It just wasn't possible. Unless you were a rabbi, maybe. Somehow she dozed off before dawn with restless dreams.

The next morning she awoke with a plan. She'd convince Michael to give up his silly fascination with fanatical beliefs. After parting with Grandfather, she worked out the details. She'd call Michael on business, they'd discuss the cup, and she'd remind him of the beauty and holiness of what she had and of what he was giving up. The strange phrase on the cup must be a hint of his wrong thinking. *I will pour out my blood for you.* How abominable! She'd heard the horrible story that the so-called Messiah had told his friends they must drink his blood. She almost gagged, thinking about it. Yes, it was up to her to rescue Michael from his folly.

Michael paced back and forth in his small office, waiting for a call from the university's Israeli Antiquities Division. Ever since he'd heard they were searching for the cup too, he'd tried to find out what they'd uncovered. They were not telling. But he had a contact who'd promised to call him when he heard anything at all. Michael was at a dead end and frustrated.

He snapped the phone up when it rang. "Van Gelder."

"Michael?" He relaxed, glad to hear from Sarah but wanting to keep it short so the line would be clear for the call he expected any minute.

"Sarah. What's up?"

"I thought we could meet this afternoon. There's something I want to talk with you about." He detected a trace of uncertainty in her voice.

He leaned over the desk and checked his calendar. Lunch with the head of security at the Pesitka Museum. "How does two-thirty at Talpiot sound to you?"

"Fine. See you there."

He rang off quickly, wondering what it was about. She was taking a risk, but it must be important. He hoped she'd taken his advice and would let the experts look for the cup. Somehow, he doubted she had.

By two o'clock Michael had not heard from his contact. He put a forward ring from his office phone to his cell phone and left.

Arriving at the site before Sarah, he waited near the parking area. *Lord Yeshua, help me find a chance to show her how You love her.* When she arrived, he felt his heart do a quick dance. She was so cute when they were young; now she was nothing less than beautiful. She wore a subdued blue dress that swirled around her legs as she walked toward him. The breeze blew a single lock of auburn hair across her cheek, and he noticed she'd put a light rosy color on her lips. Imprinted on his memory was Sarah at about eight years old with bright spots of Rachel's makeup on her young face. But that was like an old photograph. She was living and real now, and the blush on her cheeks was natural.

He forced himself back to reality and stepped forward. "Hello, Sarah."

"Michael." She smiled, but he sensed an uneasiness behind her cheerful features.

He led her up the path to the top. Tourists, speaking English, passed them. "So, little one. What's the reason for meeting? It could get you in trouble, you know."

She took a deep breath. "Yes, I know. That's precisely why I'm here." She clasped and unclasped her hands, then looked into his eyes. "Michael, you've really hurt your family. I know your mother must be grieving that you can't come home. How can it be so important that you'd give up your family and all of us?"

Thank You, Lord. Guide my words. "You really want to know?"

"I'm trying to understand without judging, Michael. I've known you a long time, and I know you're not stupid, so what is it?" There was hurt mixed with trust in her eyes.

"First of all, I haven't given up my family and all of you."

"Yes, you have! You've given up being Jewish. What are you now?" She turned to him, imploring him to explain.

"I like to think of it as being a complete Jew," he said.

"Don't make fun of me, Michael. Be serious."

"I am. You know we've been looking for our Messiah for centuries."

She nodded. "So?"

"He came two thousand years ago. His name is Yeshua."

"You actually believe that?" She looked shocked.

"I actually do. I found all the evidence in our holy books."

"Impossible!"

They paused to look out over Jerusalem. The whole city spread before them, astonishing, laid out like a great work of art.

"I love coming here," she said.

"I'm awed and grateful to call Jerusalem home." Michael enjoyed the way the sunlight touched her rich auburn hair. "Remember what we learned in yeshiva about temple sacrifices?"

"Yes. But—"

He held up a hand to stop her argument. "God said it was the only way our sins would be covered. Right?"

She bit her lower lip. "Right."

"We don't do that anymore. So, did God change his mind?"

Sarah frowned and peered at the spectacular view. "Well, I don't know about that. I suppose there's no way we can do it now, since we have no temple."

"Father Abraham had no temple. Yet he knew to sacrifice blood in payment for sins."

She released a long-held breath. "Oy! These things are for the rabbis to ponder and discuss."

"Speaking of rabbis, Yeshua was a Jewish rabbi."

Her eyes widened, and she stared at him. "No! I don't believe that."

"Well, He was. But more important, He fulfilled more than five hundred prophecies of the coming Messiah that

Moses and the prophets predicted."

"If it was so obvious, then why don't our rabbis know it? They know a lot more than you or I. Ask any of them, and they'll say your Yeshua was an impostor or worse."

"Sarah. There are more rabbis and learned men than you can imagine who know that Yeshua is the true Messiah. Many right here in Jerusalem are waiting for the right time to come forward and say so."

Sarah glanced over her shoulder as though fearful someone might hear them.

"Don't worry. Lightning won't strike if we talk of Yeshua." He leaned toward her. "You may not remember, but our prophet Isaiah said the coming Messiah would be beaten, bruised, and bloodied for our sins and diseases. Other prophets saw this too."

She stood, wringing her hands, clearly agitated. "You mustn't speak of this! It's. . .it's too horrible. I mustn't listen."

Michael gently reached for her wrist. "Relax, Sarah. Yeshua brings peace. Let's discuss this like adults."

She shook her head, the curls around her face dancing. "No more. I can't." She closed her eyes, and he watched her compose herself. She smiled without humor. "And I came to set you straight."

He put his arm around her shoulders. "I appreciate that. It shows you care."

Tears brightened her eyes. "I don't want to see you and your family hurt any more."

"Neither do I." His voice was low and sad. "But I can't ignore the truth."

He moved his arm from her shoulder and put his hand on the railing. They watched the light on the city shift and change. He glanced at her. How brave and wonderful she was, how thrilling it would be if she would follow Yeshua. Dreams of their working and worshiping side by side tempted him. But he knew he couldn't commit himself to a union that would be filled with the problems of differing faiths. Saddened, he looked away.

"Have you discovered any more about the whereabouts of the cup?"

Sarah's question brought him back to earth. "There has been some progress." He kept his answer noncommittal, hoping she'd let the subject drop.

"I found something too."

Michael stiffened, annoyed. "Please. Don't get yourself in danger. This is serious."

She rolled her eyes. "I simply did some checking on the phone and the computer. I found out something very interesting."

"What, pray tell, did you find?"

"Never mind. I think you're patronizing me."

"Sarah! Come on. I'm the one the Ben Ami family hired. Let me do my job."

"It could be dangerous for you too. Let me in on what you have, and we can work together." Her eyes brightened. "We can help each other stay out of danger."

He tilted his head, shaking it slowly. "Still the girl spy. I—" His cell phone beeped and he said, "Excuse me." He walked a few steps away, glancing back at Sarah.

"And so a special unit of the Israeli police will be closing in on them in about an hour," said the caller. Michael glanced at Sarah. She had a smug look on her face, as if she'd heard every word. How was he going to be there to stake the Ben Amis' claim on the cup without involving her?

Chapter 6

Sarah had a nagging feeling that Michael was talking with someone about the cup and was trying to keep her from finding out. He finished his call, flipped his cell phone shut, and stared out over the city.

"Is there news about the cup?"

His expression became guarded. "A friend may have a lead on it."

"It may be the same one I have. Shall we pool our information and work together?"

He shook his head. "Too dangerous. Tell me what you have, and I'll let you know if it's the same information I have."

"And have you run with it? No way, Michael. We work together. I want that cup a whole lot more than you do. It's personal."

"Sarah, this is one time you just can't follow me like you used to." He turned toward her, looking into her eyes. "Let me do this. I know what I'm doing."

Sarah thought about that for two seconds. "I'm not giving up, Michael. So you might as well let me come along." She grabbed her purse, without letting him reply, and turned to leave.

Following her, Michael didn't say anything until he opened

her car door for her. "I promise I'll let you know the minute I find anything. Give me your cell phone number."

"You won't need it." She'd be with him every step of the way, whether he liked it or not. He waited for her to drive away, but she waved him off. Finally he went to his own car and left.

Sarah had to laugh at his attempt to lose her in the heavy Jerusalem traffic. But she stuck on his trail. He parked in a bus lane near the Dung Gate, put a small sign on his car, and dashed through the gate. She parked behind his car and ran after him.

Half a block behind him, she followed him past the Western Wall, through alleys and narrow streets, onto El-Wad Road. Yes! Her information was correct. The farther they got into Muslim territory, the closer she followed Michael. She felt peril in the shadows and doorways. Old men watched her pass with blank faces, but black-robed women looked at her with disgust.

She hurried. Michael would just have to deal with the fact that she was with him. She finally got close enough to be able to reach out and grab his arm. But before she could do anything, she heard a commotion in the market square ahead.

Five Israeli soldiers held the yelling and cursing crowd back, and two more came out from the meat market, holding the arms of a Palestinian who looked to be in his thirties. She clutched Michael's arm, and he looked down at her with surprise, his eyes gray pools of quiet calm. Two more policemen emerged carrying cloth bags wrapped around bulky objects.

Sarah started after them, but Michael grabbed her arm. "Let them go. You can't get it now."

She put her hands on her hips and glared at him. "They have the cup, don't they? And you knew it!"

"I knew they had a lead, and this was the probable place, that's all." He looked over his shoulder, uneasy. There were only two soldiers left, and the crowd was restless. Sarah recognized one of them and approached him. "Where have they taken the artifacts?"

"Sarah Reuben, is that you?" Yaakov, with whom she had trained, narrowed his eyes at her.

"Yaakov. Good to see you again." She leaned close to him, so he could hear her. "One of the items was stolen from our museum, and I want it back."

"They've taken it to the Ha-Aretz Kibbutz for temporary safekeeping where no one will think to look for it."

"Thanks." She glanced nervously over her shoulder. "The people seem to be calming down."

Michael put his arm around her shoulder. "Let's get out of here."

Yaakov nodded. "Good idea." He and his partner stayed, their rifles hanging from belts slung over their shoulders.

Michael and Sarah turned onto Sheik Rehan Road, back toward the Jaffa Gate, the closest area of safety.

They'd only gone a short way, when two Palestinian men stepped out in front of them. "Stop right there."

Sarah gasped as a shiver of panic slid down her back. The hostility and hatred in their eyes hit her with an almost tangible force.

"Let us by." Michael pulled her forward. Another man blocked their way.

"Tell us where they've taken our things." Two more men appeared from the other side of the street and surrounded Sarah and Michael.

"Get lost." Michael grabbed Sarah's hand and pulled her close to his side.

One of the men grabbed Michael, and another reached for

Sarah. Frightened of being dragged into one of the nearby dark doorways, she pushed at him. Another reached for her. She did the only thing she could do. She screamed. A loud, shrill caterwauling screech.

The startled attackers fell back for a moment. Sarah glared at them and took a deep breath to scream again. They looked past her, and she turned around. A small group of European tourists had stopped and stood staring at them. When a tall, red-haired gentleman headed toward them, the cold knot in Sarah's stomach loosened a bit.

Michael pulled her toward the tourist group. When she looked back she saw an empty street where they'd been.

The red-haired man asked a question in German.

Michael answered, and although Sarah didn't fully understand that language, she knew enough of it to discern that Michael had told them there had been a misunderstanding, but that all was well.

They followed the tourists for a few minutes toward the Via Dolorosa Road. Sarah understood very little of the guide's explanation of the events that had happened two centuries ago in front of the Ecce Homo Basilica. Michael leaned close to her and told her about the sacrifice of Yeshua Ha-Masheach, the Messiah, who poured out His blood for His people, as it was written.

Still shaken, she looked into his eyes, which glowed with love and the depth of something undefinable. "Michael, everyone knows that our Messiah will come and be King."

"That's right. He'll be coming again as King. But first He had to be our *pesach*, our Passover Lamb." He pointed to the street beside the brick courtyard where they were standing. "And a lot of the story happened right here."

"Sounds like a fairy tale." The streets looked calm. People milled around, and no one even noticed them. "Let's go to the Armenian Quarter. I feel uncomfortable here."

He turned her face up to his. "Are you all right? Those hoodlums didn't hurt you, did they?" His jaw tightened, showing his anger.

"No. I'm all right. I just need to get out of here."

Michael scanned the wide street, then took her hand. "Let's go, then."

She caught her breath and started walking, feeling safe with him beside her. The pilgrims who came to see the place where their leader, Jesus, was killed had nothing to do with her.

As though Michael had heard her thoughts, he said, "The Romans and some of the Jews hated Yeshua. His followers thought he was going to kick out the Romans and establish the kingdom."

"Yes, so? That's logical. It's what Messiah is supposed to do. Not die like a criminal." Sarah wouldn't look at Michael. She didn't want to be drawn in by his expressive gray eyes.

"He will eventually. But as it was written by the prophets, He came to pour out His blood for us."

Sarah stopped and faced him putting her hands on her hips. "You mean that cup—my cup—is a Christian artifact?"

Michael smiled. "It's a Jewish symbol of what Messiah did as sacrificial lamb so we could have our sins forgiven."

She shook her head. "It's *shmeggege!* Crazy! Messiah is not a poor little lamb led to the slaughter. It's blasphemy to even suggest it."

"Would you like for me to show you sometime where it says He will die for us? It's all in the Law and Prophets."

She kept up with him as he started walking. "You can't

prove any such thing."

Sarah changed the subject. "They took the artifacts to a kibbutz." She slid an anxious glance at the darkening street ahead. Several of the Muslim shop owners had closed their doors to lay out their mats and pray to Allah.

"That's a good idea," said Michael. "A neutral place where no one can lay hands on them while the police sort out where they belong." He looked down at her as they continued walking. "Tell no one where they are. Even people you think you can trust."

"They wouldn't raid a heavily guarded kibbutz would they? That would be a suicide mission."

"These people are desperate, and those items represent lots of money. They'd do it if they thought they could get away with it. The lives of the people in the kibbutz depend on our keeping the secret."

Sarah smiled. "Spies never tell, even when tortured." She laughed up at him. "I never told when I was a child, although I was never tortured. I can still keep a secret, though."

"Good, because—" His eyes suddenly widened in alarm, and he pushed her, so hard that she almost lost her balance. "Go! Get help." When she hesitated, he pushed her again. "Hurry! Call the police!"

Four men came from the side street, and in panic she fled. She looked back once to see Michael standing between her and them. She ran through the streets with an urgency she had never before felt. She dashed behind the low wall of an outside café and caught her breath, then pulled her cell phone from her purse.

"Answer!" she whispered, looking uneasily over her shoulder as the number rang. When the police operator answered, she closed her eyes to calm herself and told them where she was and about Michael. "Hurry!"

"Stay where you are," said the operator. "Someone will be there shortly." In the gathering dusk, the café's outside lights turned on. Curious patrons looked away when she glanced at them. She stood outside the wall and scanned in every direction. Though it seemed like hours, it was less than three minutes before three soldiers arrived, two men and a woman, their guns slung over their shoulders.

She led them back to the last place where she had seen Michael. The area was semi-dark, with a mother sitting outside on a stoop, her toddler playing with colored rocks at her feet. The soldiers asked if she'd seen anything unusual, and she said no. Sarah surveyed the alleys and doorways. Smells of onion and herbs floated out from open windows in a second-story apartment.

There was nothing to show what had happened only a few moments earlier. They walked the side streets, searching for Michael.

Chapter 7

Seeing the danger coming his way, Michael deliberately pushed Sarah away, more roughly than he'd wanted, but enough so that she wouldn't hesitate. He touched a button on his cell phone which would automatically dial his contact, Ben Rossberg, to let him know there was trouble. It also emitted a signal showing his location.

Two of the attackers got on each side of him, grabbing his arms. He struggled until he felt a knife pressing into his side. "I'll go after the girl," said the third.

"She knows nothing!" Michael yelled after him. Sarah had turned the corner toward the Jewish Quarter and safety. He glanced up to see a soldier on the rooftop of the Herzl Building, hoping the soldier would notice Sarah's run for safety or even look his way. The third man decided not to pursue her and instead came back.

The man on his left yanked the yarmulke off Michael's head, making him unidentifiable as a Jew. Michael knew that if they got him into one of the nearby dark recesses, he would be impossible to find.

He struggled but felt the knife prick his side and stopped. If they stabbed him, they'd just pull him into one of the dark doorways, and he'd die. But if he told the artifacts' location, dozens in the kibbutz would die. He'd have to give his life if necessary. *Lord, help.*

"Tell us where they've taken our property."

"It isn't yours." He winced as the knife nicked him near the first scratch.

"Don't be stupid." They pulled him a few feet forward, deeper into the labyrinth of narrow streets.

"Tell us now and save your girlfriend the trouble."

Michael glanced back at the street they'd just come from. "I told you she doesn't know anything."

"So you say. We'll find out."

He said nothing, expecting the police any minute.

He had to stall for time and keep them from dragging him farther from the main street. "Why do you think I know where it is?"

"You're one of them." The dark eyes of the man on his left glittered with hatred. "You were waiting for us in the museum."

Michael looked closer. The man was shorter than he and younger.

"Enough!" The other man yanked Michael's arm, pulling him deeper into the dark maze.

"Yes." The third man walked behind them. "Let's convince him to talk."

Michael kicked the knee of the man on his left. At almost the same instant he grabbed the wrist of the other man, twisting the knife.

The third man grabbed Michael around his waist and dragged him back. The other two closed in, punching him. He lunged at one of them and turned his head to see the end of the street, hoping someone would be curious enough to investigate the commotion.

The three men, for just an instant, followed Michael's glance, so he punched one of them in the jaw and started running. He felt his jacket being pulled. Shrugging it off, he ran a few more steps until he was tackled.

Falling to the ground with the breath knocked out of him, he felt his face hit the street. He saw a door opening and a man's feet in the doorway. One of his attackers said, "Go back inside," and the door shut quickly.

He was pulled to his feet. He opened his eyes, but everything was dark and blurred.

Suddenly the men let go, and he stumbled but managed to stay upright. He could hear them running away behind him and could barely make out the people approaching him.

Thank God. Someone had seen trouble and come to his rescue.

"Michael!" Sarah's voice sounded like an angel's. He rubbed his eyes and squeezed them shut. Forcing them open, he focused on her dear face.

"Are you okay?" Her face, puckered in concern, stared back at him.

"I am now." He looked behind him. "I thought I saw four people."

"You did." She touched his cheek. "The other two went after your attackers."

The soldier extended his hand toward the main road. "Let's go."

They left the Muslim Quarter and crossed over into the Jewish Quarter to the police command post. Michael lifted his shirt and put an ointment on the cuts on his side, and Sarah tended to the scratches on his face.

A short while later, Michael called Rossberg, and Sarah called her grandfather.

"Maideleh," her grandfather said gently, "you sound tense. Is everything all right?"

"It is now. Something happened, and I'll tell you about it when I get home." She dreaded telling him she had been with Michael again. But she wouldn't lie. Just imagining his blue eyes filled with disappointment saddened her.

As they left the police, Sarah said, "I need to walk and sort everything out." She felt too keyed up to go straight home.

"Let's go for a ride. That always helps."

The walk through the cool night air to the parking lot used up some of her nervous energy. She felt glad for Michael's protective company.

As they drove out of the Old City, Sarah leaned her head back. "I prayed for your protection."

"So did I."

"Who did you pray to?" She kept her eyes closed.

"The God of Abraham, Isaac, and Jacob, of course."

After a deep sigh, she said, "Michael, why are you forsaking us? Someday you'll come to your senses, but if you wait too long it might be too late to undo the hurt."

"Sarah, if you'd only examine the evidence, you'd come to the same conclusion I have. Yeshua is our Messiah."

"A lot of good a dead Messiah is."

"He isn't dead. He rose from the grave and is alive."

"Let's not talk of fairy tales." She opened her eyes. They were heading south on the highway. More lights twinkled in the new homes on the hills. She wanted to drop the whole subject but couldn't stop trying to get Michael to come back to the truth.

"If I were a Muslim, would you examine my doctrinal books?"

"I would." He took the off-ramp, avoiding the Palestinian checkpoint outside Bethlehem. "In fact, I did study the Koran."

She gaped at him as if he'd grown two heads. "Why?"

"A friend asked me to. He felt I had no basis to refute his beliefs if I didn't know them. He was right."

Sarah didn't know what to say. He made it sound as if she were putting her head into the sand. "This is stupid. We're just going round and round. I don't want to talk about it anymore." She buttoned her sweater, watched a bus pass them, and simply let the simple act of riding through the night relax her.

"You're cold." Michael turned on the heater.

"Thanks. Why did the Ben Amis hire you to search for the cup?"

"You're welcome. It's what I do. My company, International Antiquities Service, keeps pretty busy. We fight against illegal artifact trading, stop looting of archaeological sites, and try to keep countries from being robbed of their cultural history."

She sat straight up. "I saw that name on my computer when I put the word out, searching for information."

"I saw your message, and so did others."

"But I transmitted on a secure line."

"Sweetie, any good hacker can find whatever they want on the Net." He glanced at her. "Don't worry. I got the information legally."

"That burns me up. There's no privacy."

"Not on the Internet." His cell phone jingled. "Excuse me."

Sarah looked out at the black hills dotted with lights while Michael punctuated his short phone call with one-word responses.

He flipped the cell phone shut and said, "I forgot the meeting at Joshua and Leah's tonight." Raising his eyebrows, he looked over at her. "Would you care to make a stop there for a few minutes?"

"That's fine with me." She remembered Leah's gracious hospitality and was interested in meeting Joshua. "Do you think they'll get the cup back?"

"It's theirs, and I do believe it will be returned to them."

In front of the neat sandstone house Michael parked behind a van. Before he shut off the engine, he leaned toward her and hesitated, measuring her for a moment. "Remember, these are true Israelis. They suffered through the *Aliyeh* of 1948."

He gave her hand a squeeze. His eyes still had that powerful depth that drew her toward him. She dragged her gaze away, and he got out of the car. Why had he told her of Joshua and Leah's Israeli allegiance. The Bible she'd seen beneath the glass of their coffee table? Were they also Yeshua followers?

She had no time to think because the Ben Ami door opened, and two bearded men hopped down the steps toward them. "Hey, Man. You're late!" They clasped hands and playfully punched each other's shoulders. "You brought someone!"

Sarah came to stand beside Michael. He introduced them as Avram and David. She recognized Avram, with his red hair and beard. They'd been in yeshiva together for a term when they were both fourteen. She'd seen him off and on at celebrations and parades.

Leah beckoned from the doorway, and they hurried up the steps. Avram studied her and asked, "Weren't we in school together?"

She smiled. "We were. A long time ago." Her smile died as she entered the living room and saw that it was crowded with people with open books on their laps. They'd obviously been studying something, and Sarah could guess what.

She stopped, unable to go farther into the room. Eager faces looked up at her and Michael, some she'd seen before.

She stiffened and felt her cheeks burning. She'd walked right into a den of the faithless.

Michael looked down at her. "Don't be afraid, little one."

Humiliation turned to fury so deep she could scarcely speak. She turned to the cool air outside, but Leah quietly shut the door and said softly, "Shalom Aleichem." *Peace to you.* Her look showed that she understood.

That confused Sarah more. She whispered to Michael, "You shouldn't have brought me here. I can't stay. You know that."

"Look what they're studying. It's a book by a nineteenth-century Russian rabbi named Chaim Bogdanovich."

A large man held the focus of the people sitting in a semi-circle around him. He had the powerful look of a gentle bear, a man who could either gently stroke a kitten or use his big hands as weapons. He continued teaching, with a nod toward her and Michael.

"That's Joshua," whispered Michael.

She didn't realize how tense she was until her nails dug into her palms as she clenched her hands. "Who is this Russian rabbi? I never heard of him."

"A pious Jew who wrote volumes on scriptural doctrines and the study of God's work among His people."

A heaviness sank into her chest. "I don't want to know any more. Give me his name, and I'll look up his work later. Now, I really need to get back home."

"It was a long day. We shouldn't have come. Give me a moment, and we'll leave." He caught Leah's look, and she approached. "Sarah has been through a lot today, and I need to get her back home. Have Joshua call me later tonight. I have news about the cup."

Leah's eyes lit up. "You've found it?"

"Yes. But there's a story behind it."

Leah grasped his hand in both of hers. "I can never thank you enough, Michael." She reached over for Sarah's hand and held it a moment. "Thank you for coming, even for a few minutes. You're welcome any time."

"Thank you. And I'm sorry I can't stay." Sarah found it hard to think with Leah's gaze seeing deeper than she knew. She turned toward the door. As Michael followed her, she heard Leah say, "Go with God."

Back on the road, she leaned back and closed her eyes. Exhausted, she wondered if she'd ever see Michael again. She'd failed miserably in trying to get him to see reason. Now she just wanted to give up, go back to her daily routine, sink back into the comfortable family embrace, and forget reading about religious disputes.

It was a joyless trip back. Michael walked her to the door, and it was flung open before she could say good-bye. Aunt Paula stood in the doorway, glaring at her. Grandfather, behind her, had the sad, disappointed look Sarah hoped she'd never see.

Chapter 8

Aunt Paula screeched. "Ach! See, Micah, I told you. He has cast a spell over her." She put the back of her hand to her forehead. "I am so glad your dear mother isn't here to see this."

Grandfather stepped to the door. "Come in. We don't want our business spread all over the neighborhood."

Sarah and Michael entered, and Grandfather shut the door. Aunt Paula stepped back from Michael as if he had the plague. "Stay by the door. You are defiling this good man's home."

"Aunt Paula, please." Sarah glanced from her to Grandfather to Michael.

Michael seemed to be the only one in the room unperturbed. He stood with quiet dignity. "I assure you, Mr. Reuben, it was all my fault. Something was stolen from the museum, and I followed Sarah to make sure she was all right, then brought her home." He kept his focus on her grandfather. "I am truly sorry if I've caused your family any worry. But it was all my fault. Don't blame Sarah."

"But, Michael, it was I who—"

"Who simply wanted to protect the museum's property. An admirable reaction."

"Sarah!" Aunt Paula's contempt radiated through her voice. "He is *farshikn,* banished."

Her grandfather's disappointment almost brought her to tears. "I was worried for you," he said. "I told you to avoid this person. You will tell me where you've been and everything that happened today."

"Yes, Zayde."

Aunt Paula stepped close to Sarah and put her finger in her face. "Promise that you will never, ever speak to this person again." She nodded toward Michael without looking at him.

"I can't promise that, Aunt Paula, because in my work I come in contact with all kinds of people."

"Then have someone else deal with him if your museum has to talk to his sort."

Sarah glanced back at Michael, who stood patiently listening.

"Don't even look at him!" Aunt Paula grabbed Sarah's chin and turned her face away from Michael. "You should quit that job and raise a family. When your mother comes home, we will have a meeting with Mrs. Finkelstein. She'll find a good man for you."

Michael said, "I'd better be going. I am so sorry to have troubled you."

Like velvet, his voice soothed and broke Sarah's heart.

"Just stay away from Sarah." Grandfather's stern look brooked no argument. He opened the door for Michael to leave. His gaze held Sarah's so she couldn't see Michael go.

As soon as the door was closed, all the fear, doubts, and anxieties crowded in her head, making it pound. "I need a couple aspirins," she said, heading for the kitchen.

"Just a minute, young lady—"

"Let her go," said Grandfather. "We'll talk later."

She endured their lecturing like a wayward teenager. As a

good Jewish girl, she didn't sass her elders, even though she was twenty-four years old. Aunt Paula didn't want to hear details of why and how she was with Michael. When she left, Sarah finally went to bed.

Restless, she got up to look out her window. Spotlights made the Tower of David her lighthouse. On the other side of their home, the windows were always curtained, to block the view of the Muslim Dome.

Looking out over the city, she wondered what Michael was doing. Writing his report, maybe sleeping. How did he deal with being an outcast? He, who was so loyal to his family and their traditions.

All those little-girl fantasies of being old enough to be his girlfriend had never happened. He'd gone away before she grew up. When she was fifteen, she'd played the part of Queen Esther in a play, wishing he were in the front row seeing how she'd grown up. Now he was back, but everything was different.

His faith in Yeshua hadn't made him a raving maniac as she'd been told happened to Jews who were so led astray. He was the same old Michael, except more somehow. Was it confidence in his job, maturity, or something deeper?

That got her to thinking about what he'd said about Messiah giving His life for His people. That was so ludicrous she wanted to laugh, but it made her sad. When Messiah came, He would lead their people to victory over all obstacles and would make peace with their enemies. He would not suffer and die. What about the sacrifices that were commanded? Of course, with no temple it was impossible to follow the ordinances in the Torah. But if God told them to, He must have later told them it was all right not to sacrifice anymore. But then what took away the sins? Their ritual of making everything right at Yom Kippur and starting fresh? That must be it. But it seemed much less compared to Mosaic ritual.

She reached down and ran her fingers along the window sill, feeling the cool, smooth wood. *I will be a good person, make my family proud, and be approved by God.* She said a prayer of repentance and dedication to doing better, then went back to bed.

The next day, Michael called Sarah at the museum. "Your aunt was kidding about the matchmaker, right?"

"She was not kidding." She glanced uneasily over her shoulder, as if Aunt Paula were standing behind her. "I shouldn't be talking with you."

"This is business. I'd like to have you with me when I talk with Joshua and Leah. You can tell them all you know about how their cup got to your museum, and I can tell them what I know. That way we can get everything out into the open at one time."

That sounded logical, but Sarah knew she'd be in deep trouble if she went anywhere with Michael. Then again, it was also logical that she be there when he told what he'd learned. "I'll drive my own car and meet you there. What time?"

"How about four o'clock? Otherwise we'll have to make it tomorrow."

"I'll be there."

"Good. And Sarah? I'm looking forward to seeing you again."

And I you. "Okay. See you then."

The day dragged. Sarah both looked forward to seeing the Ben Amis again and dreaded it. She arrived before Michael, and Leah and Joshua graciously invited her in.

"I am so sorry you weren't able to stay last night." Leah led them into the living room.

"Yes, well. . ."

Leah patted her arm. "I understand, Dear. I had the same problem at first too." She looked lovingly at Joshua. "Joshua was a hero, and to say I was surprised when after we'd married he decided to become a follower of Yeshua is putting it mildly."

Michael arrived, entering the room and looking directly at her as if he were burning the image in his memory. She gazed at him for a moment, thinking that he'd never looked so handsome and honorable. Looking away, she tried to stop the warmth that flooded through her. Being attracted to him was perilous.

He sat beside her, flustering her even more. Leah returned with hot chocolate, and they talked of the cup.

"The story starts with me," said Michael. "When you asked me to investigate its location, I searched the Internet and found nothing. I asked my contacts, pored through museum catalogs, and was at a standstill."

"It was turned in to our museum," Sarah continued. "A young couple found it in a box with other things left in the basement of their new apartment in Jerusalem. They brought it to us to find out if it was valuable or just junk."

"I wonder how it got there." Leah lowered her gaze. "When the rockets were fired on us a few years ago, we had to evacuate our home for a couple of days. When we returned, some things were missing, including the silver goblet."

"It's been in our family for more than a century." Joshua nodded toward Leah. "Came with Leah, actually."

Leah brightened. "I'll be so pleased to see it again."

"Me too." Michael sat forward. "You see, I found where it was when Sarah put the word out looking for background data. She included a photo, and I contacted her."

Sarah noticed he didn't say anything about the theft and subsequent pursuit.

"When it's been catalogued and proven to be yours, you'll get it back," said Michael.

"We plan on giving it to your museum," said Joshua.

Sarah sat stunned for a moment. Then happiness bubbled up, leaving her breathless.

Leah smiled. "The cup is more than a piece of silver to you."

"Oh, yes. From the moment I picked it up, I felt an odd connection to it. As though it had come to our museum and to me by some grand design."

"Of course, you read Hebrew and understood the inscription?" Joshua's bushy salt-and-pepper brows rose over his intelligent eyes.

"I read it, but I don't understand it." Sarah glanced at Michael.

Leah spoke gently. "The inscription shows that our Messiah poured out His blood for His people, like the sacrificial lamb at Passover. The lamb was merely a symbol of what was to come and what Yeshua did for us, for all time."

Sarah sat very still, her fingers tensed in her lap.

"I'm really not trying to preach to you, Dear," said Leah. "It's simply the truth."

Michael leaned forward. "Sometimes the truth isn't simple or easy to understand."

"From the mouth of God to Moses I can understand." Before they could say more, Sarah reached for her purse on the floor. "It's getting late. I need to go now."

"I'd like to visit with you again some time," said Leah.

Sarah stood. She liked Leah. She was gracious and easy to be with. But she wasn't sure if it was right. Was she being seduced away from her religion? She murmured a thank you and headed for the door.

Before she left, Joshua placed a book in her hand. "Read the first chapter and tell me what you think."

"Thank you." She took it and left.

Michael followed her down the steps to her car. "I'll call you." He closed the door after her, and she saw him in her rearview mirror, watching as she drove away. It was when she turned into the Old City that she glanced down at the book. *Studies from the Foundations of Judaism.* She slid the book under the seat, hoping to forget it was there.

Sarah hurried to the museum to tell Mr. Silverman about the cup being donated. He had just left, so she cleaned up her desk and went home.

Michael did call, two days later, while she was at work. "Something came up, and I'll be leaving for New York in the morning. I'd hoped to see you before I go."

"I don't know." She longed to see him again yet was not willing to lie to do it.

"Let's call it a business appointment. In my investigation of the Ben Amis' chalice, I uncovered the whereabouts of some artifacts that date back to the Crusades."

"Do you have photos?"

"Of some. So, how about dinner and business at the same time?"

She agreed to meet him at a local Argentinean restaurant and told Mr. Silverman of the artifacts. "Ah, I'd heard of these. I'd love to talk to the people who have them."

"A friend of mine knows about them," she told him. "I think we're at the top of the list, and I'll try to get the owners' names for you."

Sarah called her grandfather and told him she had a business meeting, a dinner with a potential donor, and would be home as soon as it was over. As she hung up the phone, she wondered if God was taking Michael out of her life. It hurt, but if it had to be, she'd cope.

The minute she drove into the parking lot, Michael got out of his car, a briefcase in his hand. He directed her to a parking spot near his. Sarah thought he looked like a movie-star hero, with his casual jeans and a black leather bomber jacket unzipped over a turtleneck dove gray sweater. His eyes glowed with promises she'd never know. She gritted her teeth, resolving to keep her heart under control. Seeing him made that difficult.

The maitre d' led them through a side door to an upstairs private room, seating them at a small table near the window. As the restaurant was on a hill, the windows looked out over city lights. Small lights around the ceiling gave the room a gentle glow.

Sarah looked over the candle on the table. "My, this is romantic."

"I wanted it to be special. I don't know when I'll see you again." He reached for her hand. "I know you took a risk to see me."

She didn't want to get on dangerous territory. "Well, as you said, this is business."

"Yes. I'll show you the photos after dessert. I'm not sure I can get all the items for you, but pick the ones you think will blend in best at your museum."

Their waiter brought water and menus, and Michael ordered for them.

The room with its soft music and the candlelight was not what she had expected. It seemed as if he was saying good-bye and making it memorable.

She didn't want him to know it affected her. Maintaining an even, casual tone, she asked, "So, what's in New York?"

"Greek treasures that have to be returned. They were looted from a Mycenaean cave and turned up in the hands of someone who is trying to sell them to a New York museum."

"The sellers aren't going to just hand them to you, are they?"

He shrugged. "They'll need persuading."

"It sounds risky."

"My job often is." He stretched out his hand and placed it on hers. "Before I go, there is something I must say. Please hear me out."

Intrigued, she looked into his gray eyes before she remembered she was trying to avoid being drawn in by them. His eyes darkened from gray to charcoal. "You've taken a big chance meeting me here. I realize how hard it is to lose your family. I miss mine very much."

"You could come back," she whispered.

"No, I can't turn my back on the truth."

Caught off guard by his intensity and the incredible notion that this proud, once loyal man would give up all he knew for a strange belief, she lowered her gaze.

"I just want you to know that while I was gone in the States, I thought of you a lot. And now that I'm back and you're all grown up and more beautiful than I ever expected—"

She raised a brow in disbelief.

"No, hear me out." He looked at her, his eyes gentle. "Sarah, if I had the chance to court you and make you mine, I'd jump at it. But as long as you reject my faith, we can never go any farther than being friends, if we are allowed even that." His fingers tightened on hers. "I beg you to at least look into the possibility that Yeshua is who He and many others say He is."

She drew her hand away. "Like I said, why should I spend time looking into lies?"

"Do you think I'd give up all my past life, my family, for a lie? And how do you know they're lies? Because someone told you so?"

"No, but—"

"All I ask is that you look at the records. Prove me wrong, then. Show me that Yeshua can't possibly be our Messiah."

She reached her hand out and touched his. "If I can show you where you're wrong, you'll deny it and come back to us?"

"If you can prove it, yes, I will."

"I'll do it. I'll show you where you're wrong." Wadding up her napkin in her left hand, she hoped she wasn't getting in over her head. Theology had never been her strong suit.

The waiter brought in their dessert, a rich, chocolate mousse layered with whipped cream. Michael opened the briefcase, and through slow spoonfuls of the rich, creamy delight, they studied his photos of ancient Israeli artifacts.

Two hours after they entered the restaurant, Michael stood with Sarah beside her car. Torn between the desire for one kiss and good intentions to not let it go any farther than friendship, he simply stared, drinking in her presence.

Her blue eyes glowed with pleasure as she looked up at him. "Thank you, Michael. I had a wonderful time." An auburn curl blew across her cheek, and he was filled with a longing to touch where it caressed her.

He dipped his head as he leaned closer. "I'm going to miss you, Gnat." Just one kiss would keep him for the rest of his life, unless by a miracle she found the same faith he had. He searched her eyes. She looked back with trust and tenderness. They stood without moving for a moment. Then he closed the gap and touched her lips with his, softly as a whisper.

A fire sprang in his heart, a desire deep within to cherish her forever, to keep her by his side. Standing on tiptoe, she reached her arms up around his neck and hungrily kissed him back. He knew kissing her would be wonderful, but he'd underestimated the force of affection that swept through him.

He touched the sides of her face to look in her eyes. She slowly opened them, and it took his breath away to see the same depth of emotion there.

"I've dreamed of this for years," she murmured. "But it's better than any dream." She lay her head on his chest, and he closed his arms around her, holding her near.

They stayed that way for a few moments until a small group came out of the restaurant. She inched back, and he took hold of her shoulders. "I'll keep in touch, if that's all right with you," he said.

"I'll need to discuss any works of art you might find for us." Her eyes sparkled, drawing him toward her again.

He resisted the urge to kiss her in front of the people passing and watching. Opening her car door, he hunkered down as she climbed in. "Good-bye," he said softly. "And remember to search the Scriptures with an open mind. I'll be praying."

A slight frown wrinkled between her brows, and he teased, "Don't see the matchmaker until you know the answer."

She rolled her eyes. "That's as good a reason as any."

He stood and closed her door. Winking at her, he watched her start her Opel and drive away. *Lord, show her truth.*

Chapter 9

A week later Michael called and told her he was working hard and wouldn't be back in time for Hanukkah. He didn't ask if she'd started studying, and she was grateful for that but decided she'd better begin. She pulled the book out from under her car seat and began taking lunch breaks to read a few pages at a time and make notes.

Was this Russian rabbi twisting the words of the Torah and Tanakh? His findings seemed to make sense. She studied deeper, looking for the flaw to prove to Michael that he should return to the God of his childhood.

At the library, she found more books on the subject of Yeshua. Most refuted his allegations to be Messiah. Sarah began to wonder if this Yeshua was crazy or a liar because His claims made no sense.

As the month of January drew to a close, she rose from her bed and padded over to the window. Gripped by a desire to be with Michael, which would not let go, she pressed her hands against the glass. The city, with muted lights, looked like a dream. King David's Tower pointed to one big star fading near the horizon.

She sighed. *Michael.* Where was he now? What time was it in America?

The next day he called again. "How's your studying? Ready to prove me wrong?"

"I'm tired of thinking about it! I'm just going round and round in circles."

"Did you read the part where the prophet Isaiah tells of His suffering for us?"

She grimaced. "That's one I do not understand. Not even the scholars' interpretations make sense."

"How about some of King David's psalms? Like the one where he describes a crucifixion, long before they were invented."

"I found that very interesting," she confessed.

"Did you read in that book Leah gave you, of the Scripture types and shadows of Messiah's life and death and resurrection?"

"I did, but still—"

"Sarah, He was crucified on Passover, as our sacrificial lamb. It was His blood that was sprinkled on the altar in heaven. For us. Pay close attention to the Seder ceremony."

"It still sounds like science fiction."

"Do you think it might be true?"

Feeling guilty, she looked over her shoulder at Mr. Silverman. "I just don't know."

"Pray about it. Ask God to show you. He will, if you really want the truth."

She was silent for a few seconds, then asked, "Are you coming back soon?"

"I've almost gotten this American Indian relic job done and should be back in Jerusalem in a week to ten days."

"Oh." She was torn between longing to see him again and the problem of disproving his beliefs in Yeshua the carpenter.

That night she opened the door at home, and her grandfather had to speak twice to get her attention. "Maideleh, what is it? You've been preoccupied for the last two months. You haven't spent time with your friends."

"It's nothing, Zayde. I have a lot on my mind."

"Your mother and aunt Paula are coming over tonight. They're ready to call Mrs. Finkelstein."

"But there aren't many men over twenty-five who are looking for a wife."

"There are a few." He tilted his head. "Not first choices, but. . ."

"Besides, I don't want to get married." Her heart turned over at the memory of Michael's kiss. There was no one like him, and he was off limits.

"Don't be sad. Mrs. Finkelstein may find a perfectly good man for you."

That night her mother and aunt Paula wheedled and cajoled, finally ordering Sarah to come to a meeting in April at her parents' home. "And wear that nice blue dress with the white belt I like so well," said her mother.

"And let him see that glorious hair," added Aunt Paula. "Just tie it back with a ribbon."

Before she went to bed Sarah prayed that God would help her sort out truth from fable. She tossed and turned, finally falling into a fitful sleep interrupted by odd dreams.

The next morning she walked to work with thoughts of Moses' tabernacle, King David, the captivities of the Jews, and references to a Messiah crowding her mind until she thought it would overload. She almost tripped over a group of girls on their way to yeshiva. Fitting the key into the museum lock, she thought of how simple her life had been before Michael returned. Now she was a mass of confusing questions. She'd asked God to show her the truth, and it still eluded her. The subject had no absolute provable answer. If only it were as simple as two-plus-two equals four, no opinions, like math.

As she booted up her computer, the phone rang.

"Sarah? Leah Ben Ami here. How are you, Dear?"

"I'm fine. How are you?"

"Good. They delivered the goblet to me yesterday, and I want to present it at a small ceremony with some of our family members."

Sarah sat straight up in her chair. She could go and talk to Leah about the ceremony. And if the subject of the Scriptures came up, she could practice her opinions on Leah before trying them out on Michael.

After work, seated at Leah's table, Sarah held the silver goblet again, turning it in her hands, marveling at its beauty and mystical appeal. "I've seen many artifacts, but this one is very special to me, and I'm not sure why."

Leah's eyes softened as she gazed at the cup. "It was used to commemorate Messiah's death for us."

"I don't understand that part of it. I've been reading the Law and the Prophets, everything I could find about Messiah, and I find conflicting reports. On the one hand, He's a king, and on the other, He's rejected and abused. I'm about to give up on the whole project and leave it to the rabbis to figure out."

"Many have come to understand." Leah poured more tea into their cups. "And those who have know that Yeshua filled all the prophecies."

"How do they know?"

Leah reached over to the bookcase and drew out a Bible. "Read the second half. This tells the life of Yeshua and has references to show how He fulfilled the Law and the Prophets foretelling His coming."

The book felt heavy in Sarah's hand. "I don't know if I really want to continue on this confusing quest. And I'm wondering if Yeshua is Messiah and He's dead, then what's the point?"

"You're almost there. Just read this, and you'll find the answers you're seeking."

They talked a little while longer, and although Sarah didn't ask, Leah told her that Michael was supposed to be back in March, in time for Purim.

Driving home, more memories that had been stored for years surfaced, carrying with them all the feelings they had held originally. Michael telling her a riddle, his gray eyes dancing with mischief when she almost guessed. The time he walked her home when a bigger girl challenged her to a fight, giving her a ride on his new bicycle. She'd thought he was the most gallant, heroic person in the world.

Then later, when she was a young teenager and feeling unattractive, he'd told her she was the prettiest girl in her class. She remembered going with Rachel and him on a ship in the Sea of Galilee. He'd brought her bread to toss to the gluttonous seagulls. She'd watched him at the prow of the ship facing into the wind and wished she could be with him forever.

She was unable to get into the Old City because there was some anti-Israel protest above the Western Wall. In a nearby parking lot she activated her cell phone. Her grandfather was all right, and Mr. Silverman, still at the museum, said all was well. The Bible was too large to put in her purse, so she walked back home holding it against her chest with her jacket closed over it.

For some odd reason, Grandfather asked what she held so tightly. She swallowed hard and in a feeble voice mumbled, "Just something someone loaned me." Hurrying toward her bedroom, she pulled her jacket tighter.

"Let me see." He reached his hand out.

She tried to be cool but felt a hot blush creep up into her cheeks. She looked the other way and handed him the book.

"What is this! How dare you bring it into our home?" He dropped it as though it scalded his fingers.

"I thought—"

"You didn't think!" He grabbed a tissue and used it to push the Bible toward the door without touching it. "No. I can't have this even close to our front door." His blue eyes crackled as he looked back at her. "I know something has been taking your interest, but this—" He pointed at the Bible without looking at it. Then he went back to his chair and sank into it. "You brought it in, now you get it out. And never bring that heathen book in here again."

"I was just trying to see why M—"

"Don't say that name. Are you going to read the Koran too? And the Buddhist books? Remember, I told you that you don't need to study counterfeits. Just learn the Law and the Prophets, and you'll have all the truth you need. You won't have to examine counterfeits to know they are false."

"Yes, Zayde." Sarah picked up the Bible and left. Tears stung her eyes as she walked back to her car. Security was tight, with soldiers on watch everywhere.

In her car, she slumped over the steering wheel, unable to stop the tears. Studying doctrines was making her crazy. If only she had someone to talk to who could logically pull it all together. The Hasidic rabbis were looking for Messiah, but what would be their proof? She couldn't talk with them; they had no respect for Jews who weren't as dedicated as they. If she talked with a Christian, the views would be biased.

She leaned back, closing her eyes. What was she going to do?

What if it was true? What if Yeshua was Messiah? One prophet said he came and the people did not value him. And others spoke of pain and suffering. She smacked the steering wheel. This was all Michael's fault. He should have simply told her and let her make her own decision. *But I wouldn't have listened.*

After a few minutes, she dried her tears and drove back to her regular parking spot. She started to put the Bible under the seat but held it suspended for a moment. Bringing it back to her lap, she opened it to the point Leah had told her to start reading. By the light of the street lamp, she read Levi-called-Matthew's account.

She put her hand on the place where Yeshua said, "Think not that I am come to destroy the law. . .but to fulfil." Pondering that amazing announcement, she stared ahead, her eyes unfocused. Many points from the Law came to mind. No, Messiah would not destroy the Law. She read farther, and for another hour she pored over the account of Yeshua from three other disciples.

She flipped the pages before closing the book and quickly opened it again. Had she seen a chapter called Hebrews? Leah had said the first four were about Yeshua's life. But Hebrews sounded interesting, so she read that too. Suddenly pieces began to fit into place. *It could be true!*

But if it was, she'd have a problem as big as Michael's. Her family would think she'd been taken in by a big lie. And like Michael, they'd disown her. If her grandfather was upset now, he'd be devastated if she turned from their religion. But she could still believe the Law and Prophets, only adding the fact that Messiah had come and would come again to fulfil all prophecies.

Thinking of all the research to learn about His kingly work

made her head throb. She slid the Bible beneath the seat and took a deep breath. *God, you know this is all confusing to me. I want to know the truth, but the fact is I don't want Michael to be right. It would be so hard for me. Help me.*

Peace filled her little car, settling over her. *Be still and know that I am God.*

"Thank You," she said as she got out of her car.

Back at the house, she and her grandfather talked. "Remember, Maideleh, Judaism is greater than any one person or any one moment, and the sadness of today will be woven into our sacred memories and joined with the joy of tomorrow." She agreed and excused herself to go to bed. There was so much to think about and pray about.

For the next few days life was more simple. From time to time connections from the Law or Prophets and Yeshua would drift into her mind. They didn't bother her as they had. She simply pondered them and refused to let confusion and worry plague her. She read the account of Yochannan-John, again, and found it oddly peaceful. There were some things she didn't understand, but they'd be explained in due time.

Seated at her computer, exploring the history of a potential artifact an hour before the museum closed, she felt a presence in the room. She turned to see Michael leaning against the doorframe, watching her with a wistful smile.

"Michael! You're back." She hurried toward him, wishing she could wrap her arms around him. But they'd agreed to be friends.

His smile was slow, but the sparkle in his eyes flashed. "Working hard?"

"No. Just doing some cross-checking. When did you get back?"

"This morning. Took a long time to get through clearance

at the airport. There was another incident."

"Tensions are mounting." She shook her head ruefully. "It's sad that some people think it's a good thing to strap a bomb on themselves and die to hurt others."

"Makes no sense to me," he agreed. "Do you have some time to talk after you're through here?"

Her spirits buoyed by his presence, she almost forgot his status. Furrowing her brow, she said, "I'll meet you in an hour."

He leaned close to her and said, "Can't be seen in the presence of a rogue, eh?" His laugh was easy and good natured as he named a place to meet and left.

Less than an hour later, Sarah almost ran to the Ron restaurant. She wanted to tell Michael about the peace she'd felt for the last two weeks. He was waiting and stood when she entered. She felt warm delight course through her.

When she was seated, they started with small talk. "What's it like in America?" she asked.

"It's a huge country, with everything from swamps to deserts, small towns to mega-cities. I never tire of seeing it."

"Someday I'm going there."

"I hope you do." He leaned forward and put his hand on hers. "Now, tell me, have you looked into the Law and Prophets and have you found proof that Yeshua is not our Messiah?"

"From all I've read and made notes on, it would seem that Yeshua does complete the Jew's search for Messiah and fulfills all requirements."

His quick intake of breath rendered him speechless for a second. "You mean—" His face lit up with a sudden smile. "You've found it's true!"

She shook her head. "I only said it would seem that He fills the requirements."

"I don't get it. What's stopping you from believing?"

Her thoughts tumbled into confusion again. "Everything is fine until I begin thinking I might be wrong."

"What if it's true, and He is the Messiah?"

She groaned. "I've asked myself that question over and over. I used to be so levelheaded, but this whole thing has turned me into a blithering idiot."

"Did you ask God to show you?"

"I did."

"And?"

She hesitated. "I felt an overwhelming peace settle over me like a warm blanket. I stopped worrying and trying to figure it all out. I was at peace, until now."

"Sarah. That was God's way of telling you He loves you, and you're on the right track. Because you asked Him to show you, if it were wrong, you'd have been uncomfortable with the facts you were uncovering. The peace is what we all feel when He confirms His presence and His blessing."

She returned his gaze, wishing she had the same assurance. "I just don't know. It seems true, but I can't give up my life, my family for something I'm not one hundred percent sure of."

"It's hard. But truth is truth, Sarah. And when you find the truth, nothing else matters." His eyes got a faraway look in them. "Other things do matter, but it's more important to live with what's true."

"You've suffered much. Aren't you a little sorry?"

"Of course, I'm sorry that my family doesn't see the truth. But more sorry that they can't accept me for who I am, not what I believe in."

Sarah looked down, heartsick about his being rejected and ostracized. He was much braver than she'd be. She couldn't imagine what it would be like if her parents, her grandfather, and all her friends refused to have any more to do with her. *But what if it's true?*

She didn't realize she'd spoken her thoughts until he answered.

"Exactly. And I'm telling you—it is true." His eyes glowed, seeming to see into her heart where a seed of belief had been sown. "You must acknowledge it, Sarah. If you see the truth, you must say so."

"I thought I was pretty brave, but I can't do that, Michael. I just can't."

His smile faded, and the glow left his eyes. "I thought you were brave too. I'd hoped you and I—" He looked away. "It doesn't matter. You have to do what you must do." When he looked back at her, sadness filled his eyes. "He who makes peace in His high places, may He make peace for you. . ."

A band of tension gripped Sarah's chest as she realized Michael was telling her good-bye. She bit her lip, wanting to believe as strongly as he did, yet not ready to give up her family, her work, and everything for him and his beliefs.

"Don't look so sad. We'll always be friends." He brushed his knuckles on her cheek. "Right?"

"Of course." Closing her eyes against the pain, she turned her head.

A few days later, her mother held her yearly scrubbing and polishing for Passover. Sarah, Rachel, and her brothers helped shampoo carpets, scrub floors, clean out drawers, move furniture, and even turn garment pockets inside out. The day before Passover they got rid of all bread and anything else that had leaven in it and put away all the regular kitchen utensils and dishes to be replaced with those specially reserved for Passover.

When Sarah and her grandfather arrived for their Seder, or Passover dinner, the house was full. Her parents, Rachel and her husband, her brothers, Aunt Paula, a widow friend of hers, and relatives from England were there. When all the greetings and hugs had finished, the service began with Mother lighting the candles and saying the *Brechat Haner* prayer in Hebrew. "Blessed art Thou, O Lord, our God, King of the Universe, who has sanctified us by Thy commandments and has commanded us to kindle the Passover Light."

As Michael suggested, Sarah was particularly watchful during the ceremony. She found the three matzos especially meaningful. When each piece was broken, then placed in a separate pocket of a three-part cloth, it spoke of Father, Son, and Holy Spirit. When her grandfather removed the middle matzah, he broke it into two unequal parts and wrapped one in a white linen cloth, similar to the Jewish burial custom. That part of the middle matzah was "hidden" away.

The four cups of wine taken during the meals stood for the four "I wills" which God spoke in Exodus 6:6-7. The Cup of Sanctification: "I will bring you out from under the burdens of the Egyptians." The Cup of Judgment: "I will rid you out of their bondage." The Cup of Redemption: "I will redeem you with a stretched out arm." The Cup of Praise: "I will take you to me for a people."

Through the meal, Sarah joined in with more fervent interest than ever before. When they recited the blessing and dipped the parsley in the salt water to represent the hyssop used to place blood upon the doorposts and lintels in Egypt, Sarah remembered something she'd read about Yeshua. A prophet said of Him, "Behold the Lamb of God which taketh away the sin of the world."

"Why is this night different from all other nights?" asked her brother.

Grandfather answered, and the ceremonial meal continued. He held up a shankbone and spoke of the lamb eaten by their forefathers as an offering to God because He spared them from the death angel. He quoted the Scripture, reminding Sarah again of Messiah being afflicted yet not opening his mouth, being brought as a lamb to the slaughter, yet saying nothing. They continued on to reading the ten plagues brought upon the Egyptians and raised the Cup of Judgment. Sarah always liked this part because it ended with singing the fun song "Dayenu" (It Would Have Been Enough).

When the youngest child searched and found the matzah that was broken and hidden, Grandfather bought it with a coin. He then broke it into small pieces and distributed it to each of them. Sarah found it very significant that the middle matzah was the one broken, hidden away, and finally redeemed and distributed. Michael said it was at this point in Yeshua's last Passover with His disciples that He had said, "This is my body which is given for you."

She looked closely at it before she ate with the rest of the family. It was pierced, as Yeshua was. She was sure the stripes and lack of leaven all had meaning too. When Grandfather lifted the Cup of Praise, representing God's promise to "take you to me for a people," her eyes filled with tears.

The chalice had that inscription, *I will pour out my blood for you.* The words didn't seem odd anymore. As a sacrifice lamb, Yeshua had poured out His blood for her. Shame flooded her that she had not acknowledged her growing belief in Him when Michael had asked her last week.

While the family sang "Who Knows One?" she joined in,

her heart mixed with happiness and more questions. After she and Grandfather walked home, Sarah went right to her bedroom and prayed, asking God to help her understand. Before she fell asleep, she decided to call Michael in the morning.

Michael sat in his small apartment, staring out the window over the city he loved. His eyes were drawn to Old Jerusalem where Sarah lived with her grandfather. Why couldn't she see the truth? He knew she'd thoroughly investigated the Scriptures. She'd told him they were swirling around in her head. Ever since she'd been a child, when she was on to something she wanted to know, she'd read everything she could get her hands on and make lists and charts to help her understand. So why didn't she see?

He missed her. The Seder with the Ben Ami family and friends was great, but he missed his family, and the day was bleak without Sarah. Being with her was like being on top of Masada and looking down across the sea and miles of valley below. An exhilarating experience. She made him laugh when they were young. Just the thought of her now made him smile.

He abruptly turned away from the view and sank into his chair to stare morosely at his four walls. He should pick up his Bible and read. That would help. The phone rang, startling him.

"Hi, Michael. This is Sarah." As if she had to tell him. He'd know her voice anywhere, even a hundred years from now. "I'd like to talk with you, if you have a few minutes."

He invited her to come and was amazed at how quickly his misery lifted. *Just be her friend,* he told himself. *It can never be anything more.* He tidied up the small apartment, which was already neat, he combed his hair, which didn't need it, and then he started a pot of coffee in case she wanted some.

So much time had passed that he began to wonder if she'd changed her mind about coming, when a knock sounded on his door. He opened it, and she stood there with two books clutched to her chest. Her eyes were alight with joy, and a secret smile curved her lips. "Come in. Sit down," he said.

She walked to his table and set the books down. "I'll come right to the point. I believe Yeshua is Messiah and want to know what I have to do next."

Momentarily speechless, Michael stared at her, his heart pounding. "You mean it?"

Frowning, she put her hands on her hips. "Of course, I mean it! What do I do?"

She stood there, looking so hopeful and expectant, he fell in love all over again. "It's so easy, my love."

"So tell me."

He gathered her in his arms and gently rocked her back and forth for a moment, then held her at arm's length. "Thanks be to God!" Looking into her beautiful blue eyes, he said, "Let's kneel." They did, and he led her in prayer, confessing her doubts and sins and asking Yeshua to come into her heart.

Afterward he saw the sparkle of new life in her eyes. "You will have to tell your family."

"I know." Concern flickered in her eyes, covered quickly with joy.

"I'll be with you. It'll be all right. I love you."

"I love you too, Michael. I always have." Her gaze met his, and he knew he would do anything, risk everything for her if she asked. "I feel so good! So new and happy."

"So do I." He laughed with her. "This is more than I'd ever hoped or wished for."

Long into the afternoon, they laughed and talked, planning their future together.

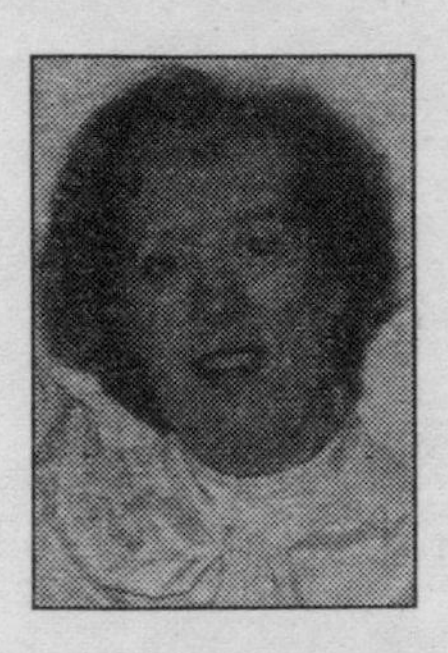

JANE LAMUNYON

Jane lives in California with her husband and designates much of her time to writing and the business of writing. She is the author of *Me God, You Jane,* her autobiography, and two **Heartsong Presents** novels, *Fly Away Home* and *Escape on the Wind*. She has written short stories for adults and children, how-tos on a wide range of topics, and a stage play. Her work has encompassed many genres, including newspaper stories, book reviews, corporate newsletters, technical manuals, and prize-winning poetry. She is a speaker and workshop leader in many different areas.

A Letter to Our Readers

Dear Readers:

In order that we might better contribute to your reading enjoyment, we would appreciate you taking a few minutes to respond to the following questions. When completed, please return to the following: Fiction Editor, Barbour Publishing, Inc., P.O. Box 719, Uhrichsville, OH 44683.

1. Did you enjoy reading *The Chalice of Israel?*
   - ❑ Very much. I would like to see more books like this.
   - ❑ Moderately—I would have enjoyed it more if ______________

   ____

   ____

2. What influenced your decision to purchase this book? (Check those that apply.)
   - ❑ Cover ❑ Back cover copy ❑ Title ❑ Price
   - ❑ Friends ❑ Publicity ❑ Other

3. Which story was your favorite?
   - ❑ *Cup of Courage* ❑ *Cup of Honor*
   - ❑ *Cup of Hope* ❑ *Cup of Praise*

4. Please check your age range:
   - ❑ Under 18 ❑ 18–24 ❑ 25–34
   - ❑ 35–45 ❑ 46–55 ❑ Over 55

5. How many hours per week do you read? ______________

Name ______________________________________

Occupation __________________________________

Address ____________________________________

City ________________ State __________ Zip __________